CALDER
BRAND

The Calder Series by Janet Dailey

JANET DAILEY

CALDER BRAND

KENSINGTON
PUBLISHING CORP.

www.kensingtonbooks.com

KENSINGTON BOOKS are published by

Kensington Publishing Corp.
119 West 40th Street
New York, NY 10018

All Kensington titles, imprints, and distributed lines are available at special quantity discounts for bulk purchases for sales promotion, premiums, fundraising, educational, or institutional use.

Special book excerpts or customized printings can also be created to fit specific needs. For details, write or phone the office of the Kensington Special Sales Manager: Attn. Special Sales Department. Kensington Publishing Corp, 119 West 40th Street, New York, NY 10018. Phone: 1-800-221-2647.

The K Logo is a trademark of Kensington Publishing Corp.

Library of Congress Card Catalogue Number: 2020945348

ISBN-13: 978-1-4967-2744-2
ISBN-10: 1-4967-2744-4
First Kensington Hardcover Edition: March 2021

ISBN-13: 978-1-4967-2750-3 (ebook)
ISBN-10: 1-4967-2750-9 (ebook)

10 9 8 7 6 5 4 3 2 1

Printed in the United States of America

PROLOGUE

JOE DOLLARHIDE STOOD ON THE WIDE, COVERED PORCH OF HIS HILL-top home, watching the season's first snowfall coat the land with white. Would this storm be a brief flurry or a full-blown blizzard that would make the roads impassable by morning? It made no difference, Joe told himself. Whatever the weather, he had to be in Miles City when the bank opened for Monday business tomor-row morning. Being first in the door was vital to his pride, his honor, and his need to avenge the betrayal he'd suffered more than twelve years ago—a betrayal that had festered in him over time, like a wound that never healed.

A betrayal at the hands of none other than Chase Benteen Calder.

The snow was falling harder now, the flakes a white blur against the darkness. Joe could hear the howling wind and feel the biting cold on his face. Maybe he should have taken a chance and left at once, as the storm was blowing in. With luck, he could have made it to Miles City, booked a room for the night, and arrived early at the bank. Take a chance—that's what Benteen Calder would probably have done. For all Joe knew, Benteen could already be there, buying drinks at the hotel bar to celebrate his victory.

But Joe's wife had put her foot down. "The storm's getting

worse," she'd insisted. "People die in weather like this. They get trapped or lost, and they freeze to death. If you go tonight, not caring whether you leave me a widow and your sons orphans, so help me, Joe, I will never forgive you."

So Joe hadn't gone. Now, as the storm gained in ferocity, he had to concede that his wife had been right, as she usually was. In his years as a Montana rancher, he'd seen blizzards come and go. This one could be a killer, the kind of storm that buried fences and left livestock frozen in the pastures. If he'd left for Miles City tonight, he would still be on the road. And in the time it took for a man to freeze to death, Joe would lose a life that had given him all the things he'd ever wanted.

At twenty-eight, he was a man in his prime, with an impressive home, a thriving business, and a fortune in land, horses, and cattle. He had a beautiful wife that he loved to the depths of his soul, and two fine young sons.

But looking back over the years, Joe realized that none of what he'd gained had come without a price. Luck and fate had played a vital role in his success. But so had sacrifice, heartbreaking effort, and backbreaking work.

As he watched the swirling snow, Joe's memory drifted back twelve years, to the beginning of his great adventure, when he'd left his family's Texas farm to join Chase Benteen Calder's cattle drive.

He'd been so young then, so full of dreams, and so eager to do his part in herding 2,500 longhorn cattle north from the dry Texas plain to the wild, rich grasslands of Montana. The journey, up through the Texas Panhandle, through the Indian Territories, into Kansas and Nebraska, Wyoming and finally Montana, took months, from spring to early autumn. By the time it was done, Joe had told himself, he would be a grown man, ready to wrest his own fortune from the wild, western land.

CHAPTER ONE

April 29, 1879, twelve years earlier

As THE SKY PALED OVER THE TEXAS PRAIRIE, JOE LAY IN HIS BEDROLL, drifting in and out of sleep. His ears caught the rustle of quail foraging in the long grass. He could hear the faint lowing of cattle, the snort of a horse, and the snores of the men sleeping around him.

Ahead lay another day on the trail—one more day of dust, danger, and unending work from dawn until dark. But for Joe, it would also be a day of secret celebration. Today was his sixteenth birthday.

He had no calendar to remind him. But he'd kept a careful count of the days. No mistake. He was sixteen for sure now—not a boy anymore but a man, doing a man's work.

Three weeks had passed since he'd left his family's Texas farm to become a cowboy on a big cattle drive—a drive owned and bossed by Mr. Chase Benteen Calder, who usually went by his middle name, Benteen. The work was filthy and grueling, the dust and rain miserable at times. But Joe was used to hard work. And even through the worst of it, there was no place he would rather be—even if he was only the wrangler's helper, the lowest job in the outfit. From the first taste of coffee in the morning to the soothing songs of the night watch as he sank into sleep, this was the life.

It was an exciting time to be a young man. The end of the Civil War, the completion of the transcontinental railroad, and the defeat of the native tribes had opened vast areas of the country to travel, commerce, farming, and ranching. The virgin prairies of the Northwest were ideal for grazing cattle, and Americans were quick to seize the advantage.

The Calder drive was one of many that moved Texas-born longhorn cattle along the trails leading north. Some herds went as far as the railroad towns in Kansas, Nebraska, and Missouri, where they were loaded onto trains, shipped east, and sold. Others, like this drive, would continue on to the untamed territories of Wyoming and Montana, where the cattle could graze on the lush, rich grasslands that were there for the taking—lands that, in their way, were more valuable than gold.

This was a time for conquest and adventure—and Joe was thrilled to be part of it.

Stealing a little more precious time, he lay in his bedroll, giving his lanky body a chance to come fully awake. In the gray light, he could see the dark outline of the chuckwagon and the sleeping forms of the men lying around it. Farther back, two covered wagons sat in the shadows. Benteen Calder and a man named Ely Stanton were moving their wives and possessions to new homes. The Calders would be starting a ranch with the cattle on their Montana land claim. The Stantons would be leaving the drive in Dodge City and heading for Iowa, where Mrs. Stanton had family.

Joe stretched, preparing to get up. Only then did he feel an unaccustomed weight across his legs. He raised his head to see a five-foot bull snake crawling across his bedroll.

With a startled yelp, Joe jerked upright. One hand fumbled for the pistol he kept under his pillow. Still groggy, he found it and might have blown the creature to kingdom come; but by the time he'd gathered his wits and cocked the gun, the snake had slithered off into the grass.

The cowboys bedded around him were awake and laughing.

"Hey, kid, you almost had yourself a bed partner there!" Shorty Niles said. "Another minute and he'd have crawled right into the sack with you."

"It's a good thing you didn't pull that trigger," Jesse Trumbo teased. "You could've shot yourself in the foot."

"You're lucky it wasn't a rattler," Yates, the wrangler said. "That was a pretty good holler you let out. Were you scared?"

"Not scared. Just spooked." Joe rubbed the sleep from his eyes. The cowboys enjoyed playing good-natured tricks on each other, and Joe, as the youngest man on the cattle drive, got more than his share. Had one of the men dropped the scary but harmless reptile on his bedroll? He'd bet against it this time. There were plenty of snakes around, and they were attracted by warmth. But he would never know.

Rusty, the grizzled cook, had risen early and was working between the chuckwagon and the campfire. The aroma of coffee mingled with the smell of bacon and sourdough biscuits cooked in a cast-iron Dutch oven made Joe's empty stomach rumble. There wasn't much variety in trail food. But at least the old man was good at his job.

The clanging of a metal spoon on a skillet shattered the peace of the morning. "Come and git it," Rusty yelled. "Git a move on, or I'll feed it to the coyotes!"

Joe sat up and hurried to pull his clothes and boots over his long underwear. Around him, the other men were doing the same, some groaning and cursing. The two who'd ridden night watch over the herd had barely managed three hours of sleep. But that didn't matter. It was time to start the long day.

Joe splashed his hands and face with a trickle of water from the barrel mounted on the chuckwagon, then hurried to get his breakfast. He knew better than to tell any of the crew about this being his birthday. The men would rib him unmercifully, and probably even play a few tricks, like throwing him in the Red River, which they'd be crossing with the herd this morning.

As he sat on the ground, wolfing down his beans, bacon, and biscuits, and gulping thick, black coffee from a tin mug, it struck him that he'd neglected to murmur a word of grace, something he'd promised his mother he would do before every meal. It wouldn't be the first time he'd forgotten. But it was too late now. He would remind himself at noon and again at suppertime.

On the far side of the fire, through the rising smoke, he could see the boss, Mr. Benteen Calder, drinking his coffee on his feet. Soon he'd be riding out ahead of the herd to plot out the best route for the cattle, horses, and wagons and choose a spot for the chuckwagon to stop and prepare the noon meal.

Benteen Calder was a tall man, broad in the shoulders with a rugged face and a trail-hardened body. Joe admired him to the point of hero worship. He was bold but prudent, tough but fair— the kind of man Joe aimed to become with time and experience.

"Joe, come here." Calder's gaze pierced the smoke. "I want to talk to you."

Joe had finished his plate and wiped it clean with the last bite of biscuit. As he rose, he slipped it into the wreck pan and strode around the fire. "Yes, Mr. Calder? What can I do for you?"

Calder finished his coffee. "This morning we'll be crossing the Red River. With wagons and animals in moving water, anything can go wrong."

"Yes, sir, I know. How can I help?" Joe could tell from the boss's slight nod that he'd said the right thing.

"We'll be taking the wagons across first," Calder said. "My wife's been driving our wagon and doing fine. But I'm not sure she's up to handling it in the river. I want you to drive her across, trailing your horse. When you get the wagon to the other side, you can ride back and help with the remuda and the herd. Understood?"

"Yes, sir." It was a big responsibility, but Joe was thrilled to have been asked. "I'll do my best."

"I don't have to tell you how important my wife's safety is to me."

"Don't worry, sir. I won't let anything happen to her." Calder's new bride, Lorna, was the prettiest woman Joe had ever seen. The job he'd been given would be like protecting a priceless porcelain doll.

He was still thinking about Lorna as he saddled his pony and rode out to help Yates, the bowlegged wrangler, round up the horses and herd them into the makeshift rope corral for the men to saddle and ride.

Lorna Calder was a true lady with sparkling brown eyes and a tumble of rich, dark mahogany hair. She couldn't have been more than seventeen or eighteen—barely older than Joe. But she was already a woman and a wife. Truth be told, Joe was more than a little sweet on her. She'd been friendly, letting him hitch her wagon team and saddle the buttermilk buckskin he'd chosen for her to ride; but he knew better than to act on his feelings. Benteen Calder was capable of killing any man who touched his bride.

After the first night on the trail, he'd made sure to lay his bedroll well away from their wagon. The faint sounds coming from under the canvas had roused forbidden images that would have shocked his God-fearing mother. As a farm boy, Joe was well acquainted with the basics of sex. But he was far from experienced. Last summer, down by the swimming hole, Betty Ann Flinders had let him kiss her and touch her breasts. The moment had strained the buttons on his trousers. But a quality girl would never let a boy go that far. And that was the kind of woman he wanted at his side someday—a real lady like Lorna Calder.

The right woman wasn't all he wanted. Someday, Joe vowed, he would have his own ranch with his own vast herds of cattle. He'd even thought of the brand he'd use—the outline of a cowhide with a dollar sign on it, for *Dollarhide*. This job was the first step toward making his dream come true.

He rode out to where the remuda was grazing and uncoiled his rope from the saddle horn. Yates was already gathering the horses. Without being told what to do, Joe made a wide circle, picking up any stragglers and heading them in with a flick of his lariat on their haunches. There were far more horses than men on the drive. Each of the hands had been assigned a string of several animals. When working cattle, they rotated their mounts every few hours to keep them rested and healthy on the long drive.

By now the horses were accustomed to the morning routine. It didn't take long to get them headed for the rope corral. Joe arrived back at camp to find Benteen Calder already gone and Lorna behind the chuckwagon, washing the last of the dishes—a job that would have fallen to Joe if she hadn't volunteered her help.

She gave him a smile as he passed her to stow his bedroll in the chuckwagon. "Good morning, Joe. My husband tells me you'll be driving our wagon across the river."

"Yes, ma'am." Joe could feel his face warming. "I promised him I'd take good care of you."

One delicate eyebrow arched slightly. "Oh, it won't be me, just our wagon. I'll be riding on the chuckwagon with Rusty."

"Oh." Joe felt the brightness drain from his special day. So Benteen Calder had changed his mind. It made sense that Calder would decide to put his wife in the safest possible place, with a driver who'd crossed more big rivers than Joe had years. Knowing the boss, it made even more sense that he would entrust her to the one male in the outfit who didn't rouse his jealousy.

"That sounds like a good idea, ma'am." Joe tipped his hat. "I'll get your wagon hitched and make sure everything's tied down tight. No need to worry about that."

She gave him another melting smile. "Thanks, Joe. I can always count on you."

"Thanks for trusting me, ma'am. It means a lot." Joe tipped his hat again and strode across the camp to the wagon. The two draft horses were grazing nearby, tied to a picket.

Mary Stanton, a plain woman who looked and talked like a younger version of Joe's mother, was hitching her team.

"Can I help you, Mrs. Stanton?" Joe asked, knowing her husband was busy with the cattle.

"Thanks for the offer, but I'm almost done." She tightened the last harness buckle. "Are you all right with driving the wagon across that river, Joe?" she asked.

"I reckon so. I've driven the wagon plenty and crossed rivers before."

"Well, the Red's a lot bigger than anything we've come to so far, and Ely says the water's high. The important thing for you will be to stay right in line with the other wagons. Otherwise you could drift off and get mired in quicksand or get carried off by the current."

"Thanks. I'll keep that in mind, ma'am." Joe hurried to hitch the horses to the wagon tongue. Mary Stanton had given him sound advice but, truth be told, he was looking forward to the crossing. It was going to be a great adventure, and he would be a vital part of it—even without Lorna on board.

By the time the wagon was ready, with Joe's saddled horse tied behind, it was time to pull out.

The chuckwagon went first, with Rusty and Lorna sharing the driver's bench. Mary Stanton's wagon pulled into second place, with Joe bringing up the rear. A few minutes later, they passed the herd. The cattle were on their feet, grazing at a distance from the water. When their time came to cross, the thirsty animals would be easy to drive into the river.

Joe could see the cowhands working the mixed herd of long-horns—steers, cows, and bulls. Rounded up wild over the winter in the thorny Texas brush, they were still apt to be skittish. Any-thing—a noise in the bushes, a clap of thunder, or even a rabbit bounding across the trail, might be enough to spook them into a stampede. It had happened before, but the quick work of the men had headed off the leaders, ending with the herd milling in a circle and finally slowing to a stop.

As the wagon passed the herd, one of the men waved to him. Joe recognized Jonesy, one of the younger hands. Over the past few weeks, Jonesy and another man, Andy Young, had become Joe's friends—not close friends, because they were usually work-ing the herd. But they sat with him at supper and shared songs and jokes. Joe looked up to them. They'd taught him a lot about being a real cowboy.

Joe liked the other men, too—Spanish Bill with his reckless, laughing ways, Wooly Willis, named for his curly blond hair, Zeke Taylor, who never seemed to stop talking, Shorty, whose mellow singing voice calmed the cattle at night, and the rest of them. They were all fine fellows. But they were seasoned cowhands, and they treated Joe like a kid. Jonesy and Andy treated him as an equal.

Joe returned Jonesy's wave, then turned his attention back to guiding the team. As the wagon crested a low rise, he saw the river for the first time. It was even wider than he'd imagined, and full to the banks. The water, mud red with spring runoff, was fast-moving and treacherous. He remembered Mary's warning. At the time, he'd dismissed it, figuring that she was being overly cautious. Now he understood.

Benteen Calder had already found the ford place and chosen the safest route across the river. Now the boss sat his horse on a high part of the bank, directing every step of the crossing. At his signal, Jesse Trumbo, the most experienced cowhand, moved ahead of the chuckwagon and rode into the water to show the way. One after another, the three wagons followed him. Joe gripped the reins as his team waded into the rushing current. The water rose around him, almost high enough to cover the horses' backs. He hadn't expected to be scared, but he was.

Clucking encouragement to the horses, he riveted his gaze on the back of Mary Stanton's wagon and followed it, pushing through the strong current. An eternity seemed to pass before the chuckwagon, then the Stantons' wagon, lurched onto the bank. Moments later, Joe, too, was out of the river, the horses dripping and snorting as water streamed off their hides. He began to breathe again.

The wagons rolled on, moving away from the river to leave plenty of room for the horses and cattle that would follow. When Rusty stopped at last, in a level clearing, Joe pulled the wagon to one side, jumped to the ground, and untied his horse from the back. As he swung into the saddle, he saw Lorna climbing down from the chuckwagon. She gave him a little wave, along with that smile of hers. He was tempted to ride over and tell her how careful he'd been, driving her wagon. But right now he needed to get back and help move the herd.

Trumbo had gone back to ride point on the herd. Joe reached the ford to find Yates bringing the remuda across. He pitched in to help. The horses were strong swimmers. They had no trouble with the deep water or the current. Within minutes they'd all made it to the far bank.

After helping Yates herd the remuda to a safe place near the wagons, Joe turned around and headed back to the river at a gallop. Already soaked to the skin, he plunged his horse into the swift-moving current and pushed for the other side.

Looking ahead, toward the far bank, he could see the cattle moving down the long slope to the ford. The riders, two on point, two on either side in flank and swing position, and three riding drag in the rear, had squeezed the herd into a ragged line, with a big brindle steer in the lead. As they reached the ford, Joe realized that the cattle would be coming straight toward him.

Spanish Bill, who was riding point with Trumbo, spotted Joe in the water. With frantic gestures, he motioned for Joe to go back. Joe got the message. With the herd surging into the river, he swung the horse around and rode back the way he'd come. Reaching the bank just in time, he reined his horse to a safe vantage point to watch the crossing.

The sight was one Joe would never forget. The first of the cattle had reached the river and stopped to drink. But more animals, with the cowboys pushing from the rear, moved in behind them, forcing them ahead. The point riders urged them forward, into the current. The flank riders, Andy and Jonesy, along with the swing riders, pressed them from the sides, keeping them to the solid bottom, away from the eddies and quicksand, while the drag riders picked up any stragglers and pressed the herd from behind.

For now, everything seemed to be going well. The cattle made a strange spectacle, with just their heads and their long horns bobbing above the muddy water. The sound of their bawling filled the air. By now, the leaders had made it across and were being herded to a safe spot half a mile beyond the river. More cattle followed behind them. On the far bank, the herd was still coming, pouring down to the water in a steady line.

The morning sun had risen and climbed the sky. Its rays danced on the water, the brightness dazzling Joe's eyes. He reached up to pull down the brim of his hat.

His pulse jerked.

His hat was gone.

Shading his eyes with his hand, he scanned the riverbank. There was no sign of his father's battered Texas-style Stetson, which he'd accepted as a parting gift when he'd left home. He must've been wearing it when he'd helped Yates with the horses. If not, he would surely have missed it sooner. But where was the hat now?

There was only one place it could be, Joe realized with a sinking heart—the river.

Still shading his eyes, he gazed out over the roiling red-brown water. There was the hat. Circling on a small eddy, it was drifting into the path of the oncoming cattle. Joe's first thought was that the hat would be trampled into the mud and lost forever. Then, suddenly, he became aware of a much more dangerous situation.

Several cattle had spotted the hat, where it twirled and bobbed on the water like some living thing. With tossing horns and snorts of alarm, they turned aside and tried to head back the way the herd had come. Other cattle followed, plowing back into the animals that were moving forward, forcing them into the mass of moving bodies.

Sick with helpless dread, Joe watched from the bank as the herd began to mill—plunging and jamming into a solid, circling, bawling mass of confusion. It crossed his mind that maybe he should ride into the river and help. But without knowing what to do, he'd only be in the way.

Was that the truth, or was he just plain scared?

Benteen Calder spurred his horse into the river as his men fought to break up the melee, pushing, shoving with their horses, and flailing with their ropes. Some of the weaker animals were already going down, to be drowned and trampled.

A panic-stricken steer slammed into Andy's horse, knocking the young cowboy out of the saddle. Seeing him go down, Jonesy charged in close to throw him a rope. An instant later, both of them were lost from sight.

Spanish Bill leaped from his horse onto the cattle. They were packed so closely that he was able to cross on their backs, beating at them with his fists as he moved toward the center to open up a wedge. A moment later, in the confusion, Joe lost track of him, as well.

Miraculously, or so it seemed, the knot of cattle began to separate. A few at first, then more and more allowed themselves to be herded the rest of the way across the river and up the bank. They left behind a mess of churned-up mud and carcasses that floated downriver on the fast-moving current.

Soaked and exhausted, the cowboys herded the last of the cattle to safety. Joe glimpsed Spanish Bill, back on his horse. The others looked to be all right, too—except for Andy and Jonesy. There was no sign of them.

Surely his two friends had made it out of the river, Joe told himself as he rode back to the wagons. Of course they had. They'd be showing up anytime, laughing and joking about their harrowing adventure.

Rusty had a fire going and hot coffee to warm the men. They drank in silence, pale and cold. Joe had set up a rope corral for the horses and was gathering dry wood for the chuckwagon when Benteen Calder rode in. His face was a granite mask.

"I need a couple of volunteers to ride downstream with me," he said. "We'll be looking for Andy and Jonesy and making a count of the lost stock. The rest of you, get those cattle ready to move out. We've got a lot of ground to cover before nightfall."

"I'll go with you, Mr. Calder," Joe said, stepping forward. Helping to find his friends was the least he could do.

Shorty offered to go as well. After saddling fresh horses, they fell in behind the boss and followed him back down to the ford.

With Joe bringing up the rear, they rode single file, saying little. Downriver, the buzzards were already flocking in to feed on the dead cattle. Calder had asked Joe and Shorty to keep their own count, to compare with his when there were no more to be found. Joe was already coming up on fifty—every one of them his fault for losing his hat in the river.

The sun beat like a hammer on his bare head. Nobody had said a word about his hat being gone, but surely the men had noticed. Some, at least, might've even guessed what had happened.

Should he open his mouth and own up to it? The question clawed at his gut.

At the river's edge, he noticed something brown caught on a snag. Pausing for a closer look, he recognized his waterlogged hat. The very sight of it made his stomach roil. But he couldn't work without a hat, and there was no place to get another one. Reaching down from the saddle, he hooked it with a finger, squeezed out the worst of the muddy water, and tucked it under his vest before catching up with the others.

A mile downstream, where the river curved in its channel, they found Andy and Jonesy in a clump of flooded willows. Their bodies lay in shallow water, coated with mud and battered from tumbling in the swift current. Joe had fooled himself into believing his friends were safe. He should have known better.

He felt the soggy lump of his hat beneath his vest—the hat that in all likelihood had caused their deaths. It was his fault that two young lives were gone. And there was nothing he could do except try not to disgrace himself by being sick.

Calder's jaw worked before he spoke. "Get them out of the water, boys, and lay them behind your saddles. I'll ride back and let the others know. We'll be moving out as soon as they're in the ground. Never mind lunch—we'll eat tonight."

Andy and Jonesy were laid to rest on a nearby bluff. Once the graves were dug, the ceremony was brief. Ely Stanton fashioned two crude crosses to serve as markers. Benteen Calder offered a few words. Mary laid a sad little bouquet of wildflowers at the foot of each cross, and Lorna took two of the precious rose cuttings she'd brought and planted them in the fresh earth.

Then it was time to move the herd.

The chuckwagon was already heading out. Lorna and Mary followed, driving their wagons. With his wet, shapeless hat jammed onto his head, Joe took his place behind the remuda, keeping the horses together and making sure none were left behind.

Silence hung like a haze of dust over the drive. The cattle trailed along, kept in line by the mounted cowboys. Seventy animals had been lost in the river, along with two fine young men.

But there was no point in mourning or counting the cost. There was nothing to do except keep moving.

As the sun dried his hat to the shape of his head, Joe struggled to clear his mind of the morning's awful images. But the guilt that gnawed at his insides wouldn't go away. His carelessness had triggered the disaster that left his two friends dead and cut deep into the value of Benteen Calder's herd.

And he hadn't said a word about it—not to anyone.

His mother had raised him to be honest. But would fessing up be honest or just plain stupid? What would the boss do to him if he confessed? Fire him and leave him alone on the prairie? Maybe take his earnings in payment toward the lost cattle? And what about the men? Surely they'd turn their backs on him, or do far worse, for what he'd caused to happen.

But how could anyone feel more contempt for him than he already felt for himself?

By the time the herd caught up with the chuckwagon, the sun had set. As the cattle bedded down, the savory aromas of beans, bacon, and fresh biscuits drifted on the air. The cowboys, who'd missed the noon meal, were ravenous. But the usual camaraderie around the fire was absent tonight. There were no tears and no mention of losses suffered, but gloom and grief hung over them all.

Joe had to force himself to swallow his beans and biscuits. By the time he'd finished the meal and returned his plate, his stomach was already churning. He fled to a thicket of bushes, a stone's throw from camp, where he doubled over and lost everything he'd eaten.

Moving to another spot, he hunkered into a ball of misery. His shoulders shook with silent sobs. Tears he could no longer hold back squeezed from his eyes and trickled down his cheeks. This morning he'd congratulated himself on becoming a man. But he'd never felt less like a man than he did right now.

"Hey, *amigo.*" The voice, coming from behind him, was Spanish Bill's. "What are you doing out here? Are you sick?"

Joe was too choked up to answer. He shook his head, but Bill wasn't convinced. Dropping to a crouch, he laid a hand on Joe's shoulder.

"It's all right," he said. "I know those two boys were your friends."

Joe shook his head, the words breaking loose and spilling out of him. "It's not just that. What happened today—it was all my fault. My hat—"

"I know about your hat. I saw it in the water. I couldn't reach it in time. But you don't hear me saying it was my fault, do you?"

"That's not the same." Joe wiped his eyes on his sleeve, ashamed of his tears. "I was the one who dropped it. I killed them—Jonesy and Andy and all those cows. I killed them, as sure as if I'd took a gun and shot them."

"No, *muchacho.*" Bill's big hand squeezed Joe's shoulder. "You didn't mean for it to happen. You were only trying to get out of the way. And the hat . . . It could've floated anywhere—down the river or to the bank. But it went the wrong way. It was a terrible thing to happen. But it was an accident. I know that. All the boys know that. Even the boss knows it."

"Even the boss?" Joe lifted his head and stared at the Mexican cowboy.

"*Sí,* even the boss. So, will you now come back to the camp with me?"

Joe hesitated, thinking how his tear-streaked face would make him appear to the men. "You go on," he said. "I'll come back in a bit."

Spanish Bill nodded and rose to his feet. "One more thing. When you're a cowboy, you learn that bad things happen on the trail. If they do, you don't judge and you don't look back. You just move on. That, my young friend, is what these men have done for you today. Don't forget."

As he walked away, Joe settled back to wait for the darkness to deepen. A waning moon rose above the distant hills. The melancholy cry of a coyote echoed across the prairie.

Joe rubbed his tearstained face with his sleeve. Spanish Bill had delivered a message of acceptance and forgiveness. But Joe would never forgive himself for the careless mistake that had set off a tragedy.

Going forward, he vowed, he would do everything in his power to make up for what he'd done. He would be the first man on the job, first to help, first in the rush to head off a stampede. That was how you became a cowboy. That was how you became a man.

CHAPTER TWO

Three weeks later

JOE WALKED ALONG THE RIVERBANK, PICKING UP FIREWOOD AND PILING it in his arms. Spring floods had ebbed on the Arkansas River. The receding water had left the banks littered with sticks and branches. It was Joe's job to gather them up and stow them in the calfskin sling, known as the cooney, that hung like a hammock below the frame of the chuckwagon. Extra wood was piled next to the campfire. Even with the herd at rest for a few days, there was always a need for fuel.

Joe was grateful for the easy work. The past three weeks on the trail had pushed men and animals to the edge of endurance. After the debacle at the Red River, the drive had left Texas and crossed into Indian Territory. At first, Joe had been nervous about the so-called savages, but the Comanches, Kiowas, and others who approached had appeared more ragged and hungry than warlike. For the price of a few beeves, which Benteen Calder had paid after some dickering, the herd was allowed to move on. Still, the threat of Indians stampeding the cattle and running some off for themselves had been a constant worry. No one had slept well at night.

But the worst was yet to come—the hundred-mile waterless cut-off to Dodge City. The boss had doubled the pace of the herd. But five days of blistering heat with little or no water had been torture for man and beast. Joe would never forget the sight of stumbling, thirst-blind cattle and horses, or the line of men and women sharing a single cup of murky water drained from the bottom of the barrel. He'd been hungry before; he'd been cold, tired, and in pain. But until then, he'd never known raging thirst and what it could do to a man's mind and body.

When the cattle had caught the scent of water in the Arkansas River, more than a mile off, it had taken every man, riding hard, to hold back a stampede and slow them down. Even then, when the cattle finally reached the riverbank, a few had literally drunk themselves to death.

Joe had heard men talk about seeing the elephant—a metaphor for the realities of death and hardship on the trail. Now he could claim he'd seen the elephant, too. He was lean and hard, his skin burnished by sun and wind. In the weeks that had passed since his sixteenth birthday, he felt as if he'd aged years.

Benteen Calder had settled his herd north of the river and declared a three-day rest while he took his wagon and his bride into Dodge City to buy more supplies and sell off three hundred steers to pay for the remainder of the trip.

Even at rest, there was plenty of work to be done—cattle to tend, horses to shoe, harnesses to mend, meals to cook, dishes and clothes to wash. If there was any talk of the men going into Dodge City for a good time, it was only that—just talk.

From the riverbank, Joe could see all the way to the railhead town. In his mind, the jumble of clapboard buildings, stockyards, and railroad cars shimmered like a distant mirage. To a farm boy who'd only heard the stories, it was a place of legend—gunfights in the streets, outlaws and lawmen, fancy restaurants and saloons with gambling, whiskey, and loose women.

According to his mother, Dodge City was the Sodom and Gomorrah of the West. But the memory of her words only sharpened Joe's curiosity. He didn't have the money to try so much as a sip of whiskey. But he'd jump at the chance to look around.

"Hey, Joe!" Zeke Taylor, one of the younger cowhands, reined in his pony as he passed. "Want to go into town with me?"

At first Joe couldn't believe what he'd heard. "Go into town? You're joshing me, Zeke."

"Nope. When the boss was here yesterday, sellin' off them steers, he asked for somebody to help load supplies in the wagon and keep an eye on it overnight. I volunteered, and he said to bring somebody else to help. So I'm bringin' you. Throw down that wood, man, and saddle yourself a horse. I'll wait, but not for long."

Barely able to believe his good luck, Joe dumped the wood onto the stack, caught one of the horses in his string, and saddled it. Zeke was waiting for him by the river. Side by side, they nudged their mounts to a trot and set out across the expanse of yellow-brown grass. Dust from the horses' hooves trailed behind them as they rode.

"Have you ever been to Dodge?" Joe asked.

"Yup." Zeke grinned. He was young, maybe nineteen, a talker who was known to be lazy. Joe liked him well enough. "I was there with a drive last summer," he said. "I got to know the place pretty well. I can show you a good time."

"I can go along and look," Joe said. "But I can't pay for anything. I don't have any money."

"I've got a little cash saved up," Zeke said. "Take my next night watch, and I'll treat you. Deal?"

As a lowly wrangler's helper, Joe had never been asked to take the night watch. But how hard could it be? "Deal," he said, accepting Zeke's handshake.

Joe was all eyes and ears as they rode into Dodge City. After weeks away from civilization, the noise and activity rocked his senses. From the nearby railroad yards, the hoot of train whistles, the hiss of steam, and the clickety-clack of iron wheels mingled with the bawl of cattle and the shouts of the drovers herding them up the chutes into the railway cars.

A haze of dust, raised by horses and wagons, hung over the unpaved streets. Cowboys sauntered along the boardwalks or stood in groups, smoking, watching the passersby, and catcalling any woman who caught their fancy. From the swinging doors of a saloon came the tinny music of an untuned piano and the sound of raucous laughter.

Joe nudged his companion. "Where are we supposed to meet the boss?"

Zeke grinned. "At the livery stable, where he left the wagon. But we don't have to be there till three o'clock, and it's barely lunchtime. We've got half the afternoon to enjoy ourselves. We can do anything we want to."

For the first time, Joe felt a prickle of unease. He'd wondered why Zeke had invited him to town instead of asking one of the older, more experienced men. Now the answer slid into place. A man like Shorty or Spanish would have kept Zeke in line. With a young greenhorn like Joe along, Zeke could be the one in charge. He really could do anything he wanted.

In his head, Joe could hear his mother's cautioning voice. He willed himself to ignore it. Here in Dodge City, adventure waited around every corner. As long as he was here, damn it, he might as well have a good time.

They dismounted, tethered their horses to a hitching rail, and stepped up onto the boardwalk. Joe had to remind himself not to stare at the people they passed—rawboned, weather-burned men whose bearing exuded danger; women dressed for seduction, walking in pairs or groups, smiling boldly, as if daring the world to judge them; cowboys like Zeke and Joe, gawking at the sights; settlers' wives in bonnets and plain dresses, keeping their husbands and children close.

They passed the hotel—probably where the boss and Lorna were staying. The smells wafting from the dining room made Joe's stomach rumble. "I could use some lunch," he said.

"If we spend money on food, we won't have enough for fun," Zeke said. "Come on. I know just the place to start."

Two doors past the hotel, Zeke stopped outside the swinging doors of a saloon.

"We're going in here?" As soon as Joe spoke, he realized he'd asked a stupid question.

"Hell, yes, we're going in here." Zeke leaned closer and lowered his voice. "Now, don't you go crawling through the door like a scared puppy. You walk in like you own the place. And if anybody asks, you're eighteen."

Joe followed his swaggering companion through the door. The place appeared as dark as a cave to Joe, after he'd spent hours in the glaring sunlight. Murmured voices and the slap and shuffle of cards blended with the odor of stale tobacco. As his eyes adjusted to the dimness, Joe could see a long bar on one wall. The shelves behind it were stocked with an array of glass liquor bottles.

Four men played cards at one of the round tables in the room. Joe glimpsed a whiskey bottle and a stack of bills before he tore his eyes away. The men didn't look like the sort who'd take kindly to his watching their game.

The other tables were empty. A piano sat in a shadowed corner. A stairway at the back led to a second-floor balcony.

"You should see this place at night," Zeke muttered in his ear. "Talk about a hot time . . ." His voice trailed off as he moved toward the bar, strutting like a rooster with his shoulders unnaturally squared.

The bartender, a stocky, balding man, was polishing glassware. "What'll it be, gents?" he asked.

"Two whiskeys. One for me and one for my friend here." Zeke fished a handful of coins out of his pocket and counted them in the palm of his hand before laying his money on the bar. "Whatever kind is cheapest," he said.

"I figured as much." The bartender took a plain bottle off the shelf and poured three fingers into each of two glasses.

Zeke slid one glass over to Joe. "Drink up," he said.

Joe eyed the whiskey in his glass. His mother had warned him about the evils of strong drink. And the yellow liquid in the murky glass looked about as appetizing as horse piss. But he was a cowboy and a man, and he knew what was expected of him. Bracing himself, he lifted the glass and took a swallow.

The cheap whiskey burned its way down his throat. The taste was sharp and bittersweet, but strangely compelling. He took another swallow, feeling the subtle heat spread through his body. By the time he'd emptied the glass, he felt strangely light-headed and mellow.

"More?" Zeke looked at him and grinned.

Joe nodded. Zeke laid a few more coins on the bar, and the bartender poured them another three fingers of whiskey. The second glass went down easier. Joe belched, then laughed at himself. His saintly mother, bless her, clearly didn't know the meaning of a good time.

Zeke leaned over the bar and spoke to the bartender in a low voice. "Maybe you can tell us where to find some, uh, good-lookin' ladies."

The bartender sighed. From out of a box on the shelf behind him, he took two round copper medallions. "These will get you a dollar off at Madame Lulu's, across from the railroad station. The house has a red door. You can't miss it."

The medallion warmed in Joe's palm as they walked out of the saloon. He knew what Zeke had in mind, but things were happening too fast. He didn't feel ready. Maybe he should just give his medallion to Zeke and wait for him outside while his friend got his money's worth.

But the cheap whiskey was singing in his blood. He remembered lying next to the Calder wagon in camp, hearing the creak of the boards and the unmistakable sounds coming from under the canvas. He recalled the images in his mind and the strange yearnings that had tugged at him until he'd had to block his ears.

If he let this chance pass by, he'd be kicking himself all the way to Ogallala. And if Zeke let it slip that Joe Dollarhide had gotten cold feet, Joe could just imagine the snickers from the men.

So why was he still dragging his feet?

Following the bartender's directions, they walked down the street to the railroad depot at the end. The Atchison, Topeka and Santa Fe had just let off passengers and was backing into the yard to take on water and hook up a string of cattle cars before continuing on the long run to Pueblo. The few arriving passengers were already leaving the platform. Farther back, empty cattle cars waited on sidings. A small station house, set back from the tracks, stood farther down the platform.

On the nearest corner, separated from the platform by a dusty street, stood a tall house with a second-floor balcony. Covered steps led up to a plain door with a brass knocker. The paint on the door was peeling, but the crimson color was unmistakable.

Grinning, Zeke looked the house up and down. "This has got to be the place," he said, walking Joe to the steps. "Are you ready for a good time?"

Joe didn't reply. He had turned away, distracted by a ruckus on the platform.

Three big, dirty-looking cowboys were closing on a petite young woman. Surrounded, with no one there to help her, she was doing her best to fight them off. Her only weapon was the carpetbag she carried. She swung it like a club, landing harmless blows that only made the cowboys laugh.

At first they'd appeared to be teasing her. But then, with the platform left empty, their mood changed. The biggest man grabbed her arm, twisting it, ripping the sleeve and forcing her to drop the carpetbag. Joe knew what was about to happen, and he knew he had to stop it.

Tossing away the medallion, he plunged into the street. His boots left a trail of dust as he raced for the platform. He'd hoped that Zeke would follow him to help, but a swift backward glance told Joe otherwise. Zeke was already knocking on the red door.

"Come on, honey. Time for some real fun." The man began to drag the girl, kicking and struggling, across the platform, back toward the line of empty cars. The other men followed, closing in behind.

Alone and unarmed, Joe sprang onto the platform and kept running. He didn't have a chance against three big men, but he could at least distract them long enough for the girl to get away.

"Leave her alone!" he shouted, trying to get their attention. The cowboys gave him a glance, then returned their attention to the girl. Moving fast, Joe crashed into the nearest man and started swinging. As the first blow landed, he glimpsed a pair of startled violet eyes. Then the cowboys began to fight back. "Run!" he gasped as a heavy fist crunched into his jaw. "Get away from here!"

But the girl didn't run. She grabbed her carpetbag and jumped back into the fray, swinging it like a club with both hands. Even when one of the men twisted it away from her and tossed it aside, she kept up the fight, punching their bellies and kicking their shins. The men, who reeked of whiskey, were laughing, enjoying the sport for now. But they were bound to run out of patience. When that happened, Joe knew that he'd be powerless to stop them.

Damn it, why didn't she break loose and run? The bastards would beat him half to death if she got away, but at least he'd go down knowing she was safe.

Joe aimed a punch at the biggest cowboy, who'd grabbed the girl's arm again. The blow landed hard enough to bloody the man's nose. With a grunt of pain and rage, he let her go and turned on Joe. His huge fist slammed into Joe's face. Joe's knees folded. *"Run!"* He mouthed the word as everything went black.

The world swam back into focus. Joe blinked. Only one of his eyes would open. The other eye was swollen shut. His face felt as if flesh and bone had been tenderized like a slab of beef.

As his mind cleared, he became aware of his surroundings. His body was lying on the hard boards of the platform, but his head, partly elevated, rested on something lumpy.

He groaned, remembering it all now—the girl, the cowboys, and the punch that had blown out his lights. Pushing with his arms, he struggled to sit.

"Don't get up yet. You need to take it easy for a bit." Kneeling beside him, the girl sponged his face with a cool, damp cloth. "Hold still. You've got a little cut on your chin. It's bleeding, but I think I can stop it." Joe sank back onto what he realized was her carpetbag, which she'd used to pillow his head.

He'd sensed that she was pretty; but only now, as she pressed the small cut with the bandanna, was he able to study her. She was young—close to his own age—with delicate features and stunning eyes, fringed by long, golden lashes. They were the color of the little spring violets he remembered from back home in the Texas hills.

Her gingham dress appeared clean and well-made, but one sleeve was torn at the shoulder. A streak of dirt smudged her cheek, and the combs had come loose from her hair, freeing her light brown curls to fall around her face. Her straw bonnet, which must have fallen off earlier, sat askew on her head.

The last thing he remembered was telling her to run.

"Are you all right?" he demanded. "Did those bastards hurt you?"

"I'm right as rain." Her voice had a childlike quality, small but throaty, like the purr of a kitten—and she'd been about as much use as a kitten in fighting off those drunken cowboys. Even the thought of what they might have done made him want to shake some sense into her.

"If you're all right, you're damned lucky," he snapped. "You could've been raped, maybe even murdered. I told you to get away. Why didn't you?"

Her eyes narrowed. "I did it for the sake of my own conscience. If those awful men had killed you, I'd have felt guilty for the rest of my life."

"Well, I can't say you were much help. If you'd gotten away, I could've looked out for myself instead of worrying about you."

She gave a dismissive little huff. "As you see, I'm fine. And I did my best to help you. If you're waiting for an apology, you're not going to get one."

Joe sighed. Clearly, this was one argument he wasn't going to win. "Well, at least, those drunks are gone, and you're in one piece. But I can't believe you fought them off by yourself. If you've got a story, I'm ready to hear it."

She settled back onto her heels, laying the wet cloth—his own red bandanna—on the platform to dry in the sun. "One of us must have a guardian angel," she said, thrusting out her hand. "I'm Sarah Foxworth, by the way. Pleased to meet you."

Joe introduced himself and accepted the shake from her small, strong hand. What was he supposed to make of this bold-spoken girl who, when she should have saved herself, had fought like a wildcat at his side? He was slightly dizzy and more than a little befuddled. Just one thing was for sure—he wanted to know more about her.

"All right, Sarah Foxworth," he said. "Tell me what happened after I went down. You said something about a guardian angel."

"Yes. Do you believe in guardian angels?"

Joe shrugged. "My mother does. But if I've got one, he pretty much leaves me to fend for myself. What did this angel look like? Did he have wings?"

She laughed, showing small, perfect white teeth. "No, silly. He had a mustache and a badge and a gun. He came out of the station house, and when those cowboys saw him, they took off like they'd just seen the devil. He stayed around long enough to make sure they were gone, and that you were coming around. I had to explain that you'd tried to help me. Otherwise, you could be waking up in jail."

"You say he had a badge. Did he tell you his name?"

"No. But when the men saw him, one of them yelled, 'It's Wyatt Earp!' Does that mean anything to you?"

Wyatt Earp. Joe nodded, amazed that the girl hadn't recognized the name or the face of the man who was already a legend. "What did he say to you?"

"Not much. Only that Dodge wasn't safe for a young woman alone. He offered to walk me to the hotel, but I turned him down. How could I just go off and leave you lying here?" She straightened her bonnet on her head. "Anyway, I won't be needing a hotel. My train will be leaving again in about an hour. I'd planned to buy some lunch in town, but maybe I should just go inside the station house and wait."

Joe reached for his hat, which had fallen nearby, and tied on his bandanna, which was still damp. He still felt as if he'd been run over by a freight wagon, but now that he'd met her, he wasn't ready to let Miss Sarah Foxworth walk out of his life.

"There's a restaurant in the hotel. If you don't mind the way I look, I'd be happy to walk there with you."

"Thank you for your offer." Her tone was cool as she rose and brushed the dust off her skirt. "But didn't you have other plans?"

"Other plans?" Joe asked, puzzled.

"As I got off the train, before those hooligans showed up, I saw you and your friend walking up to that house across the street. I know what kind of place that is. If you want to go back there, I certainly won't stand in your way."

Joe's cheeks flamed. He stared down at his boots, unable to face the honesty in those stunning violet eyes.

"You don't have to explain," she said. "Just go. I'll be fine."

Joe forced himself to meet her gaze as the words came stumbling out. "That's not how it was. It was my friend who wanted to go there. I was hoping for a reason not to go with him. I swear, I've never been inside one of those places in my life, and I don't want to go now."

It was a lame explanation, especially since Zeke hadn't exactly dragged him up to that house. But it was the best Joe could do. He waited in silence, desperate for her to believe him.

Her smile was like the sun coming out. "Well, then, I accept your invitation. I have plenty of time, and I could use some lunch. Let's go."

Joe picked up her carpetbag, which was surprisingly heavy, and fell into step beside her. His heart soared, then sank like a stone. What if she was expecting him to buy her lunch? What would she think of him when he told her that he didn't have any money?

Should he offer her his arm? But no, he decided, that would be too forward. He would just walk beside her, carrying her carpetbag and enjoying the company of a pretty girl who, once she learned that he couldn't afford to treat her, would probably never speak to him again.

As they walked, he stole glances at her—her profile with its pert nose and stubborn chin, the golden highlights in her sunlit hair, and the way her womanly little breasts shaped the front of her dress. She was beautiful—even more beautiful, in her own way, than Lorna Calder.

"Do you live here in Dodge?" she asked, making conversation.

"No, I'm just passing through with a cattle drive," he said. "We're taking the boss's herd all the way to Montana."

"Goodness, that sounds like an adventure," she said. "If I'd been born a boy, I'd sign up and go with you."

"Driving cattle is hard, dirty work. And I'm really glad you weren't born a boy. I like you fine just the way you are." Maybe he shouldn't have said that. Except for his sisters, he didn't know much about talking to girls. Especially classy girls like Sarah.

She walked with him in silence for a moment. "I never thanked you for rushing to my rescue," she said. "You risked your life for me. I'd like a chance to repay you. Would you let me buy our lunch?"

Relief was like a cloud lifting. But he didn't want to appear too eager. "Well, I don't know about that, you being a lady and all," Joe said. "But if you're sure, and if it won't be a hardship . . ."

"Oh, please let me," she said. "When my uncle sent me money for the trip, he gave me extra for meals. I can certainly afford to treat you."

"Then thank you." Joe's step lightened. This had to be his lucky day. But he made a silent vow that when he got paid at the end of the drive, he would set money aside so that he would never be embarrassed by empty pockets again.

The waiter seated them in an out-of-the-way corner of the restaurant. Joe suspected it was because of the way he looked, with his trail-worn clothes, battered face, and swollen eye. But that didn't matter because he was with the prettiest girl in the room, maybe the prettiest girl in Dodge City.

He ordered the cheapest item on the menu—a plain cheese sandwich. Someday, he promised himself, when he had money, he would put on a fine suit, find Miss Sarah Foxworth, wherever she might be, and buy her dinner in an elegant restaurant.

"You mentioned that you had to be back on the train," he said. "Where did you come from, and where are you headed?"

"That's a long story." She gave her chicken soup a moment to cool. "I was raised by my grandmother in a little town this side of

Kansas City. She passed away last month. Now I'm going to live with her brother. He's a doctor in Ogallala, Nebraska."

"But how are you getting to Ogallala? There's no railroad going north from here, and the country between is pretty rough. I know because that's the way we'll be driving the herd."

"I'm aware of that," she said. "I'll be taking the train from here to Pueblo and then another train to Denver. My great-uncle will be meeting me there. We'll spend a couple of days in the city, then catch a different train back to Ogallala."

"I've never even ridden on a train," Joe said. "What's it like?"

"It's about like the way you described driving cattle—noisy and dirty and uncomfortable—especially if you're riding third class. I'll be glad when the trip's over."

"But hey, you'll likely be in Ogallala when we get there with the herd. If the boss will let me go to town, maybe I could stop by and see you."

As soon as the words were out of his mouth, Joe feared he'd said too much. He was nothing but a poor, barely educated cowboy without a cent to his name. Why should a classy girl whose uncle was a doctor want to see any more of him?

Her smile deepened the dimples in her cheeks. "When you come—and I hope you will—just ask someone for directions to Dr. Blake's house."

"If you see cattle with a triple C brand, and a boss named Benteen Calder, you'll know we've arrived."

Joe was still walking on air when he escorted Sarah back to the train station. He was already counting the weeks until the cattle drive reached Ogallala, a railhead town that would be the last chance to rest the herd and the men and to stock up on supplies before the long push to Montana.

Somehow he would find a way to see Sarah again. This time, even if he had to beg Benteen Calder for an advance or take extra shifts, he would make sure he had enough money to take her out.

Her train was waiting next to the platform. Joe helped her mount the steps and passed her the carpetbag. He felt the weight of it as he lifted it into her hands. "What have you got inside here, anyway, anvils?" he joked.

"No. Just a few things to wear and my favorite books."

So she was a reader. Joe made a mental note of that. He had never read anything but a few primers in school and his mother's Bible. If he wanted to impress this girl, it wouldn't hurt to educate himself some before he saw her again. Maybe Lorna Calder would have a book or two he could borrow.

"Thanks again for lunch," he said. "Have a safe trip—but be careful. Don't let yourself get caught alone, like you did here. Stay where there are plenty of people. Promise me you'll do that."

"I promise. And I'll see you in Ogallala." Her hand brushed his cheek. Then she was gone.

As the train pulled out, she waved at him through the dusty window. Fingering the cut on his chin, which had stopped bleeding but still stung, he watched the train disappear from sight. The smile she gave him would brighten his days and warm his nights until he saw her again.

But right now it was time to find Zeke, meet Benteen Calder at the livery stable, and get back to work.

CHAPTER THREE

WHEN SARAH COULD NO LONGER SEE THE LONE FIGURE ON THE platform, she settled back in her seat, took a book from her carpet-bag, and opened it to the page she'd marked with a gray feather she'd found on the porch of her grandmother's house.

Written for students, the book told the story of Elizabeth Blackwell, America's first licensed woman doctor. Sarah had saved her meager allowance to buy a copy of the book, which she was now reading for the third time.

For years she'd dreamed of becoming a doctor. With little money, an ordinary education, and no helpful connections, that dream had seemed far out of reach. But now that she was going to live with her great-uncle, Dr. Harlan Blake, a glimmer of hope had surfaced. Maybe she could learn by watching him. Maybe, in a few years, he might even help her get into medical school.

She read until her mind began to wander. Closing the book, she gazed out the window at the bleak, yellow prairie, which stretched into the distance as far as her eyes could see. What would it be like for Joe Dollarhide, driving cattle across that country, with little water and no shelter from storms?

She remembered how the young cowboy had charged to her rescue without a thought for his own safety. His reckless act of bravery had touched her in surprising ways, as had the sight of his swollen eye and battered face. The rough-edged young trail hand had literally put his life on the line to save her. His manners had been awkward. But afterward, as he'd walked her to town and back, he'd done his best to treat her the way a gentleman would treat a lady.

Would she see him again in Ogallala? She wanted to, Sarah conceded. Her dream of becoming a doctor didn't include romance. But she liked the boy. She liked the sound of his voice, his clean-chiseled features, and his lean-muscled frame that was still growing into manhood. And she'd liked the protected way he'd made her feel, as if she were something rare and precious. She wouldn't mind feeling that way again.

As the prairie rolled endlessly past the window of the train, she dozed lightly, read, chatted with the middle-aged couple sitting across from her, and tried her best to stretch her cramped legs. As darkness fell, she tried resting her head against the jiggling, rattling window, but between the discomfort and the clatter of iron wheels on the track, sleep was impossible. She could only hope that there was a room with a cushiony bed waiting for her in Denver—as well as a good meal and maybe even a night at the theater, something her uncle had suggested. Sarah had loved her grandmother and wept when the kind old woman passed away. But now she couldn't help feeling buoyed at the prospect of an exciting new life.

In Pueblo the next day, she had to wait several hours for the train to Denver. She'd settled for a breakfast of lukewarm coffee, stale biscuits, and canned sardines in a café next to the station. Her experience in Dodge, along with Joe's warning, had taught her a lesson: Stay with other passengers, and don't go off alone, not even for food. She'd also found a ladies' room where she freshened her face and pinned up her hair. She wanted to look presentable when she met her great-uncle in Denver. He had her photograph, and she had his—a studio portrait of a distinguished, silver-haired gentleman in a gray suit. They should have no trouble recognizing each other.

On this short final leg of her journey, there was more to see—ranches and farms, small towns and stockyards, wagons, coaches, and buggies on the roads. Sarah's pulse quickened as the train sped through the outskirts of the city and headed into the bust-ling heart of Denver.

Because the Atchison, Topeka and Santa Fe ran through her hometown, she'd been able to board the train there. Before that, Sarah had never even been away from home, not even as far as Kansas City. Denver, with its crowded streets and sidewalks, seem-ingly endless blocks of dwellings and businesses, and its constant barrage of sights, smells, and sounds, was a thrilling new world, where everything seemed to be fashioned on a grand scale.

The most imposing structure of all was the railroad station. On approach, it appeared vast enough to cover a large field, its walls rising skyward and topped by an ornate cupola on the roof. In-side, the cavernous space dwarfed the trains and the people who swarmed the platforms like bees in a hive.

Clutching her carpetbag, she stepped down from the car. She'd hoped that her uncle Harlan would be waiting to meet her. But as her eyes scanned the crowded platform, there was no sign of the gentleman in the photo she carried. Maybe he was still looking for her.

Finding an open spot where she could be seen from more than one direction, Sarah rested the heavy carpetbag against her legs and stood still. Surely, at any moment, Dr. Harlan Blake would come rushing along, apologizing for making her wait.

Minutes passed, then half an hour. Between the hot sun on the roof and the steam and fire from the trains, the air inside the depot was stifling. Sarah could feel the sweaty dampness under her clothes. Her feet felt like swollen lumps in her boots. Maybe Uncle Harlan was waiting for her somewhere else. Wherever he was, it wasn't here. She needed to move.

Lugging the heavy carpetbag, she wove her way through the crowd. Nobody paid her any heed as she sank onto a bench, too tired to go another step.

What could have happened to him?

What would she do if he didn't show up?

Uncle Harlan had mailed her the train ticket to Denver along with ten dollars for food. But he'd planned to buy their tickets to

Ogallala when they left here together. If she couldn't find him, the only safe option would be to get to Ogallala on her own.

In her head, she counted the money remaining in the small purse she kept pinned inside the pocket of her dress. Between the lunch she'd shared with Joe Dollarhide in Dodge and the breakfast she'd bought in Pueblo, she'd spent a little more than three dollars. Would the money she had left be enough for the ticket she needed?

What would she do if it wasn't?

The railroad line that would take her from Denver to Ogallala was the Chicago and North Western. Lugging the heavy carpetbag, she trudged along the line of ticket windows, looking for the right one while she continued to watch for her uncle. She'd been tempted to wait for him a little longer. But if he didn't come, and waiting caused her to miss the next train, she could be stranded here all night.

The people she passed paid her little attention. If Sarah had been less tired and less worried, she might have enjoyed the colorful parade around her—wealthy women in stylish summer traveling ensembles, cowboys fresh off the cattle drive, businessmen wearing suits and hats and carrying leather briefcases, ragged boys with shoeshine boxes, nannies with baby carriages, and Chinese porters laden with baggage. The air rang with the sounds of hissing steam and train whistles, the shouts of conductors urging all passengers to board, and the newsboys' cries of "Denver Po-AY-ost" as they hawked their papers up and down the platform.

Sarah passed a vendor with a tray of sandwiches. By now her stomach was growling with hunger, but she knew better than to spend another cent before knowing how much her ticket would cost.

At last she spotted the ticket window for the Chicago and North Western. Clutching the carpetbag in her aching arms, she took her place at the end of the line. There were five people ahead of her. By the time she reached the window, more passengers had queued up behind her. Sarah took her small purse out of her pocket and opened it. Inside, she had six dollars and fifty-two cents. "One third-class ticket to Ogallala," she told the ticket agent.

The agent, a thin man with spectacles, tore the ticket off a roll and prepared to stamp it. "That'll be seven dollars even."

Sarah's heart dropped. She dumped her money on the counter and pushed it toward the man. Maybe he'd take pity on her. "Please, I'm here alone, and this is all I have."

He counted the money and shoved it back at her. His eyes were cold behind the thick lenses. "Sorry. If you want a ticket, you'll need another forty-eight cents. Next?"

"Wait!" Desperate now, Sarah dropped her carpetbag on the platform, opened it, and took out one of her favorite books— Jane Austen's *Pride and Prejudice*. Turning back to the people in line behind her, some of whom were getting impatient, she held up the book. "Fifty cents. Wouldn't somebody like it? It's a wonderful story."

"I'll buy it." A well-dressed woman opened her handbag and took out some change. "I could use something to read on the train. Here you are, my dear."

Sarah took the money and handed the woman the book. "I hope you'll love this book as much as I have," she said.

Shaking with relief, she turned back to the window and bought her ticket—just in time to make a dash for the train.

The sun was going down when the train pulled into Ogallala, a cattle and railroad town much like Dodge—smaller, perhaps, but by reputation, every bit as wild. Tired and hungry, Sarah stepped down from the third-class coach and made a beeline for the station house. Maybe someone there could help her find out what had happened to Uncle Harlan. At least, if he'd gone to Denver, there should be a record of his buying a ticket.

The station agent, a white-haired man with a kind face, had just lit a lamp on the counter. He gave her a concerned look. "Can I help you with something, miss?" he asked.

"I'm looking for my great-uncle, Dr. Harlan Blake," Sarah said. "Do you happen to know him?"

"Sure, I do. Everybody in town knows the doc."

"Then maybe you can tell me this. Did he take the train to Denver anytime in the past few days?"

The man shook his head. "Can't say as he did. And I would know. I'm always here when the train stops to pick up passengers, going either way."

"Did he buy a ticket?"

"No record of it. Come to think of it, I haven't seen the doc since last week."

Worry tightened a knot in the pit of Sarah's stomach. "Could you show me the way to his house?"

"It's not far. But it'll be dark soon, and you shouldn't go alone. It isn't safe. I'll have my grandson take you. Ezra!" he called, turning toward a partition behind the counter. "Put down that blasted book and come out here. I need you."

The boy who stepped into sight appeared to be about twelve, thin, with freckles and an unruly thatch of red hair. "What do you need, Grandpa?" he asked.

"Make yourself useful," the older man said. "This young lady—sorry, miss, I didn't catch your name."

"It's Sarah. Sarah Foxworth."

"Well, Ezra, Miss Sarah, here, needs a trustworthy young man to carry a lantern and walk her to Doc Blake's house. Don't come back until she's safely inside. Hear?"

"Yes, sir. I'll get the lantern." The boy ducked behind the partition and returned with a glowing lantern, which he may have been using to read. "I can carry your bag," he said to Sarah. "I'm really strong."

The old man caught her eye. A slight shake of his head signaled her that she wasn't to take the boy up on his offer.

"Just carry the lantern. I'll be fine, thank you." Sarah followed the boy out the door and into the twilight. The train was gone, the platform empty. A wide street paralleled the tracks on the far side.

"That's Railroad Street," Ezra said. "The north side, where we are now, is pretty quiet. But things get wild on the south side, where all the saloons and dance halls are, especially when the cattle drives are coming through. You shouldn't go down there alone, but we'll be all right here."

Sarah walked beside him, clutching her bag as she followed the circle of light from the lantern. "Your grandfather mentioned a book," she said. "What are you reading?"

"*Tom Sawyer*. It's about this boy who lives by a river and has all kinds of adventures. I can't put it down—not even when Grandpa scolds me for reading instead of working."

"I read it last winter," Sarah said. "It's a wonderful book, so exciting. I'll bet reading it will make you want to go out and have adventures, too."

The boy sighed. "I'd give anything to have adventures like Tom Sawyer. But I had rheumatic fever when I was nine. The doctor says it made my heart weak, so I need to be careful. I can't let myself get too tired. But it doesn't stop me from reading."

Sarah felt a stab of empathy for the boy. "I love to read, too. Maybe we could share some books and talk about them. Would you like that?"

"You bet. I've got friends, but they mostly just like to play. None of them like to read. Does that mean you're going to stay here?"

"That's my plan." Sarah followed the bobbing light of his lantern down a narrow street lined with small, dimly lit homes. Behind a fence, a dog barked. Ezra shushed it with a word. Evidently the boy knew the neighborhood well.

The house at the far end of the street was dark. The sight of it triggered a spasm of uncertain dread. Sarah took a deep breath and willed herself to stay calm. "Is that my uncle's house?" Sarah asked the boy. "It's so dark."

"Uh-huh. Maybe he's asleep. Or maybe he isn't home."

"You must know him pretty well." Sarah slowed her steps, stalling for time to work up her courage. "What can you tell me about him?"

Ezra shrugged. "He's nice. And he's a good doctor. But the last couple of times I saw him, he seemed really sad."

"Sad? Do you know why?"

"Not for sure. But it might be because his wife went away. She was a lot younger, and she was pretty. Maybe she thought he was rich and found out he wasn't. I don't know much about things like that."

They had reached the front gate to the dark house. Using her free hand, Sarah lifted the latch. "Stay with me, Ezra," she said.

"Do you think he's dead?" The boy raised the lantern to illuminate the sidewalk and porch.

"I don't know. We'll just have to find out."

The door was unlocked. Lowering the heavy carpetbag to the floor, Sarah took the lantern from Ezra and raised it high. The front room ran the width of the house, with the kitchen at one end, a table in the middle, and a sitting area with chairs and a settee in front of a stone fireplace. The air was warm and stale, as if the house had been closed for days. Unopened mail and unread newspapers were scattered on the rug, and dirty dishes were piled in the sink. But so far, there was no sign of Harlan Blake.

There were three doors along the back wall, all of them closed. "The middle one is his office," Ezra said. "The one on the left is his surgery. The one on the right is his bedroom."

"Let's try the bedroom." Pulse slamming, Sarah walked toward the door on the right and opened it.

The air inside reeked of urine, whiskey, and unwashed bedding. A trapped fly buzzed in the darkness. As Sarah stepped across the threshold, her foot stubbed an empty bottle. It rolled away, clattering against a leg of the bed.

Raising the lantern higher, Sarah saw the fully clothed figure of a man sprawled facedown across the unmade bed. He was tall and sparely built, dressed in a black vest, rumpled white shirt, and gray woolen trousers. She recognized the clothes and the silver hair from the photograph. There could be little doubt. She had finally found her great-uncle, Dr. Harlan Blake.

Handing the lantern to Ezra, she bent over the man. The smell of whiskey was strong enough to make her recoil. His skin was warm to the touch. A barely audible snore escaped his lips.

Behind her, Ezra held the lantern high. "Is he dead?" the boy asked.

Sarah's sigh blended relief and despair. "No, he's not dead. Just dead-drunk."

The Kansas prairie shimmered in the heat of the torrid July sun. The parched grass, which covered the land as far as the eye could see, crumbled under the hooves of two thousand cattle. Churned into dust and stirred by the furnace-like blast of the wind, it billowed in a vast yellow cloud behind the herd.

Moving cattle was not what Joe had imagined. Because beef cattle were priced and sold by the pound, the aim was to get the animals to where they were going with as little weight loss as possible. Running them, or allowing them to stampede, burned precious pounds off their bodies, and every pound was money lost. So cattle on the trail were taken at an ambling pace, moving at a stroll, even allowed to graze along the way. Herding them was mostly slow, boring work. The dust and heat made it even worse.

Joe's hat brim was pulled low against the burning sun. He wore his bandanna over the lower half of his face to keep from breathing the dust into his lungs. But there was little he could do about his stinging, watering eyes or his thirst-parched throat.

Three days ago, Benteen Calder had promoted him from wrangler's helper to full-fledged cowhand. Joe was a real cowboy at last. But so far, he'd spent his days riding drag behind the herd with another man, picking up stragglers, and eating dust all the way. Riding drag was essential, but it was the job that nobody wanted. It could even be doled out as punishment.

The heat-seared days were their own kind of hell. But the nights were even worse, with dry lightning flashing across the sky, frightening men as well as animals. With stampedes a constant threat, no one slept well at night.

Just one thing kept Joe's spirits buoyed. Days from now the drive would be coming up on Ogallala, Nebraska. When they arrived, the first thing he meant to do was find Sarah.

He knew better than to leave things to chance. That morning, as he helped hitch the Calder wagon, he'd confessed his hopes to Lorna. Delighted to aid the cause of young love, the boss's wife had agreed to work on her husband and make sure Joe was sent into town alone—perhaps with a small advance on his pay.

The next night, he had the watch, along with Wooly Willis and Spanish Bill. By now, Joe knew what to do. It was the cowboy's job to circle the herd, riding at an easy pace, making sure the cattle were bedded down and safe from any disturbance. Singing to the animals, which helped to keep them calm, was part of the job. Some of the men had fine voices and knew some great trail songs. Joe could barely carry a tune, and the only songs he knew by heart were the hymns his mother had sung as she went about her daily work. But he sang them as best he could, even though his serenades to the cattle drew some good-natured ribbing from the other cowboys.

On clear, calm nights, Joe didn't mind the watch. It was a peaceful time, with the cattle bedded down and the stars shining overhead—a time when he could be alone with his own thoughts, most of them about Sarah.

But tonight was different. Thick clouds, blown by a bracing north wind, poured across the sky. Sheet lightning danced and flickered, painting the landscape with eerie blue-white light. Thunder echoed like the sound of distant cannon fire.

Above the farthest horizon, a solid mass of clouds, blacker than sin, swirled and grew. Lightning bolts cracked like whips as the storm swept closer.

The cattle were nervous, still lying down, but snorting and testing the air. An icy sense of dread crept over Joe, but he continued to ride and sing.

"Rock of Ages, cleft for me, let me hide myself in Thee . . ." He thought of his mother and how she'd promised to pray for him every night. He could only hope she was praying for him now.

The darkness seemed to thicken around him, tingling with a strange, electric energy. He could hear shouting voices, Benteen Calder's among them, and he realized that more men had ridden out to help with the herd. Joe glimpsed other riders as he kept to his counterclockwise path, with the cattle on his left, but in the darkness that swirled around him, he could no longer be certain where he was going. From somewhere in the middle of the herd, he could hear Spanish Bill singing in his native language, his fine tenor voice rising above the wind.

"Si a tu ventana llega una paloma, trátala con cariño . . ."

The cattle were lurching to their feet now, first one, then two or three more, until the whole herd was up, shifting and bawling. Lightning crackled overhead in the sky, but the air closer to the ground was eerily still. Turning in the saddle, Joe saw a sight that made his blood run cold. A glowing thread of light danced along the tops of the cattle's horns—every single one of them, four thousand horns, glittering in the dark. Joe had never seen anything like it. He didn't know what it was or what it meant. He only knew it was the most terrifying thing he'd ever seen.

Spanish was still singing when a huge, blue ball of lightning ripped out of the sky and struck the ground with an earthshaking boom. As the sky split open, spilling torrents of rain, the cattle were off like a shot, thundering across the prairie in a wave of sheer, blind panic.

Wheeling his horse, Joe bolted after the stampede. He'd been told what to do in case something like this happened—catch up with the leaders and force them to turn aside. The herd would follow, milling in an ever-tightening circle until they had to stop.

With a deafening boom, a lightning bolt struck the ground less than twenty yards away. As his horse reared and bucked, Joe clung to the saddle. The cattle were all around him now. If he let the horse throw him, he'd be trampled to death.

With a strength fueled by desperation, he sawed at the reins and managed to get the horse under control. But in the seconds that passed, the stampede had left him behind. Spurring the horse, he raced to catch up. He had no chance of stopping the cattle, but at least he could try to be where he was needed.

Rain and darkness swallowed him. Guided only by the sound of the bawling herd, he took the horse at a gallop, flying blind over the trampled ground.

A lightning flash revealed a jagged wash, gouged out of the

earth by spring floods. Joe had been riding alongside it, on a parallel course, but the horse had veered too close to the rim. Reflexes slamming, he jerked the reins sharply to the left, but it was too late. The rain-soaked edge crumbled under the pounding hooves. Horse and rider went over together, screaming through wet, black space to land, with a shuddering crash, on the steep, muddy slope below.

The last thing Joe remembered before the world caved in and disappeared was the sound of rushing water.

Joe opened his eyes. A bloodred dawn was just visible above the dark, tight space he was in. His head throbbed, and every breath shot agony through his body. But at least, the pain told him he was alive.

Clenching his teeth, he struggled to free himself from whatever was holding him prisoner. Only after several tries that hurt like hell and got him nowhere did he realize his predicament. He was lying facedown, wedged partway under the trunk of a massive dead tree that must've been carried here by a flood. The lifeless body of the horse lay on its side against the tree, almost on top of him. He had just enough room to breathe. Otherwise he could barely move.

As his mind cleared, he remembered the stampede and the storm. He remembered racing to catch the herd and the moment the horse had broken through the edge of the wash and carried him over. He must have been thrown past the horse, then rolled or slid under the tree, which had caught the animal's weight before it could crush him. Now he was walled into a space as tight as a coffin, with the horse's eight-hundred-pound body as a lid.

This would be a hellish way to die, Joe thought. But he wouldn't dwell on that. The men would be out searching after last night's storm. They would see the horse and find him. Everything would be all right.

He could hear voices already, mingled with the sounds of horses and cattle. The boys must be rounding up the scattered herd. They'd be looking for him, too.

"Help!" He tried to shout, but his voice was weak, and the effort

stabbed pain into what felt like broken ribs. He would wait until he knew the men could hear him before he tried again.

A short time later, from farther down the rim of the wash, he heard voices, coming closer. Joe's pulse surged with hope as he recognized them. Jesse Trumbo and Benteen Calder were probably looking for him, searching along the wash. Any minute now, they would spot the horse and find him.

As they rode closer, taking their mounts at a walk, Joe could hear their conversation.

"Never seen anything like that damned storm," Jesse was saying. "Poor Spanish never saw that lightning bolt coming. Hell to see a man die that way."

Spanish Bill was dead? Struck by lightning? Joe thought of his friend, so wise and so fearless. He wouldn't believe the man was gone. Not until he could see the proof of it.

"Well, at least Wooly's broken leg will mend," Benteen Calder said. "Though he won't be much use till he can ride. It's young Dollarhide's death that's hardest to take. Just a kid, gone without a trace. Those damned cattle didn't even leave enough of him to find and bury."

Joe's breath stopped. Did the men think he'd been trampled in the stampede? That was pretty much what the boss was saying.

"You'd think we'd have found his spurs, at least, or his gun," Jesse said.

"With all the lightning out there, he probably took them off, like most of the men did."

"Well, at least we could've found his horse."

"Hell, the horse probably ran off when Joe went down," Calder said. "It could still be out there. Maybe one of the men will catch it and bring it in. Shame to lose a good horse."

"No. By God, look!" Jesse exclaimed. "There's Joe's horse down there by that big snag, dead as a doornail. It must've panicked and gone over the edge here after Joe fell off." Jesse had stopped his mount above the place where Joe was trapped. Joe could hear the man's voice clearly.

"Help! Somebody help me!" Joe tried to shout, but his voice

emerged as something between a gasp and a groan. With cattle bawling around them, there was no way the two men could hear him. Still, he tried again.

"Help! I'm down here!"

There was no reaction from either of the men.

"Come on. Let's go," Calder growled, losing patience. "We've got cattle to round up."

"It wouldn't take me long to go down there," Jesse said. "I could look around for any sign of the kid's body, even get the saddle and gear off the horse if you want."

Joe tried to shout again, but he knew he was wasting his breath. The men couldn't hear his weak voice over the bawling of the cattle. Jesse's offer to climb down into the wash was his only hope. But the cowhand wouldn't do it without Calder's permission.

Time seemed to stand still as Joe waited for his boss's reply.

"Don't bother," Calder said. "That old saddle was junk when I gave it to him. And if we don't get those cows rounded up, they'll be all the hell over Kansas by the end of the day. The buzzards can have what's left of that dead horse. Come on. Let's get moving."

Turning their horses, the two men rode away.

Feeling as if he'd been kicked in the gut, Joe lay still. Nobody was going to find him. Nobody was going to help him. If he couldn't get free by himself, he was going to die a slow, miserable death right here. The buzzards and coyotes would finish off what was left of him. And all his dreams—his own brand, his own ranch, and Sarah, or a woman like her, as his wife—would be nothing more than dust.

And Benteen Calder didn't give a damn. *Don't bother*, he'd said. All he cared about was those cattle and the God-cursed money they would make him.

As Joe lay there, battling self-pity, a new emotion took root in him and began to grow. It was hot and bitter, searing his soul like iron fresh out of the branding fire.

It was rage.

From their first meeting Joe had worshipped Benteen Calder. He had wanted nothing more than to be like him, to have the kind of things he had. But Calder had betrayed him. The soulless bastard had ridden away without a second thought and left him to die.

Fury surged through Joe's veins, fueling his determination. Whatever it took, he would get free of this hellish trap and move on.

Whatever it took, he would survive to face Benteen Calder and make the man pay for what he'd done.

CHAPTER FOUR

*T*HE LAST SOUNDS OF MEN, HORSES, AND CATTLE DIED AWAY IN THE distance, leaving nothing to hear but the wind. Utterly alone now, Joe took stock of his situation.

The ground beneath him was muddy from the storm. His clothes were damp as well. He remembered hearing the rush of water as he fell. He could hear no water now. But last night's heavy rain could have created a flood that ran its course through the wash. It was possible that only the massive tree stump had saved him from being swept away and drowned.

What if he was trapped here, with no way to get free? How long would it take him to die?

But he wasn't going to let that happen, Joe told himself. He had too many things to live for—finding Sarah again, building a solid future, and avenging himself on Benteen Calder, who'd cared more about his damned cattle than about taking time to save a man's life.

Joe knew that if he wanted to get out of this death trap, he would have to act soon. The longer he lay here, the more his strength would be sapped by thirst and hunger, until he became too weak to move.

He heard the flapping wings as the first buzzard settled on the body of the dead horse and began tearing at its tough hide. A second bird lit next to it, and the two began to squabble, hissing and grunting as they fought for the choicest spots. It occurred to Joe that between the feasting birds and the hot, drying rays of the sun, the horse's body would become lighter over the next couple of days—perhaps light enough for him to shove aside.

But the notion of waiting for that to happen, under awful conditions, was unimaginable. There had to be another way.

Think!

Joe cursed out loud. His mind was dulled by pain and exhaustion, but waiting wasn't going to make him any sharper. He needed to focus his scattered thoughts and come up with a plan.

In a fury of frustration, he struck the damp mud with his fist. The surface softened under the blow, leaving the imprint of his knuckles in the russet earth.

Suddenly everything became clear.

Ignoring the pain that shot through his body with every move, he began clawing away the sandy soil with his bare hands.

By the time Joe had finished digging himself free, the broiling Kansas sun had reached its zenith. His hands were raw and bleeding, his skin salty with sweat under his muddy clothes. The pain around his ribs was so severe, it was all he could do to keep from screaming.

Exhausted, he forced himself to stay on his feet. He couldn't remain here. He had to get out of the wash and find some kind of shelter. But right now, what his body needed most was water.

More buzzards had gathered on the dead horse. Picking up a rock, Joe flung it into their midst. They scattered, lifting off on their wide, black wings to circle overhead or perch nearby, watching him with curious, beady eyes.

His canteen was on the horse, the strap still looped over the saddle horn. He took it, along with his rope, then rummaged through the saddlebags for anything else that might be of use. There wouldn't be much. His gun and knife had been left behind in camp because of the lightning. His clothes and other personal items were in his bedroll, stowed in the chuckwagon.

In one of the saddlebags, he found a soggy biscuit and a thin slice of jerky wrapped in a bit of cloth. There was nothing else worth taking—not even the saddle, which he was too weak to carry. He took a careful swig of water from the canteen, which was less than half-full. Then he bound his ribs with his shirt, leaving his underwear to protect him from the sun. His hat was long gone. All he had was the bandanna around his neck. Pulling it off, he tied it around his head. It wasn't enough to keep his face from burning, but it would have to do.

Leaving the horse to the buzzards, he forced himself to walk. As the sun crawled across the sky, he trudged along the bottom of the wash, looking for a place where he could climb out. He could see the high-water marks on the walls. Those marks told him he wasn't in a safe place. Another rainstorm, even far upstream, could send enough water gushing down the wash to drown him.

Here and there, in low spots, drying puddles of water remained from last night's storm. Since the water appeared clean, he drank as much as he dared, then splashed his face, cleansed his bleeding hands, and soaked the bandanna before retying it around his head. The coolness helped the pain, but it didn't last long.

After filling the canteen, he plodded on. Stumbling over rocks and flood debris, Joe lost track of time and distance. He could feel his meager strength flagging. His pain-wracked body pleaded for rest, but he feared that if he paused to lie down, or even sit, he wouldn't be strong enough to get up again. The sky, what he could see of it, was blazing blue above the wash. But the past few days had taught him how fast storms could move in over the Kansas prairie.

His mind wandered in and out of dreams. Shadows became faces. Sounds became voices. The path through the bottom of the wash had begun to wind and twist. Joe was stumbling along when his boot struck something soft. A pungent but familiar odor flooded his senses. Startled, he looked down, stared, then laughed out loud. If there was anything a wrangler could recognize, it was horse shit.

Suddenly alert, he studied the ground. The horse droppings were fresh; and there were hoof prints, in different sizes, leading along the floor of the wash. But the hooves that had made them were unshod. These horses were wild mustangs.

Moving cautiously now, he rounded the next bend in the wash. There they were—two spotted mares and a chestnut foal, drinking from a rocky pool.

Sensing his presence, they raised their heads. Their ears pricked. Their nostrils flared. Then, with snorts of alarm, they were gone, thundering up a narrow trail to vanish over the top of the wash.

Joe's gaze followed the way they'd gone. Veiled by shadow, the trail was almost invisible. If the mustangs hadn't gone that way, he would have missed it.

At last he had a way out. But his ordeal was far from over. Surviving on the open prairie would raise a whole new set of challenges—no shelter from sun, storms, or predators; no food unless he caught it; no water unless he was lucky enough to find it; no tools or weapons except the rope he had coiled and slung over his shoulder.

His best hope—maybe his only hope—would be to find a cattle trail and follow it. There were plenty of outfits driving stock from Texas to the railhead towns or the free grass in Wyoming and Montana. His rescue would depend on being in the right place at the right time. But that would be mostly a matter of luck. For now, all he could do was point himself north and try to stay alive.

Stumbling forward, he sank to his knees at the water's edge, drank as much as he could safely hold, then refilled the canteen and splashed his face and clothes. That done, he took time to rest on a boulder at the foot of the trail. His injured ribs shot agony through his body, but aside from trying to adjust the makeshift wrapping, there was nothing he could do except get up, clench his teeth against the pain, and move on.

At the top of the trail, he emerged to a view of rolling prairie, as vast and as empty as the sky. There was no sign that any cattle had been here. Even the horses he'd seen were gone. The only sign of life was a buzzing fly that landed on his arm. Joe brushed it off, feeling more alone than ever in his life.

The sun had passed the peak of the sky. Keeping it on his left,

Joe headed north, tramping through the long, dry grass. Walking would be cooler at night, if he could keep moving that long. Spanish Bill had shown him how to navigate using the North Star as a true compass. Learn to find it, Spanish had said, and he would never lose his way.

The thought of his wise friend and the awful way he'd been taken stirred a deep sorrow in Joe. He remembered other friends—Andy and Jonesy, who'd died in the Red River. He could only hope they were somewhere happy, where the grass grew tall and the streams ran clear, with old friends and loved ones close by.

But Joe wasn't ready to give up and join them. While there was breath in his body, he would keep moving north. North to Ogallala; north to Sarah. She would be his compass, his North Star. And when his legs grew weary, the thought of her would give him one more step, and then another.

These were his thoughts as he trudged along, half-blinded by the glare without a hat to shade his eyes. He yearned to lie down in the shade and rest, but there was no shade to be had, only this beastly, burning sun from which there was no escape.

Had he gone miles or only a few hundred yards? His mind had lost track of time and distance. His limbs had grown leaden. His eyelids drooped, refusing to stay open. The empty canteen dropped into the grass, to be left behind. He took one more step, then another, until the toe of his boot stubbed a badger hole. Joe stumbled and pitched forward, facedown into the long grass. He didn't get up.

Three days later

Sarah filled a plate with scrambled eggs, bacon, and beans, and placed it on the table for her great-uncle. He gave her a smile. "My, but that looks good," he said. "I'll have some more of that coffee, too. Then sit down and have some breakfast with me. I enjoy seeing a friendly face across the table."

Sarah refilled his cup and poured another for herself before she sat down across from him. Once she'd gotten him sobered up, Dr. Harlan Blake had turned out to be kind and generous, even charming. He'd apologized profusely for failing to meet her train in Denver and had even offered her a trip back to the city, to have a nice dinner and go to the theater as he'd promised. Sarah had thanked him and turned him down. Such a trip would be a needless extravagance, especially now, when what the good man really needed was to get his life in order.

While he recovered from his bender, she'd cleaned the house, thrown out his liquor stash, and used what little cash she'd found to buy a supply of nourishing food. Other aspects of his life, including his medical practice and his finances, were in even worse condition than the house. But she couldn't just step in and take over. Uncle Harlan needed to pull himself together and take responsibility for his own affairs.

"Aren't you going to eat something?" he asked. "Coffee's not much of a breakfast for a young lady."

"I'll eat later," she said. "This morning I've got too much on my mind—like the notice I put up in the post office yesterday, to let folks know you're accepting patients again. As the only doctor in Ogallala, you're bound to get plenty of business. Are you sure you're ready to get back to work?"

"I'll be fine," he said. "But before the day gets busy, there are some things you need to understand."

He really was a dear man, Sarah thought. But there was a great deal she didn't know about him. What he had to say might be brutally honest. She had to be ready to hear it.

"I'm listening," she said.

He took a deep breath. "I've never told you why I missed your train in Denver, or why you found me passed out drunk," he said. "I've always had a struggle with alcohol. For years now, I've managed to keep the craving under control. But then, some things happened."

Sarah sipped her coffee and waited for him to go on.

"Your grandmother probably told you that my first wife, Annie, died in childbirth years ago, and the baby with her. Annie was the love of my life. After I lost her, that was when I started drinking. I had a position as a surgeon in a prestigious New York hospital. But showing up drunk on the job got me fired."

"I'm sorry," Sarah said.

He shook his head. "No need for pity. It was my own damned fault. With the help of some friends, I finally managed to get sober and stay that way. But no hospital would have me. That's how I ended up here, at the end of the line, in Ogallala."

"But you've been needed here, and you've done a lot of good." Sarah had talked to people in town and knew this to be true. "Doesn't that give you some satisfaction?"

"I tried to tell myself it did. But something was missing from my life, and I didn't know what it was—not until last year when I met Lenore."

"Everyone needs love." Sarah remembered Joe, and the way she'd felt when she was with him. She couldn't call it love, but she'd liked it. She'd liked it a lot.

"That's true, my dear. It's also true that there's no fool like an old fool. Lenore had come to stay with her uncle, who owned the dry goods store. She was working there when I came in to buy a case of soap and some towels for my surgery. She was a beauty, with long, black hair and porcelain skin—and those gypsy eyes that seemed to look right into my soul. When she smiled and touched my hand, I fell for her like a load of timber. It didn't matter that she was young enough to be my daughter. It didn't even matter when her uncle took me aside and warned me that she'd been sent here by her family after a scandal with a married man. I was as smitten as a seventeen-year-old schoolboy.

"We were married a month from the day we met. She wanted a honeymoon in New York City, so that's what I gave her—nights at the theater, dinners at the best restaurants, the bridal suite at our hotel. . . ." He sighed, remembering. "The trip cost a fortune, of course, along with all the new clothes and jewelry I bought her. But all I could think of was wanting to make her happy.

"We came home, I had patients to see, work to do, and my bank account was down to almost nothing. My bride complained because she wanted new furniture, and because we couldn't afford a housekeeper to cook and clean." His sad-eyed gaze met Sarah's across the table. "You can imagine where this is leading. She ran off with a gambler who promised her pretty things and a good time."

Sarah reached across the table and laid her hand on his. "I'm sorry, but that strikes me as good riddance."

"I told myself the same thing," he said. "Even so, the loss was devastating, because I did love her. I thought a couple of drinks might ease the pain—and it might have, if I could've stopped at that. But there was something else, and this is what I need you to understand."

"So you didn't just get drunk because of Lenore leaving you?"

"No, this happened more recently."

A chill of foreboding passed through Sarah, as if she'd already sensed what she was about to hear. "Tell me," she said.

"I'd been having some headaches that I shrugged off at first. But then, just a few days after Lenore left, I started having optical symptoms. I'm a doctor. I knew what I was facing. It was time for the denial to end." He took a deep breath. "I'm a coward at heart, and I took the coward's way out. I drank myself senseless."

Sarah gazed at him, her throat so tight that she couldn't have spoken even if she'd known what to say.

"In case you haven't already figured it out, Sarah dear, I have a brain tumor," he said. "Sooner or later I've no doubt that it's going to kill me."

She let her silence ask the question.

"I'm guessing I've got about six months—maybe even a year, not much longer. But the end, when it comes, won't take long. If you stay, you'll need to be prepared for that."

Sarah found her voice. "Of course I'll stay, Uncle Harlan. You're going to need me."

The ghost of a smile flickered across his thin face. "In that case, I've got more to say to you. My sister told me you wanted to become a doctor. I was hoping that, when the time came, I could help pay for your training. Unfortunately, Lenore, and my own foolishness, took care of that plan. She left me with little more than the house, my medical equipment, and my horse and buggy, which I keep at the livery stable. And in the time that's left, I can't hope to earn much more than what we need to live."

Sarah swallowed her disappointment. Why mourn the loss of something she'd never had? "Thank you, Uncle Harlan. I know you meant well," she said. "If there's another way, I'll find it. If not, maybe it wasn't meant to be."

"No—you mustn't give up. I can still help a little. While I'm here, if you're willing to work with me, I'll teach you what I can, hopefully enough for you to pass the entrance exam. And when I'm gone, this house will be yours. You can sell it for enough to get you started in school, at least."

"Oh—" Sarah was out of her chair, rushing around the table to put her arms about the old man. "I'll be here for you. And I'll do my best to make you proud."

"You've already done that, my dear." He patted her hand. "Now let's finish our breakfast and hope we get some patients today."

Sarah finished washing the breakfast dishes, dried the plates and cups, and placed them on the shelf above the sink. That done, she put fresh coffee on the stove to boil. When it came to keeping Uncle Harlan's alcohol craving in check, she'd found that lots of hot, strong coffee was the best medicine.

As she worked, she pondered their earlier conversation. She was still coming to grips with his condition, and the fact that she was going to lose him. But it was what he'd said a little later, after breakfast, that had shaken her even more deeply.

"Now that you've agreed to stay, I need to make you aware of something else," he'd said. "When my headaches come on—the worst ones—my sight goes dark. If people know about it, I'll be in danger of losing my practice—or worse, losing a patient. That's why I really need you here. If I go blind at the wrong time, I'll need your eyes and your steady, young hands. Do you understand?"

Sarah understood. But the enormity of what he wanted left her paralyzed with self-doubt. She'd expected to watch, listen, and learn. But what he'd asked of her was far beyond that. What if she wasn't up to the task? What if she failed?

Drying her hands on her apron, she walked out onto the shaded front porch to clear her thoughts. The doctor was wrapping a sprained ankle and didn't need her help. For now, at least, she had a few minutes to breathe fresh air and think.

The July morning was already hot. Powdery dust coated the cottonwood leaves and swirled under the wheels of the wagons that passed. From the railway yard, a few blocks distant, came the lowing protests of cattle being loaded into boxcars. The sound reminded Sarah that the Calder cattle drive was due to reach Ogallala soon, maybe even today. Would she be seeing Joe, or had he already forgotten her?

Only now, after Uncle Harlan's startling revelations, did Sarah realize how much she needed a friend to talk to. She'd only spent a short time with Joe, but thinking of him this morning, she felt as if she could tell him anything, and he would understand. She remembered his bravery, his gentleness, and the special way he'd made her feel. He might be just a poor cowboy, but he had a kind and honest heart. She trusted him—and today she needed him.

Sarah's musings were cut short by the sight of a woman coming up the sidewalk toward the house. She was slender and appeared young—perhaps a little older than Sarah herself. The hair that showed beneath her bonnet was a rich, dark brown. Her calico dress was worn but well-made. The most striking thing about her was the way she carried herself—like a lady.

As she opened the gate, Sarah came down the front walk to greet her. "Good morning, ma'am," she said. "If you're here to see the doctor, he's with a patient now. But he shouldn't be long. You're welcome to come inside where it's still cool. I can make you a cup of tea."

Up close, the woman was stunning, with flawless skin and expressive brown eyes. "Thank you," she said, "but I'm not here to see the doctor. If your name is Sarah Foxworth, I've come to see you. My name is Lorna Calder. Please call me Lorna."

Sarah's knees went liquid as she recognized the surname. A

sick premonition crept over her. Who else could the woman be but Benteen Calder's wife? And why would she have come here except to bring bad news?

She took a deep breath and forced herself to say the words she dreaded. "This is about Joe Dollarhide, isn't it?"

Lorna nodded toward a wooden bench, set against the house in the shade of the porch. "Why don't we sit down over there, where we can talk out of the sun?"

"Of course." Heart pounding, Sarah ushered Lorna to the porch and sat down beside her. She had yet to hear the awful news, but she was already fighting tears. Joe wouldn't be coming by to see her. She would never see his eager grin or hear his voice again.

"You don't have to tell me, Lorna," she said. "I knew as soon as you told me your name. He's gone, isn't he?"

Lorna reached over and took her hand. Her palm was like smooth leather. "Joe was my friend," she said. "He always saddled my horse and helped me hitch the wagon. Sometimes we talked. I know how much he cared about you. He even made sure that, when we got to Ogallala, I'd find an excuse to send him into town. I'm just sorry that it had to be me who walked through your gate, and not him."

Sarah willed herself to take a deep breath. It hurt, the air going in and out of her tight chest. "What happened?" she asked. "Tell me the truth."

"There was a stampede, in a big lightning storm. We think he was thrown from his horse and fell under the cattle."

Sarah struggled, and failed, to block the image from her mind—the helpless terror Joe must've felt. She could only hope the end had been swift, and that he was at peace now. "Can you tell me where you buried him?" she asked.

Lorna hesitated, then shook her head. "I'm sorry. The men searched, but all they found was his dead horse. There was nothing left of Joe to bury."

Sarah almost broke then. But she managed to hold back until Lorna had said good-bye and was headed back downtown to join her husband before she collapsed on the bench, shuddering with shock and grief.

She couldn't say she'd loved Joe Dollarhide. She hadn't known him long enough for that. But if he'd lived—if he'd come back to her—it might have happened. He might have been the love of her life. But now he was gone, leaving nothing behind.

All she would ever have of him was the memory.

The wind that stirred the prairie grass brought clouds and a passing sprinkle of rain. The man lying facedown on the earth didn't stir, not even when a rattlesnake slithered across his water-warped boot and crawled away. Not even when a curious raven lit on his shoulder, pecked at his sunburned ear, and flapped off into the sky.

Joe Dollarhide was alive, but barely. His battered body lay as still as death, drained of the strength to move. His clouded mind wandered in and out of dreams.

His most vivid dream was of wild horses. Timid but curious, they came to stand around him. The two spotted mares and the chestnut foal he had seen in the wash were there, along with others—bays and pintos, buckskins, grullas, and sorrels; mares with their foals, and yearlings nearly grown to size. They gazed down at him with their velvety eyes, nuzzling his skin and clothes, tasting his hair. They nickered softly as if conversing in a secret tongue.

The band stallion, a magnificent blue roan, kept his distance. Head high, his splendid mane streaming in the wind, he kept watch from a grassy knoll. His nostrils flared as he tested the wind, ex-pectant, like a general preparing for battle.

A powerful black stallion galloped into sight, an outsider, charging in to steal mares and foals to add to his own harem. Ig-noring the blue roan, the big black horse moved in among the mares, shoving and nipping to cut out one, then two more, sepa-rating them with their foals from the rest of the band.

The blue roan's shrill challenge echoed across the prairie as he charged his rival. The black horse wheeled as the blue stallion crashed into him, the impact so violent that the ground seemed to shake under their hooves.

Biting, kicking, and slamming with their massive bodies, the two stallions grunted and screamed as they battled for dominance. In size and strength they were a close match, but the blue roan was defending his family. He had more to lose.

Slate-colored clouds rumbled across the sky, darkening the sun. Sheet lightning etched the horses in electric blue and white. Both stallions were bleeding now, from the strikes of their slashing teeth. They were nearing exhaustion, but the fight went on. Suddenly, the black horse went down, hooves flailing, neck straining. The blue roan poised over his rival as if readying a final blow.

At that instant lightning split the sky. Rain poured out of the clouds. Taking advantage of a moment's distraction, the black horse scrambled to his feet and loped away, favoring an injured leg. As the blue roan shrilled his victory call, the horses melted into the rain and vanished, leaving nothing in the dream but wind, thunder, and rippling grass.

"Check his pockets, Clem. Maybe the poor bastard's got some cash on him."

The words penetrated the fog in Joe's mind. He smelled wet earth and the pungent odor of tobacco smoke. From somewhere nearby came the snort of a horse and the faint metallic jingle of bridle hardware. He lay still, too weak to move, let alone resist whatever was about to happen.

Where was he?

How long had he been here?

But the answers to those questions would have to wait.

"Don't look like he's been dead long. The buzzards ain't even got to him yet." The gritty voice was close by. "Don't see no bullet wound neither." Rough hands fumbled in the hip pockets of Joe's pants. "Empty as a granny's tits."

"Well, turn him over," said the nasal voice. "He'd better have somethin' worth takin'."

Big hands gripped Joe's shoulders, lifted them slightly, and wrenched him over onto his back. The pain stabbed like a hot knife through his ribs. Shocked awake, Joe groaned and opened his eyes.

Startled, Clem, a husky, coarse-looking man with a stubby black beard, cursed and let him go. Joe fell back onto the ground.

"Holy hell, the bastard's alive," Clem said. "What do we do with him now, Slinger?"

The nasal-voiced man, mounted on a good-looking bay, was weasel thin. Otherwise, he looked enough like Clem to be his brother. He shrugged. "We could leave him. Don't look like he'll last long out here. But on the chance that he could live and turn us in for the reward, it might be smart to shoot him."

Joe's mind was still foggy, but he'd heard enough to surmise that the two men must be outlaws. He was too weak to fight or run. All he could do was keep quiet and trust to luck.

Clem scowled down at him. "Aw, Slinger, he's just a kid. Not much older'n Benjy was. What do you say we haul him home and let Pa decide what to do with him?"

"Doesn't look to me like he'd last that long," Slinger said. "Here." He lifted a canteen by its strap from the saddle horn and flung it down to his brother. Clem twisted out the stopper, lifted Joe's head with one hand, and tipped the canteen to Joe's mouth. Joe gulped the cool, fresh water. He was still weak, but at least he was becoming more aware.

"So . . . Can you talk now, kid?" Clem replaced the stopper in the canteen.

Joe nodded. "Yeah, a little."

"What's your name?"

"Joe." He was about to give his last name, then hesitated, suddenly cautious. "Joe White."

"Well, Joe White, do you think you can ride?"

"Sure." The motion of the horse would be agony on his ribs, but it would be better than being shot or left out here to die.

Slinger frowned down at Joe from the saddle of his tall buckskin. "You can ride behind me. But you'd damn well better hang on. If you fall off, nobody's going to stop and pick you up again, hear?"

"I hear." Teeth clenched against the pain, Joe let Clem help him to his feet and boost him up behind Slinger's saddle. When the horse began to move, at a brisk walk, every step made him want to scream. But he hung onto Slinger, biting back the urge to cry out.

Whatever happened next, he swore silently, he would get through it. He hoped to see Sarah again, but even if he didn't, he would survive to confront Benteen Calder, the soulless bastard who'd gone off to find his cattle and left him to die in that wash.

CHAPTER FIVE

THE TWO OUTLAWS RODE AT A STEADY BUT UNHURRIED PACE, SLINGER in front with Joe clinging on behind the saddle, and Clem bringing up the rear. When they finally came to a halt, the sun hung low in the western sky.

By then, Joe was almost unconscious from pain and fatigue. Only the awareness that if he slid off the horse, he'd be left behind, had given him the strength to lock his fingers onto Slinger's belt and keep them there. He was so weak that once the horse stopped and the outlaw moved forward, forcing his grip loose, Joe slid down the horse's flank and collapsed on the ground with a grunt of pain. As he lay there, too spent to open his eyes, the conversation seeped through the fog in his mind.

"What the hell's this?" The gravelly voice belonged to an older man. "I send you off to scout for a herd, and you bring me back somethin' that looks like a dead squirrel."

"We didn't see no sign of a herd, Pa," Clem said. "But we found this kid half-dead on the prairie. Since he seen us, we figured we'd best not leave him there."

"Shit, Clem, you coulda shot him and saved yourselves the trouble."

"I told him that, Pa," Slinger said. "But Clem said to bring him in and let you decide what to do with him."

"He ain't much older than Benjy was," Clem said. "I figured maybe we could put him to use."

"If he don't die on us first." The old man cursed. "What the hell. Lay him out on one of the beds, and let's have a look at him. Help me with him, Clem. Slinger, you put away the horses."

With one man taking his legs and the other his shoulders, Joe was carried through a narrow doorway and dropped onto what felt like a frame strung with rawhide strips, with a thin blanket laid on top. He moaned as pain rocketed around his ribs.

"The kid's hurtin' some," Clem said.

"Looks like he might've fell off his horse and cracked a rib or two," the old man said. "See how he's tried to wrap 'em with his shirt? Leave that be for now. Get some water down him first, and then some of that soup on the fire. I'm goin' out to see what your brother's got to say."

As the cool water trickled down his throat, Joe opened his eyes. His head was elevated on what felt like a rolled-up coat. Clem was holding the rim of a tin dipper to his mouth.

"Not too much," he said, taking the dipper away. "You don't want to heave it up again."

"Where am I?" Joe's eyes took in the rough walls and ceiling of a sod cabin.

"We brought you home, Slinger and me. Right now, that's all you need to know."

"And the other man I heard? Is that your pa?"

Clem nodded, stood, and took a chipped bowl off the plank table. A charred iron pot nestled in the coals of the fireplace. "Pa said to give you some soup." He ladled something liquid out of the pot and into the bowl.

"I keep hearing about somebody named Benjy," Joe said. "Who's that?"

"Benjy was our little brother. He died of snakebite last spring. It about killed Pa. Benjy was his favorite. Ma passed away years ago, so there's just the three of us here—and now you." Clem sat on the edge of the bed and spooned the soup into Joe's mouth. The broth and meat—whatever animal it had come from—had a rank, gamey taste, but the soup was warm and nourishing. Joe was still in pain, but he could feel his body stirring to life.

"What are you going to do with me?" he asked.

Clem set the bowl and spoon aside. "That's up to Pa," he said. "I'm thinkin' he wants to keep you—otherwise he wouldn't be wastin' good vittles. But it's up to you, too. Now that you've got a look at us, we can't just turn you loose. If you want to live, you'll have to stay and help us out."

"And if I've got someplace else to go?" Joe thought about Sarah and about his vendetta with Benteen Calder.

Clem shook his head. "Try leavin' and you'd best start sayin' your prayers. Even if you sneak off at night, Slinger will track you down. That man can track a lizard over bare rock. And when he finds you, he'll kill you."

Joe took a moment to ponder what he'd just heard. Not that he was surprised. He'd heard one of the brothers mention that there was a price on their heads. If he tried to escape, he had little doubt that the threat of being tracked down and killed was real.

"You mentioned helping you out," he said. "What is it exactly that your family does?"

"Nothin' that hurts folks," Clem said. "All we do is round up a few stray cows and horses that wander off from the herds. Finders keepers, right?"

"So what do you do with the stock you, uh, find?"

"There's a man that buys 'em from us and sells 'em somewhere else. Good business. Everybody's happy."

"I understand," Joe said. And he did. He understood perfectly. He had fallen in with a family of stock rustlers. And rustling, in cattle country, was a hanging offense.

Within a week's time, Joe was healthy enough to work. Pa, whose real name was Ambrose McCracken, declared that if he wanted to live, it was time he started learning the family trade.

There was plenty to be learned. The easiest way to find "stray" animals on the prairie was after a stampede. Lightning storms, like the one that had scattered the Calder herd, made for easy pickings. Even after the drovers had collected the herd, there were bound to be a few cows and horses they'd missed. Joe had even noticed some steers with the Calder brand in the McCrackens' corral.

Clem's specialty was altering the brands. In a shed behind the sod house, he kept a collection of branding irons he'd fashioned himself. When a new batch of livestock came in, he would make a fire, heat up the irons, and go to work.

Joe, whose job it was to rope and help hold the animals for branding, found it fascinating to watch him. Outlaw or not, Clem was a master craftsman. When he finished changing a bar to an arrow, a *C* to a circle, adding a rocking symbol, or making other alterations, the change was undetectable.

Much of the time they talked as they worked. Ambrose was taciturn; Slinger was aloof; but Clem's easygoing manner made him the closest thing Joe had to a friend. By the time he'd been with the family a month, Joe had told Clem about the stampede and how Benteen Calder had turned his back, ridden off, and left him for dead.

"So I'm guessin' you'd like to get even with the sonofabitch." Clem lifted a glowing iron out of the charcoal fire, positioned it perfectly, and pressed it to the hip of a bawling steer. The odor of charred hide filled the air as the steer scrambled away.

"You bet your life I would." Joe singled out a branded calf, roped its legs, and dragged it to the fire.

"Well, there's just one way to do that. Calder's drive is likely crossing Wyoming by now. They're out of our reach. But if Benteen Calder's as ambitious as you say, he'll be bringin' more cattle north. Next time he drives a herd through Nebraska, we can stampede the stock and rob him blind. Calder won't know what hit 'im. How does that sound?"

"It sounds fine." Joe held the calf down, while Clem changed the brand. He wasn't crazy about waiting for the next Calder cattle drive, which wouldn't happen until the following spring, at the soonest. Worse, from the way Clem was talking, it sounded as if the McCrackens planned to keep him around as a permanent part of the family operation.

He'd already stepped into young Benjy's job, just as he'd

stepped into Benjy's clothes and boots, which fit him well
enough. Benjy's, and now Joe's, specialty was close-up scouting—
how many hands were on a cattle drive, how many cattle and
horses, and where were the most vulnerable spots to pick up a few
animals. Once Joe had made his report, Slinger would plan and
carry out the theft, with as much help as needed from the rest of
the gang.

The McCrackens avoided any confrontation with the cowboys.
Although they carried guns, Joe had yet to hear them fire a shot.
Their method was to steal in under cover of darkness and make
off with a few cattle and horses that might not even be missed
until later.

They were good at what they did. And as long as he did as he
was told, they treated Joe decently enough. But Joe's mother had
raised him to be honest. He was tormented by guilt. And the
dread of being arrested and hanged kept him awake at night. He
was tempted to find an unguarded moment and try to run. But if
caught by the outlaws, he'd likely be killed. Even if he escaped,
he'd still be in danger from the law, or from angry cattlemen
who'd string him up on the spot.

He was trapped, with no way out. Finding Sarah was out of the
question now. So was going home to his family in Texas. At the
age of sixteen, Joe Dollarhide had become an outcast.

Summer passed into autumn. Autumn gave way to a frigid, miserable winter the likes of which Joe had never experienced in
Texas. Aside from tending to the horses and other chores, much
of the time was spent either huddled in the sod house, with the
fire burning dried cow chips and a norther howling outside, or
hunting for game to supplement the meager stores in the cellar
under the floor. When Slinger found a cow, recently dead from
hunger and cold, he dragged the carcass home to be butchered,
keeping them in meat for a few more precarious weeks.

"Why in hell's name do you live like this?" Joe asked Clem as
they broke the ice on the horse trough one morning. "Hiding out
here in the middle of nowhere, stealing stock, afraid to even go
into a town because of the price on your heads—there's got to be
a better way."

Clem emptied the bucket of water he'd carried from the crude well behind the house. "It was Pa's idea. It come to him after our ma died. When he sells the stock, he hides most all of the money—Slinger and me don't even know where. When we get enough, he says, we'll pull up stakes and head down to Mexico. We'll be safe from the law, and we can live like kings. I reckon you can come with us if you want."

Joe had doubts that the McCrackens would live long enough to make it to Mexico. Truth be told, he had the same worries for himself. But at least Clem's words held out a glimmer of hope. One way or another, this mess he'd gotten himself into would have to end.

By the time spring crept over the prairie, Joe was restless and ready for change. By now he was seventeen, and still growing. Benjy's ragged shirts and pants, which had fit him last fall, now left gaps above the wrists and ankles. After a winter of near starvation, he was thin, but his muscles were hard and strong. His body was a man's body now, his mind a man's mind.

With the change in season, the cattle herds were moving north again in even greater numbers than before. Joe and the brothers stampeded the first outfit, made off with eleven longhorn steers, and they were back in business. The man who bought them would pay part in cash and part in much-needed food and supplies.

As spring wore into blistering summer, Joe watched the trails for any sign that Benteen Calder was moving another herd up from Texas. To his disappointment he saw no trace of Calder cattle or any of the cowboys he remembered. If they'd made another drive, he'd missed it.

Day after day, his frustration boiled. If his old boss had taken extra minutes to rescue him, he'd be in Montana now, working to build his own future on the land. Instead, he was an outlaw, stealing to survive and living every day in fear for his life and freedom. As the weeks passed, the anger in his heart froze into cold rage— a rage that refused to be sated by anything less than vengeance.

One morning, after scouting a herd most of the night, Joe was riding back to the sod house, hidden from distant view by the bank of a dry riverbed. Bone-tired, saddle sore, and discontented to the core of his being, all he wanted was to fling himself onto his bunk, pull the smelly woolen blanket over his head, and shut out the world for a few hours.

Last night he'd gotten close enough to the camp to see the cowboys sitting around the fire before bedtime, talking, laughing, and singing. He'd remembered such times with the Calder outfit, the good men, the easy camaraderie, the trust that had bound them together. Somewhere below his heart, an ache festered like an abscess. He had never felt more alone.

He'd even toyed with the idea of walking into the camp and asking for a job, or even turning himself in and asking for protection. But caution had warned him off. The cowboys hated rustlers. Likely as not, he'd become the guest of honor at a hanging party.

Dark emotions swirled around him as he crossed the plain of parched grass. Dawn was breaking in the east. As the sun rose, ribbons of flame streaked the sky, casting a glow over the flatland.

That was when he saw them—the wild horses, galloping over the horizon with the blue roan stallion in the lead, and the mares, foals, and yearlings streaming behind him. Joe's breath caught. He'd assumed that he'd dreamed those horses. Maybe he was dreaming now.

The horses had been coming right toward him. Now, as if suddenly wary of the stranger, they veered to one side and thundered past at an angle. Seized by a sense of awe, Joe gazed after them as they raced away. How could anything in this miserable world be so beautiful, so wild and free?

After the horses had vanished from sight, Joe began to wonder if his exhausted mind had been playing tricks on him. But no, he could still see tracks—the dry grass flattened by their hooves, and the hazy film of dust that lingered where the band had passed.

Nothing had changed for him. He was still part of an outlaw gang, going home to a place and a life he detested. But for a moment he had seen beauty and known wonder. And somehow, it made a difference.

* * *

Joe should have known that his time with the McCrackens would come to an end. But when that end came, on a clear September morning, the suddenness of it left him in shock.

With winter approaching and the cattle drives thinning out, Ambrose had been pressuring his sons to bring in more stock. They were hitting every outfit that came up the trail and driving off more cattle than ever before. It would only be a matter of time before they went too far.

It was early dawn when the mounted vigilantes came thundering over the rise. Joe was out beyond the corral gathering sticks and cow chips to fuel the morning fire. When he heard the riders coming, he dived behind a big clump of sagebrush, burrowed into its shadow, and lay as still as stone, his heart drumming in his ears.

From where he lay, he could see what was happening in the yard. Ambrose, still in his long johns, had just come out of the privy. A volley of gunfire cut him down where he stood.

One of the men dismounted, kicked open the front door of the house, and lit a kerosene-soaked torch that he tossed inside. As the blaze caught the house's contents, they waited, pistols cocked to shoot anybody who came running out.

As the roof began to smolder, Clem and Slinger came busting out of the house's rear, through a section of sod they'd weakened for this very purpose. Running for their lives, they made it to their horses, which were still saddled from last night's raid. Before the armed riders could gather their wits, the two brothers were mounted and tearing across the plain.

Whooping and shooting, the vigilantes charged after them. As they disappeared over the horizon, Joe realized he was alone.

But he wouldn't be alone for long. Whether they caught the brothers or not, the riders would soon be back for the stolen cattle and horses, and to salvage anything useful that the outlaws had left behind. He had to get out of here now.

His first impulse was to saddle a horse. But no, that would be a mistake. A horse could be tracked and spotted at a distance. He'd be less visible walking. For that matter, he'd be better off not even setting foot in the yard. If the vigilantes saw any evidence that another person had been there, they would never stop hunting him.

Go. Don't take anything—not a gun, not even water. Just go.

After a swift, backward glance to make sure the horizon was clear, Joe broke into a run.

Dr. Harlan Blake passed away sometime before dawn on the last day of September. When he didn't appear at the breakfast table for his morning coffee, Sarah went to his room and found him lying with his eyes closed and a peaceful expression on his face, almost as if he'd arranged himself that way.

Numb with shock, she leaned over him, kissed his waxen forehead, and pulled the sheet up to cover his head. Then she walked into the kitchen, sat down at the table, and buried her face in her hands.

At least the end had been gentle. And at least, in the fifteen months they'd shared, he'd done his best to ready her for this day. He'd even left instructions for his funeral and paid the undertaker for the coffin and burial expenses.

But nothing could have prepared her for his absence. He was gone—simply gone, never to return in this life. She was utterly alone, with no family or close friends to share her grief.

What now? She and Uncle Harlan had talked about the future—the one she hoped to have after he was gone. She was to sell the house and use the money toward medical school. The experience she'd had working with him—serving as his hands and eyes when the headaches struck—should serve her well when it came time to apply for admission, as would the letter of recommendation an old friend of his had agreed to write. But even with that, as a woman, Sarah knew she'd be fighting long odds.

Uncle Harlan had given her the names and addresses of schools she could contact for applications. But to write those letters while he was still alive struck her as monstrously cold. Now that he was gone, she faced a long period of trying and waiting. Even if she managed to get accepted, the process could take months. Meanwhile, she needed a plan to survive.

Selling the house wouldn't make sense until she had her acceptance, especially given the letters and paperwork that would need to go back and forth with every application. She would stay here through the winter. By spring, if all went according to her best hopes, she would be ready to sell the house and begin her new life as a medical student.

Meanwhile, she would need to make a living. She wasn't a real doctor, but she knew how to deliver babies, set broken bones, stitch up wounds, and treat fevers. With no other doctor practicing in Ogallala, she would still be needed, and hopefully paid.

Rising from her chair, she walked back into her great-uncle's bedroom. Lifting his cold hand in hers, she pressed it to her lips. As the loss became real, tears welled in her eyes and trickled down her cheeks.

"Thank you for giving me my chance, Uncle Harlan," she whispered. "I'll do everything I can to make you proud."

Turning away, she tied on her bonnet, squared her shoulders, and left the house to fetch the undertaker.

The doctor was laid to rest two days later. The graveside service was a simple one, as he'd requested, but a good number of townspeople turned out to pay their respects and to offer Sarah their condolences, including her young friend, Ezra, and his grandfather, the stationmaster.

When the grave was filled in, Sarah laid a bouquet of autumn daisies and sunflowers on the sad mound of earth and went home to an empty house. She was footsore from standing and wrung out from the sad farewell to a good man she'd come to love. His presence seemed to linger in every room—his instruments in the surgery, his clothes and shoes in the closet, his books beside hers on the shelves, his favorite blue coffee cup on the kitchen counter.

Tomorrow she would roll up her sleeves and try to make the place seem more like her own. For now, all she wanted to do was rest.

Sinking into the rocker that faced the empty fireplace, Sarah leaned back and closed her eyes. She'd begun to doze when she was startled by a sharp rap at the front door.

Forcing herself to her feet, she smoothed the skirt of her black mourning dress and hurried to answer the knock. Maybe someone needed her help.

She opened the door to find two people standing on the porch. One was a small man with a narrow ferret's face, wearing a tobacco brown suit and carrying a briefcase. Slightly behind him stood a tall, stunning brunette wearing a blue-gray traveling suit with white gloves and a chic matching hat. Neither of them was smiling.

Sarah found her voice. "Can I help you?" she asked.

"Allow me to introduce myself," the small man said. "I'm Phillip Roxberry, attorney-at-law. This"—he nodded toward the woman behind him—"is my client, Mrs. Lenore Blake, widow of the late Dr. Harlan Blake. We've come with legal documents in hand, supporting Mrs. Blake's claim to her late husband's property."

Dumbfounded, Sarah stared at them. "I don't understand. I thought—"

"It's like this, honey." The woman's voice and manner belied her elegant appearance. "I never signed any divorce papers, so the marriage is still legal. As Harlan's widow, this house is mine. So get packing, and make sure you don't take any valuables— believe me, we'll check. You've got twenty-four hours."

After an hour of sprinting, ducking, and scanning the empty horizon behind him, Joe allowed himself to feel hopeful. Maybe he wasn't being trailed. Maybe he'd gotten away clean.

Using the skills he'd honed as a scout for the McCracken gang, he'd cut a zigzag course, doubling back in some places, and keeping to short grass and bare rock where he could find it. An expert tracker might still be able to follow him, but the vigilantes struck him as nothing more than a bunch of riled-up cowboys, out to kill off a nest of rustlers. A lawful posse would have arrested Ambrose for trial, not shot down an unarmed man in his underwear.

He couldn't help hoping that Clem and Slinger would get away. They might be outlaws, but they'd treated him decently. They deserved better than the bloody, brutal death they would suffer if they were caught. As for their father's hidden money stash, it was probably gone for good—either burned in the fire or buried and lost. One thing was for sure—Joe would never go back there to look for it.

Setting a course for a distant outcrop of badlands, he began walking again—at a measured pace now, to conserve his remaining strength. Even with nobody tracking him, he was still in danger. He had no food, no water, no weapon, and no way of knowing where he was headed. Men had died on the prairie under similar conditions. If he was to survive, he would need to be strong and smart.

Water was the most critical thing. As he walked, Joe scanned the ground in search of animal tracks—cattle, sheep, wild horses, or even buffalo, what few were left. If he could find several sets leading in the same direction, there was a chance they would take him to a water hole. But he couldn't depend on that alone.

He could see an outcrop of barren hills floating like a mirage above the distant horizon—a streak of badlands cutting like a wrinkle across the flat prairie. If there was water to be found anywhere in this sunbaked hell, it would most likely be there.

He was already thirsty. Picking up a pebble from the ground, he put it in his mouth to keep the moisture flowing around it. As he walked, the sun beat down on his head. He'd left his hat in the soddie when he'd gone out to gather fuel at dawn. That hat was probably burned to a cinder by now.

Stripping off his shirt, he tied it around his head and kept walking. His undershirt would protect his body, but none of that would matter if he couldn't find water.

The distant hills were getting closer. He could see that they were the color of baked clay with no sign of anything growing on them. Not good. But he had no choice except to keep moving. If he stopped to rest, he would never get up again.

By the time the sun sank out of sight, leaving a bloodred sky in its wake, Joe's feet were dragging. The autumn air had become chilly. As he walked, he untied the shirt from his head and slipped it back on. The hills loomed ahead of him, bigger now, but still out of reach. His throat was as dry as dust, his vision so blurry that he could barely see.

As moonless dark fell around him, the coyotes began to call. Joe wasn't afraid of coyotes, but there were wolves out here, too. The cattle drives had drawn them onto the plain. Hunting in packs, they picked on the weaker animals, bringing them down and feasting on them where they lay. Wolves were one of the main reasons why the night guards on a drive carried guns.

Joe swore as he stubbed his foot on a sharp rock. He reeled, barely catching his balance. Hellfire, in his weakened condition it wouldn't take even one wolf to bring him down. He'd be dead meat by the time he hit the ground.

As if the thought could conjure it up, he heard something in the darkness. The low, animal sound was neither whimper nor growl, but it raised the hair on the back of Joe's neck and made his blood run cold.

With no more warning than that, a large, furry shape came hurtling out of the night. Too weak to defend himself, Joe went down under the impact. Flat on his back, he struggled against the warm, smelly weight, felt the heated breath against his throat, the wetness of a tongue, licking his face. His flailing hand made contact with a thick leather collar.

Sonofabitch! It wasn't a wolf. It was a blasted dog.

CHAPTER SIX

Now other sounds reached Joe's ears—the nicker of a horse, the creak of a wagon wheel, then a voice.

"Festus! Come here, you crazy mutt!"

The dog turned and trotted back in the direction of the voice. A lantern flickered, moving closer as Joe struggled to sit up.

"What the devil are you doing out here, you young fool?" The lantern light revealed a man who appeared to be in his sixties, with a stern face and long gray hair, worn in braids that hung over his chest.

"*Water.*" Joe's throat cracked as he spoke.

"Here." The man uncorked the canteen he carried and tilted the mouth to Joe's lips. The water was lukewarm and had a slightly metallic taste, but Joe couldn't get enough. After several deep gulps he forced himself to stop. "Thanks. I'd better leave some for you," he muttered.

"Drink it all if you want. We're not an hour from home, and there's plenty water there." The man spoke with a flat cadence that sounded strange to Joe, and yet somehow familiar. "Come climb on the wagon." He extended a hand to help Joe up. "You can tell me your story on the way."

But how much of his story could he safely tell? Joe asked himself as he followed the lantern to a good-sized wagon loaded with hay and several crates of supplies. His rescuer appeared to be a kindly man. But that could change if he discovered he was harboring a fugitive cattle rustler.

The man climbed onto the wagon seat and reached down to give Joe a hand up. The dog jumped up behind them, and they set off, the sturdy, two-horse team moving the loaded wagon at a cautious pace on the uneven ground. A narrow moon had risen above the hills, helping to light the way.

"Elijah Hawkins is the name. You can call me Elijah." His gaze remained focused on the team. "I don't believe I caught yours."

"It's Joe." Joe hesitated, then made a swift decision to be truthful, at least about the name. "Joe Dollarhide."

"I don't recollect knowing any folks by that name. I'd remember if I did."

"My family's in Texas. I came here with a cattle drive." Had he already said too much? Every new revelation made him nervous.

"Well, Joe Dollarhide, maybe you'd care to tell me how you ended up out here by your lonesome, with nothing but the clothes on your back."

Joe squirmed inside. Lying would have been safer. He should've been thinking up a convincing tale while he was walking. But he hadn't planned on being rescued. And something in Elijah Hawkins's forthright manner told him that the man wouldn't be easily fooled.

"It's a long story," he said. "I got lost after a stampede. The folks who took me in, a father and two brothers . . . well, they weren't the best."

Elijah gave him a knowing glance. "It strikes me that you've got a talent for getting lost and found."

"I guess maybe so," Joe said. "I wanted to leave. But they said they'd kill me if I tried. So I stayed, for almost a year."

Elijah nodded slowly, as if pondering what he hadn't heard. "A whole year and you didn't leave?"

"I was too scared to try. I knew they'd do what they said. But this morning I was out gathering wood in the brush when vigilantes showed up. I ducked down until they left. Then I took off running, as fast and as far as I could go."

"The vigilantes didn't come after you?"

"They shot the father, then they rode off after the brothers. I don't think they even knew I was there."

"I see." Something in Elijah's voice told Joe he'd already filled in the missing parts of the story. "How old are you, Joe?"

"Seventeen. I'll be eighteen come spring."

In the long silence, the only sounds were the creak of the wagon wheels and the muted plodding of horses' hooves in the dust. At last Elijah spoke. "I can offer you a meal and shelter for the night. After that, we'll see what happens."

"Thank you, sir," Joe said. "Whatever you might be thinking, I won't cause you any trouble."

Elijah didn't reply.

Now that the moon had risen, Joe could see the patch of badlands up close. Erosion had carved the hills into a maze of miniature mesas and canyons, their shapes unearthly in the faint light. The wagon entered a narrow passage between cliffs and emerged into a moonlit clearing with a cabin, a set of corrals, and a small barn. Willows grew around a gurgling spring. From somewhere out of the darkness came the snorting, nickering, stamping sounds of horses.

As Elijah pulled the wagon up to the barn, Festus the dog jumped to the ground and began racing around the yard, stopping here and there to sniff a spot and lift his leg. Elijah took a moment to study the sky. "It's a clear night," he said. "The unloading can wait till morning. But I'll need to put the horses away before supper."

"I'll help. I'm feeling stronger." Joe fudged the truth as he climbed down from the wagon. His legs almost buckled as he walked around to unfasten the traces, but he needed to show that he was willing to do his share.

After the two bay horses had been fed, watered, and rubbed down in the barn, Joe followed Elijah to the cabin. The man hadn't said much about himself, but Joe was burning with curiosity. Who was Elijah Hawkins? A hermit? An outlaw? A friend of the vigilantes who'd raided the McCrackens? Would he be safe here, or was he setting himself up to be killed or arrested?

Joe had sensed Elijah watching him, taking his measure as they rubbed down the horses. But there was no way to know what the man was thinking. There was something in his taciturn nature, the way he wore his hair in long braids, and the flat tone of his speech, that reminded Joe of the Comanches and Kiowas he'd met when the drive was passing through Indian Territory. But Elijah was pale-skinned and blue-eyed; and his silvery hair showed reddish glints in the lantern light. He was clearly a white man. But what sort of white man was he?

Joe followed him out of the barn and waited while he closed the door. Now that the moon was higher, he could see beyond the barn to a stout log corral with shapes moving behind the rails, shifting like grass in the wind. *Horses. Wild horses.*

"I catch them and break them for sale," Elijah said. "Kiowa breaking. That's what they call what I do. You'll see more in the morning."

They crossed the clearing to the cabin, which was made of adobe, not the usual sod. The place was spare and neat, with everything in one room. Clothes and tools hung from pegs around the walls. A shelf above the bed held a lamp and a half-dozen books.

Books. A memory flashed through Joe's mind. Sarah, lugging her carpetbag, weighted down with her precious books. Where would Sarah be now? Probably married. Such a pretty girl and so full of spunk. Surely, by now, some man would've sweet-talked her into becoming his wife. Whoever it was, he'd damn well better treat her right.

Joe's one regret was that he hadn't pulled that girl into his arms at the train and kissed her good-bye. Even after all this time, he thought about her at night, imagining how those full lips, sweet and ripe as summer cherries, would have tasted pressing his. Knowing Sarah, she probably would've slapped his face. But the memory would have been worth it.

Elijah stirred the coals in the fireplace and added enough cow chips to make a cheering blaze. Within a few minutes, he'd heated some coffee, warmed up some beans, and added a few stale biscuits that were wrapped in a cloth.

The table was a board resting between two wooden crates. Two more crates served as chairs. The plates were leftover pie tins. The cups were tin as well, like the ones from the cattle drive. The knives and forks were old and tarnished.

The food couldn't compare to Rusty's chuckwagon meals, let alone Joe's mother's cooking; but he hadn't eaten all day, and Joe was starved. The beans, with dry biscuits dipped in the sauce, tasted good; and he was grateful for anything that would fill his belly and restore his strength.

So far, at least, Elijah didn't seem to be much of a talker, especially while he was eating. But Joe was curious about the man, and he might not get a better chance to learn more.

"You mentioned Kiowa breaking," he said. "What does that mean? How is it different from regular breaking?"

Elijah washed down his biscuit with a swig of coffee. "When a cowboy like you breaks a horse, he does it with force and fear. By the time the horse is ready to ride, it behaves because it doesn't want to be punished. Kiowa breaking is a whole different way. It's done with gentleness and trust. The horse obeys because it wants to. A man who's learned to ride a Kiowa broke horse will never be satisfied with the other kind. I can show you tomorrow."

"But I can see that you're not an Indian. How did you learn?"

Elijah helped himself to more beans. "My folks settled in western Missouri—pretty wild country back in the day. As one of seven kids, I was pretty much left to my own devices. When I was about twelve, I was fishing along the creek that ran past our farm when a couple of Kiowa braves snuck up behind me, threw a blanket over my head, and rode off with me. I never saw my family again."

"What happened to your people? Did the Kiowas attack them?" Joe asked.

Elijah shrugged. "To this day, I don't know. I never found them. Never tried." Elijah's mouth tightened for a moment. "The chief had lost his own boy to the whites, and he took me in the lad's place. For nine years, I lived as a Kiowa—hunted with them, raided with them, starved with them during the rough winters. I even had a pretty, young wife, but she died, along with our baby.

That's a part of the story I choose not to tell. Anyway, since you asked, that was how I came to learn their way of breaking horses."

"But how did you come to be here? How did you escape?"

"Escape?" Elijah's expression darkened. "I was Kiowa. The end came when the army wiped out our band. Most of my people, the ones that didn't get away fast enough, were killed. The soldiers would've killed me, too, if they hadn't noticed my blue eyes and red hair. They took me back to the fort and gave me clothes to wear. I knew better than to misbehave." A bitter smile teased his lips. "However, I did threaten to kill anybody who tried to cut off my braids.

"They asked me about my family. I said I didn't remember their names. The truth was, I knew that if they were alive, they wouldn't want me. And if they were dead, I didn't want to know. I took the name Hawkins because the translation of my Kiowa name was Red Hawk. Since I was old enough to be on my own, all the soldiers could do was turn me loose."

"So you went to work breaking horses?"

"That's right." Elijah refilled his coffee cup and, at a nod from Joe, filled his as well. "A rancher—best white man I ever knew—hired me when I showed him what I could do with wild mustangs. He treated me well, and we made good money selling the horses. But I always wanted a place of my own, where I could live by myself—live in peace. When I discovered this spot, he helped me file a claim on the land. He's gone now, but I still work with his son. I catch and break the horses. He sells them and keeps me in supplies. I was on my way back from his ranch with a wagonload when I found you."

"And the books?" Joe glanced up at the shelf above the bed. "Is there a story behind those?"

Elijah nodded. "The rancher I worked for—his mother was a retired schoolmarm. She took a shine to me and decided to give me an education. I could read a little before the Kiowa took me, but I talked like a cracker. She took me through those books, and when she died, her son gave them to me."

"So you've read them all?"

"Every one, more than once. They make good company on long winter nights." Elijah stood. "I need to check the stock. You can clean up here. Give the scrapings to the dog on the porch. I'll give you a warm blanket to sleep in, but the floor will have to do for your bed."

"It'll be fine. I'm much obliged for your hospitality." Joe murmured the polite phrase his mother had taught him. Another question rose in his mind as Elijah went out the door and closed it behind him. He'd mentioned raiding with the Kiowa. Did that mean the man had raided white settlers, even killed them and taken their scalps?

He decided not to ask. Everyone had a right to their secrets.

The wild mustang, a handsome chestnut, stood alone in the training pen quivering as Joe approached. The horse had been gelded a few weeks earlier, by means of a wet rawhide string wound tightly above the scrotum. The string had tightened as it dried, cutting off the blood supply and causing the testicles, over time, to shrink and fall off.

"Is this how the Kiowas gelded their horses?" Joe remembered asking as he'd steadied the horse in the narrow chute while Elijah did the delicate work.

"It was one way," Elijah had answered. "Sometimes they'd just cut with a knife, depending on the horse and other things. But this is how my grandfather taught me."

"Your Kiowa grandfather."

When Elijah hadn't replied, Joe had realized it was a needless question. Now the horse was healed and ready for training. And, after some careful schooling, Elijah had given the job to him.

It had taken time for Joe to gain the old man's confidence. One turning point had come when he'd told Elijah about seeing the blue roan stallion and his band.

"I have never seen such horses," Elijah had said. "Surely, if I had, I would remember. Maybe you were the only one who could see them."

"Are you saying those horses might not be real? Do you think I'm crazy?" Joe had demanded.

"Not at all. I only mean that there might be some reason you were meant to see them. My grandfather might have told you that the horses were a vision—but I can't say I'd go that far. All I can tell you is that if you see them again, pay attention and ask yourself why they have come to you."

Perhaps this so-called vision was the reason Elijah had invited Joe to stay and work with the horses. He'd started by cleaning up after them and filling their water troughs, then feeding them and helping to geld the young stallions. Only now, after weeks of teaching, would he finally be allowed to break a horse in the Kiowa way.

Pushing the memory aside, Joe focused his energy and attention on the beautiful gelding in the pen. For several days now, it had been separated from the other horses. Joe had walked around it, first outside the pen, then inside, talking to it, getting it accustomed to his presence, giving it hay and water, and finally feeding it pieces of carrot from the outside of the fence. Today, for the first time, he would lay his hands on it.

Elijah stood outside the fence, watching. "Remember, a horse is a herd animal," he'd told Joe. "Its instincts are to follow the herd leader. What you want is to become the leader for this horse, so he will want to follow you. To do that, you must first win his trust."

As Joe walked toward it, the horse twitched its ears, showing uncertainty, as if sensing that something new was going to happen. Stopping a few paces away, Joe held out a piece of carrot on the flat of his hand. The horse snorted, fearful, but clearly wanting the treat.

Standing motionless Joe held out his hand and made a coaxing sound. The horse inched closer, snatched the carrot, then snorted and danced away.

"Try it again," Elijah coached him from outside the corral. "Give him time to feel safe."

On the third try, the horse came without hesitation. As it

munched the carrot, Joe laid a gentle but firm hand on its withers. A shudder passed beneath his palm as he stroked the satiny coat. The horse was trembling, but Joe was able to run his hand down its neck and over its shoulder before its fear got the best of it. It jumped away and trotted out of reach.

Tomorrow he would try again. Once the horse became accustomed to being handled, it would be introduced to the blanket, the halter and lead, the bridle and saddle, and finally to a rider on its back. The training would take weeks.

"That's enough for now," Elijah said. "Come on out. It's getting late."

They walked back to the house, with the dog tagging at their heels. Joe was becoming fond of the chestnut gelding, but he knew the horse had already been bought by a wealthy rancher. Once it was ready, after weeks of training, the new owner would spend time learning to handle the horse before he took it away. If all went well, the man would have a superb mount that would respond to his most subtle cues, a horse he could ride anywhere.

Joe hoped to train his own horse one day. For now, he rode one of Elijah's older work animals, a sturdy buckskin named Flint. It was a good horse, but even that one wasn't his to keep.

"You did a good job today," Elijah said. "It takes a lot of patience to win a horse's trust."

Joe shook his head. "I've watched cowboys break ten horses in a day—just by riding them till they gave up and stopped bucking."

"But those horses are just that—broken. They have no trust, no loyalty, and if they obey, it's only because they know they'll feel pain if they don't." Elijah paused on the porch to scratch the dog's ears before opening the door. "I wish you could've seen a Kiowa ride after buffalo—bareback, single rein with a piece of rawhide for a bit, shooting arrows with both hands while the horse galloped among the herd, dodging and chasing. You might think that the rider was guiding the horse with his knees—but you'd be wrong. There was no time to think about that. It was up to the horse to know exactly what his rider needed."

"Did you ever ride like that?" Joe asked.

"Yes, a long time ago. But those days are gone now. And there are no more buffalo to hunt." Elijah went inside to check on the beans that were simmering over the fire.

As usual, Elijah was worn-out by the end of the day. After supper, he stripped down to his long johns and eased his tired, old body into bed. Soon the sound of his snoring filled the small house.

Joe cleared the table and washed the dishes. Then, too restless to sleep, he wandered outside and settled on the front stoop. The day had been warm, but with the sun gone, the early November night was chilly. The dog trotted over and lay down next to him. Its shaggy coat smelled of damp earth and grass. Its tail thumped as Joe scratched its ears.

A full moon rose out of the prairie, flooding the corrals and outbuildings with light. From somewhere beyond the clearing came the wail of a coyote.

This was a good place, Joe told himself. Here he felt safe from the law and the vigilantes. He was doing honest work and learning from the kind old man who'd taken him in.

It was a good place. But not his place.

Outside these confining canyon walls lay the world he really wanted—the chance to build his life and make something of himself, and the chance to do the one thing he wanted most—to get even with Benteen Calder for destroying his life. Until he achieved that satisfaction, he would never know peace.

The roof was leaking, this time over the kitchen table. Sarah set out a dishpan to catch the drops that fell through the cracks in the water-stained ceiling. Each drip made a *ping* that plucked at her nerves as it struck the metal surface.

At least, when the weather turned frigid, this icy rain would turn to snow and give her some relief. But then, of course, she would have other problems.

Last summer, after Uncle Harlan had died and she'd lost his house to his faithless widow, this deserted place, little more than a shack on the road out of town, had been all she could afford. After she'd chased out the mice and spiders, scrubbed it from top to bottom, and made a place for her books, she'd told herself it would do well enough. But then the season had changed, with the cold November wind whistling through the cracks, and the outside pump frozen in the mornings. That was when she'd realized that conditions were only going to get worse.

Wrapping her woolen shawl more tightly around her shoulders, she stood by the window, watching the raindrops slide down the glass. She was shivering, but the wood supply for the stove that heated the place and served for cooking was getting low. She'd need it even more when the cold front moved in. Besides, she'd soon be needing to put on her slicker and go out. Becky Poulsen's baby was due, and Sarah had promised to look in on her.

When Lenore had claimed Uncle Harlan's house, the woman had never meant to live there. Instead she'd put the place up for sale. The buyer had been another doctor, moving to Ogallala with his young family. Unfortunately for Sarah, he'd taken all the patients who wanted to be treated by a "real" doctor—at least the ones who could pay. Since he only accepted cash, that left the others to Sarah.

She took in enough money to pay rent on the house—mostly from women who preferred a midwife to a male doctor. But most of her patients paid her in such items as eggs, chickens, fresh and bottled produce, baked bread, milk, butter, cheese, chopped firewood, and hay for Ahab, the irascible old mule who pulled her two-wheeled cart when she made house calls.

One old woman had paid her with a warm quilt. A seamstress had made her a dress. Some folks even paid with labor. Maybe, when the weather cleared, Becky's husband would mend her leaking roof as the price of delivering the baby.

Through the blur of the rainy window, Sarah could see the mailbox on its post next to the road. Despite the setback in her fortunes, she hadn't given up on her dream of becoming a doctor. Money would be a problem now. But she had to keep trying. Last month she'd written to several medical schools for application forms. She had yet to hear back from any of them. But maybe today would be the day.

She would wait for the postman to pass by—or to stop if he had anything for her. After that, she would put on her boots and slicker, take Uncle Harlan's old medical bag, and travel two miles through the rain to the Poulsen farm. In this mud, the cart would only bog down. She would saddle Ahab and ride him.

She was still waiting for the mail when a buggy pulled up in front of the house. Recognizing it, she battled mixed feelings while she waited for the knock at the door. She hated being dependent on anyone, especially when she had so little to offer in return. But on a day like today, with rain pouring down, the roof leaking, and the stove running out of firewood, Everett Hamilton deserved a warm welcome. Hearing the light rap, Sarah hurried to open the door.

The man who stood on the porch, shaking water off his slicker, was in his mid-thirties. Widowed last year, with no children, he owned one of the more respectable saloons in Ogallala. He was as handsome as he was prosperous, and a number of women had set their sights on him. But for whatever reason, he had singled out Sarah.

He gave her a winning smile. "I saw you at the window. Were you watching for me?"

"I was watching for the mail. But I'm glad to see you. Can I take your slicker?"

He shook his head. With the slicker hood thrown back, his blond hair lay in damp curls against his skull. "I can't stay long. But I brought you more firewood. My new hired boy is unloading it in the shed. It looks like you could use some here, too. I'll have him bring a few logs inside."

"Thank you, Everett. I'm beholden to you." Sarah hated being in anyone's debt, but she would freeze without the wood.

"Don't be silly. It's my pleasure. I only wish you'd let me do more." He glanced toward the window. "You said you were waiting for the mail. Were you expecting something?"

Sarah forced a smile. "Only the same old thing. I keep hoping I'll get an application for at least one medical school."

He sighed. "Sarah, I know you have this crazy dream of being a doctor. But what are the chances of it coming true? You would be happier if you gave it up and let me take care of you."

Sarah gazed past him, through the window, as the postman's buggy passed on the road—once again—without stopping at her mailbox. "I've never wanted to be taken care of," she said.

"Maybe that's what makes you different from every other woman I've known." He took a step closer.

"Maybe you've just known the wrong women." She gave him a smile as she turned away. "Speaking of women, I need to be going. Becky Poulsen is due to have her baby anytime now. I promised her a visit today."

"You're not going out in this weather!"

"I'll be fine. My slicker will keep me dry. Ahab won't be too happy, but I'll give him a good rubdown and some oats when we get home."

"You'll catch your death. Let me drive you in the buggy."

"It's a tempting offer. But if Becky is going into labor I could be stuck there for hours. And I'll need my own way home afterward."

His simmering impatience exploded in a sigh. *If I were your husband, I could forbid you.* Sarah could almost read his thoughts, but Everett had enough sense to keep them to himself.

"You're the most stubborn woman I've ever known, Sarah Foxworth," he said. "But I've always enjoyed a challenge. Maybe that's why I can't stop coming around to see you."

"You can come and go as you like, Everett," she said. "And now if you'll excuse me, I really need to get on the road." She reached for her slicker, which hung on a peg by the door.

"Wait." He stopped her with a touch. "Before you go, there's something I came to say. Just hear me out—it won't take long. And I'm not asking for a decision now. Just promise me that you'll think about it."

"I'm listening." Sarah's smile masked the sense that she was being backed into a corner.

He cleared his throat. "Some important folks have been talking to me. They want me to run for Keith County commissioner in the next election. I've already said yes."

"Congratulations—assuming you win, which I'm sure you will. You'd make a fine commissioner, Everett."

"Thank you. But a single man is at a disadvantage in an election. To help me win voters, I'm going to need a woman at my side—an attractive, charming, intelligent woman with a spotless reputation . . . like you."

An awkward beat of silence followed in which Sarah struggled for the right words. She hadn't been expecting this.

"Was that a proposal?" she asked.

"Only if you want it to be." When she didn't reply, he plunged ahead. "How much longer can you spend writing letters and waiting for answers that don't come? You don't have to be a doctor. There are other ways to do good in the world, Sarah. I'm offering you one. What do you say?"

"You said you didn't need an answer right away—that you'd give me time to think about it," she reminded him. "I may need a lot of time. Months, even."

His sigh carried an undertone of impatience. "I won't start serious campaigning till summer. But I hope you won't take that long to decide."

"I'll keep your timing in mind," Sarah said. "But meanwhile, don't consider yourself bound by any promise. If you find someone else—"

"I'll take that into consideration. But it's not likely to happen." He caught her waist and pulled her against him. His kiss was perfectly timed and flawlessly executed. Sarah allowed it, even though it left her with no more than a pleasant tingle.

A rap on the door broke them apart. Sarah hurried to answer it. A youth in a ragged coat stood on the porch with his arms full of cut wood. "Do you want this inside, miss?" he asked politely.

"Yes, thank you." Sarah stepped aside for him. As the boy piled the wood next to the stove, she reached for her slicker, found her gloves and medical bag, and made herself ready to leave.

"I'll walk you to the shed," Everett offered. "I'd saddle old Ahab for you, but last time I tried, he bit me."

"It's all right. I'll manage fine." Sarah gave the boy two cookies from the batch someone had brought her to pay for a headache remedy. She held one out to Everett, but he shook his head.

"It's time the two of you were getting back to town. Thank you again for the wood." Sarah watched them leave as she stepped outside into the drizzling rain. At least the cold, wet ride would give her time to think.

But as she saddled the grumpy old mule and mounted up, Sarah's mood was as gloomy as the weather. There was just one thing she wanted. And thinking wasn't going to make it happen. Only luck, and maybe a small miracle, could do that.

CHAPTER SEVEN

AFTER A LONG AND DREARY WINTER, SPRING HAD COME TO THE prairie. New grass sprouted under the melting snow to spread a fresh, green carpet over the land and sprinkle it with the earliest wildflowers. Ducks and geese, migrating north in long *V*s, filled the air with their cries. Meadowlarks and blackbirds marked their nesting territories with their songs.

Far to the south, on the Texas plains, new herds of longhorn cattle had begun the long push north to the grasslands of Wyoming and Montana.

By May, the first herds were passing through Kansas and Nebraska. Joe, now a strapping eighteen-year-old, watched them from a distance as he scouted for wild mustangs. He knew better than to venture close. He worried less about being arrested as a rustler these days, but why take chances?

All the same, every time he saw a herd of cattle, he couldn't help wondering if Benteen Calder would be moving more longhorns to his Montana kingdom. Nearly two years had passed since Calder had ridden away and left him to die under his horse. In that time, Joe's bitterness had festered like an infected wound. Once he'd dreamed of going to Montana, getting some land of his own, and starting a prosperous future. But the act of riding out in a storm to save Calder's damned longhorns had cost him everything.

And Benteen Calder hadn't cared enough to save his life.

Someday, Joe vowed, he would get the justice he deserved. But right now, he had wild horses to find.

Using binoculars, he scanned the prairie for flattened grass, where a herd might have grazed or bedded down. Elijah had taught him where to look and what to look for. Wild horse bands tended to avoid cattle country—the two mares and the foal that had guided him out of the wash were probably drawn to the water there. But this spring, there was no water shortage. The wild horses were free to run wherever their band stallion led them.

Joe had kept his eyes open for the big blue roan, imagining the thrill of catching, breaking, and riding such an animal. But the wily stallion kept his band out of sight—that, or maybe they hadn't survived the hard winter.

When Joe located a band, he would let Elijah know their general whereabouts. With the help of cowboys from Elijah's partner's ranch, they would surround the mustangs and run them into a corral. The choicest horses would be chosen for breaking. The rest would be set free.

Elijah had taught him everything he knew about tracking, catching, and breaking horses. Joe enjoyed the work, and he was good at what he did. But he was coming to realize that his future was limited here. He had nothing of his own. In a sense, he was Elijah's partner, and he shared in the profits from the sale of the horses. But he had no ownership of land or livestock, no home of his own, no wife, or even a best girl, no friends except the old man. And as long as he stayed here, that wasn't likely to change.

Now, reining in his horse, he paused to study the ground. Mixed with the grass, he could just make out the prints of unshod hooves. Not fresh, they were maybe a day old. But at least the mustangs had been here. Nudging the bay, he moved forward to follow the trail.

He was riding with his gaze fixed on the ground when he happened to look up. There, on the horizon, coming toward him, was a lone rider.

Joe had a loaded Winchester rifle slung from the saddle. He lifted it free as the rider came closer, but lowered the weapon as the newcomer hailed him with a wave. They were less than fifty yards apart when Joe recognized him.

Even with his black beard grown long, there was no mistaking Clem McCracken.

Joe's emotions clashed as he waited for Clem to approach. Relief at seeing the likable outlaw alive was mixed with caution and worry. The fact that Clem had tracked him down could only mean trouble.

Clem greeted him with a grin as he brought his horse in close. "I'll be damned, kid. You're a grown man!"

"How did you find me, Clem?" Joe asked, still uneasy.

Clem laughed. "It weren't easy, I can tell you that much. But it came down to askin' the right people, and then keepin' my eyes open."

"The last time I saw you and Slinger, you were riding off with the vigilantes on your tail. What happened? Did Slinger get away, too?"

"Yup. We managed to outrun the bastards and join up with some friends. Slinger got hit, but he's better now. Say, kid, you're talkin' different. You sound like a damned professor."

"I spent the winter reading a shelf full of books. I guess some of what was in them rubbed off on me. But I can't say it makes much difference. I'm still poor and single."

"Well, how'd you like to be rich and single?"

Joe's instincts prickled in warning. "What happened? Did you find your father's stash?"

"Never did. We even went back and dug around. We reckon he must've hid it in the mattress or somewhere like that, and it got burnt up. No, this is somethin' different. Me and Slinger figured you'd be interested."

Joe shook his head. "Stop right there. That vigilante raid cured me of ever wanting to break the law again. Whatever you two are planning, you can count me out."

"Count you out?" Clem's eyes narrowed. "Even if it means getting back at Benteen Calder?"

Joe's pulse slammed. The voice of wisdom whispered that he should turn around and ride off. But the desire to get even with his former boss had been gnawing at his gut for two long years. He could at least listen. "Tell me more," he said.

Clem leaned closer in the saddle. "Calder's bringin' a big herd up from Texas. They passed by Dodge City a few days ago, so they should be up this way afore long."

"How did you find out about it?"

Clem grinned. "The man that buys our stock pays this madam in Dodge to talk up the cowboys. When she finds out what outfit they're with and where they're headed, she telegraphs our buyer in Ogallala. He gets word to us. Beats the old way where we just rode out and looked for 'em."

"What about the brand changes? Do you still do those before you deliver?"

"No, the buyer takes 'em to his ranch, and I do it there. Easier and safer, and you wouldn't have to go along. Just help us get the cattle."

"Is Benteen Calder with his herd?" Joe's jaw tightened as he spoke the name.

"Don't rightly know. But it's his cows and his money. You'll be hurtin' him the same whether he's there or not."

"One last question. I can't imagine you're out to do me any favors. What do you need me for?"

"Fair question," Clem said. "It's a big outfit, and we want to hit 'em hard. Since the last man we had helpin' us got hisself strung up, there's just Slinger and me. We'll need help roundin' up the stock."

"Anybody can do that. Why me?"

"You know the Calder outfit—how they run, when they change shifts, who's in charge, who's a greenhorn. With you scouting for us, we can make a solid plan."

"It's been two years since I was with them. A lot of things could've changed, especially the men."

"True. But you're the best chance we got of doin' this up right. And with you wantin' to get back at Calder, we figure you'll want to do it up right, too. Hey, it'll be like old times, only better. What d'you say?"

"I'll need time to think it over." Joe sensed that he'd be smart to walk away. But maybe if he did this just one time, and got back at Benteen Calder, he could put his anger behind him and move on.

"One thing," he said. "If I say yes, I'm not going to hang around waiting for the stock to sell. I'll want my money as soon as we get the cattle away from the herd."

Clem mulled for a moment, then nodded. "We could manage that—though you'd get more if you waited. Twelve dollars to you for each critter we take. How does that sound?"

"Sounds fair enough." Joe did some mental figuring. The money would be tainted, but what the hell, he was owed. His share from even a few cows would get him to Montana. And if they managed to run off fifty, even a hundred head of cattle, he'd have enough to buy a parcel of land. More important, he'd be hurting Benteen Calder in that pocketbook the sonofabitch wore under his vest in place of a heart.

"How soon will the herd be coming through?" he asked.

"In the next few days. We'll need time to scout and plan first. So, are you with us?"

Joe hesitated. He could still do the sensible thing, walk away, and go back to chasing mustangs for Elijah. But the mention of Calder's herd had lit a fire inside him. The choice he made here and now could change his life forever. As a man, he had to throw his dice into the ring. He had to take this chance.

"Tell me where to meet up with you," he said.

"A man came by asking for you this morning," Elijah remarked over supper. "Husky with a black beard. I didn't have a good feeling about him, but I told him where to look for you."

"He found me." Joe dipped a biscuit into the stew on his plate. It wouldn't be easy, telling the old man he had someplace to go. Elijah wasn't easy to fool. He would know that something was afoot.

Joe cleared his throat. "I'll need to be gone for a few days. You've got new horses to break. You should be fine without me."

"Does your disappearance have anything to do with that man who was here?"

Joe hesitated, then slowly nodded.

"I thought so. And I can tell from that look on your face that you'll be up to no good—no, don't tell me. The less I know, the better."

"So you're all right with me going."

"Hell, no!" Elijah's fist came down hard on the plank table. "Hang around with that sort, and you'll end up dead or behind bars. You're a man. You'll do what you want. But I'm telling you this one time, don't go."

"I've got to." Joe stuck to his resolve. "I gave my word. Don't worry. I'll be back in a few days."

"No, you won't," Elijah said. "You've got till morning to make up your mind. Ride out through that gate, and you're gone for good. I figure your back wages will about pay for the horse you're riding and the saddle you're using. But the rifle stays here."

So it had come to this, as Joe should have known it would. "I'll be gone at first light," he said. "Want me to do the chores before I leave?"

"Don't bother." The old man stood, holding his fork and plate. "Reckon I'll go out on the porch and eat with the dog."

The two of them didn't speak again. Joe gathered up what little was his and rode out before dawn the next morning. It wasn't the way he wanted to take leave of the man who'd treated him like a son, but he'd made his choice—and Elijah had made his. For better or for worse, it was time to move on.

As he rode south onto the open plain, the sun came up, flooding the prairie with its golden rays. Dewy blades of grass glittered where they caught the light. A flock of blackbirds rose from the ground in a circling cloud and vanished into the blue sky.

That was when Joe saw them, galloping over the horizon—the blue roan stallion and his band. As he paused to watch them, they moved in his direction, then, still keeping their distance, veered away and vanished, leaving him to wonder if he'd seen them at all. Maybe he'd only dreamed or imagined them. Maybe, as Elijah had suggested, they were spirit messengers sent to guide him, or even to warn him. But now they were gone, leaving only a mystery in his mind. Nudging his horse, he moved on.

By now Joe knew the country well enough to locate the camp where Clem and Slinger would be waiting for him. He could see the thread of rising smoke from a half mile off. As he rode closer, the smell of coffee and bacon guided him in.

"You're early." Clem greeted him with a grin. "Have some vittles. You look like a starved coyote. Where's your shootin' iron?"

"The one I had wasn't mine. Hope you've got an extra."

"I've got Pa's old .44 in my gear. You can use it till you get your own."

"Thanks." As he helped himself to coffee, bacon, and eggs, Joe hid a sudden unease. Hadn't he told Clem that he only meant to join them for this one job? Clem was talking as if they planned for him to stay.

Huddled by the fire drinking coffee, Slinger gave him a nod. He looked older and thinner than Joe remembered. When he stood, with effort, a grimace of pain flickered across his face. Clem had mentioned that his brother had been shot escaping the vigilantes last fall. Slinger appeared to have been badly wounded. And Joe would bet that he hadn't been treated by a doctor.

No wonder Clem had come to find him, Joe realized. Slinger didn't look strong enough to be much help in a dangerous situation like a cattle stampede. The brothers had needed at least one more able-bodied, experienced man to pull off this big job.

If the raid was successful, maybe the brothers would take their share of the money and head to Mexico. They might not have enough to live high, the way their father had planned, but it wouldn't take much to get by in some small pueblo. And it would certainly be better than the life they had here.

But why did he care? Joe asked himself. These men had held him against his will and forced him to commit crimes. Now here he was, against his better judgment, joining up with them again. Only the thought of getting revenge on Benteen Calder kept him from mounting up and riding away—that, and the strong hunch that he'd be shot in the back if he tried.

"So tell me the plan so far," he said. "Where's the Calder herd now, and how are we going to hit them?"

They crouched around a patch of smooth ground, using the sharp point of a knife to draw a crude map and plot lines of attack. The cattle drive had last been reported four days short of Ogallala. The raid needed to happen soon, before the herd got close to the town.

Joe argued that they should wait for a storm. The weather had been unsettled for the past few days, with rain and lightning bursts sweeping across the prairie. The dark, the noise, and the rain would offer the best chance of stampeding the herd and using the confusion to make off with a good number of animals. It might even be possible to blend in with the riders who were rushing to round up the cattle. Stampede the remuda as well, and any cowboys chasing the stolen stock would be riding worn-out horses.

"And if it doesn't rain?" Slinger demanded.

"Then everything gets a lot riskier, and we won't take as many cattle," Joe said. "I say we trail the herd and wait for a storm as long as we can."

"We can't wait too long," Clem argued. "If they make it to Ogallala, we've lost 'em. Beyond that point, we'd be too far from our buyer, and we don't know the country. We could even run into renegade Cheyenne or Lakota. The ladies like how I look with my scalp on my head. I'd just as soon keep it there."

"So what if we don't get a storm?" Slinger asked.

"Then we make a new plan for going in on a clear night."

"Makes sense to me," Clem said. "Slinger?"

Slinger managed a nod before he was seized by a racking cough. Blood drops dotted his beard as he doubled over with pain.

For the next two days and nights, the three men trailed the Calder herd. The air smelled of rain. Sheet lightning flashed among the clouds that roiled along the horizon. But the hoped-for nighttime storm had yet to come.

Joe had plenty of time to study the cattle and the crew. The herd was about the same size as on the first drive—close to 2,500 steers, cows, and calves, all wearing the triple C brand of the Calder Cattle Company.

There was no sign of Benteen Calder. This time the trail boss was Jesse Trumbo. Joe still had mixed feelings toward Jesse, the man who would have found him under his horse on that fateful morning if he hadn't obeyed Calder's order to leave. The boss was the man who gave the orders—but if Jesse had insisted on taking five minutes to check the wash and offered to catch up afterward, Calder would probably have let him.

Rusty was still manning the chuckwagon. The rest of the cowhands were strangers—all to the good. Even if one of them saw his face, he wouldn't be recognized. And if, God forbid, he had to shoot somebody, at least it wouldn't be somebody he knew.

By the third day, Clem and Slinger were getting impatient. So was Joe. But the advantages of a storm held him in check. The memory of that awful night with the lightning, the rain, and the stampede still haunted his dreams. But when he thought of how easy it would have been for someone to make off with part of the herd, he knew that a storm, if it came, would be worth the wait.

On the last possible night, after the three had already agreed on a dry weather plan, the storm moved in. Sweeping across the sky, boiling black clouds exploded overhead in earthshaking bursts of lightning and thunder.

With no time to lose, Joe and the brothers moved in to carry out their plan. Remembering the tragic death of Spanish Bill, Joe had cautioned the brothers against wearing metal that might attract lightning. His words were wasted breath. They would all need their guns. But with luck, out of the same fear, the cowboys guarding the herd might leave their weapons in camp tonight.

The plan was for Joe to sneak up close and spook the remuda. The bolting horses would trigger a cattle stampede, or at least a distraction. Clem and Slinger would flank the west side of the herd. Once the stampede started, they would drive as many cattle as possible in an eastward direction before the animals could start to mill. Once Joe got the horses running, he would cut around and join them. They would ride off together, driving the stolen cattle ahead of them.

If all went as planned, no shots would be fired, and no one would be hurt. But as Joe left his companions and rode through the black rain, with blue lightning crackling across the sky, he sensed that this was a night when nothing could be planned.

The remembered terror of that other storm—the unearthly glow on 2,000 pairs of horns, the tingling air, and the deadly bolt that had killed his friend crept over him. A knot of cold fear tightened in his gut. Joe forced himself to think about Benteen Calder and how the arrogant bastard had left him to die. Tonight was about the revenge he'd dreamed of for two long years. This was his chance. He had to keep going.

The cattle were on their feet, shifting and snorting. Most of the hands had ridden out to the herd. Joe could hear them singing to calm the restless animals. Anything—a lightning bolt, an unexpected sound, or a movement in the dark—could trigger the stampede.

Despite the cold storm, Joe was sweating under his clothes. Rain streamed off his slicker and ran down the horse's flanks. Ahead, through the murk, he could see the camp. Set on a low rise, it was marked by glowing lanterns that hung from the chuckwagon. The horses would be nearby. On most nights, they would have been turned loose to graze. Tonight, they were bunched inside a rope corral to keep them where they might be needed in case of a stampede.

The corral, which could be put up anywhere, was nothing more than a long rope strung in a circle, supported by a few stakes hammered into the ground. Pulling it down with the horse would be easy. The only challenge would be not getting caught.

Slipping out of the saddle and dropping the reins, he looped one end of his lariat around the nearest stake and wrapped the other around the saddle horn. He was so close to the camp that he could recognize Rusty's square-built shadow cast by the lanterns against the cover of the chuckwagon.

Joe was about to mount his horse again when, from the rainy darkness beyond the herd, his ears caught a popping sound. For an instant he hoped it might be thunder. But he knew better. It was pistol fire.

One shot, then a second. A pause, then two more, then silence. Not a gunfight. An execution.

Even before he'd thought it out, the nauseous weight in his gut told him the truth. Clem and Slinger were dead. All he could do now was try to get away and save himself.

Chain lightning zigzagged across the sky, striking close. As the thunder boomed, Joe leaped into the saddle. The horse surged forward, jerking out the stake that anchored the rope fence and pulling down one side of the corral. Snorting and whinnying, the horses in the remuda poured through the opening and plunged downhill toward the herd. Spooked by the gunfire and the lightning, the cattle were already stampeding. As they spread over the prairie in a dark wave of thundering hooves and bobbing horns, the men raced to catch the leaders and turn them aside.

Left in the open, Joe was still dragging the stakes and the rope from the corral. He paused to free his lariat from where he'd twisted it around the saddle horn. The water-swollen rope refused to come loose.

Pausing the horse for an instant, he used both hands to attack the tangle. That was when something seemed to explode inside his head. The horse reared and bucked. He felt a burning sensation above his ear and then another, like the stab of a red-hot knife, going through his shoulder from the back. For an instant he fought the blackness that was swirling around him. Then, as another burning jab struck his side, he tumbled through space and into the dark.

Joe hovered on the edge of unconsciousness, his slow awareness coming and going like the open spaces in a cloudy sky. There was pain—deep and throbbing—in his head and through his body. And he felt cold, as if he were lying on wet ground. He could no longer hear the sound of the rain or feel it on his face. Maybe the storm was over.

He could not summon the will or the strength to open his eyes, but he sensed a bright light, like a lantern, shining down on him. And he could hear men's voices, fading in and out, but strangely familiar.

"Looks like we got a live one here, Jesse." Joe recognized the voice of Rusty, the cook.

"Well, we can turn him over to the sheriff with the two dead ones tomorrow, if he lives that long. Looks like he's shot up pretty bad. Were you the one who hit him?"

"Hell, Jesse, you know I can't shoot for sour apples. It was Mike, come up to change horses, that plugged him. Good thing you told the men to keep their guns handy tonight."

"Well, there's been a lot of rustling in these parts. Maybe now there won't be so damned much. And we got the stampede stopped, too. All in all, the night could've been worse. Hell, there might even be a reward for these three buzzards—that would make a nice bonus to split among the men."

The talk faded. The next thing Joe became aware of was a damp cloth sponging his face, wiping away something sticky. Was it blood? It seemed he'd been shot. That would explain the pain. Pain everywhere . . . and a strange numbness setting in. Was he dying?

"This one's not much more than a kid," Rusty said. "I'm bettin' he fell in with some bad company. Maybe we oughta try and save him."

"You could try. But he looks pretty near gone. And even if he lives, it'll only be to hang."

"I could wrap him to slow the bleeding. The head wound's just a crease. But the other two . . ." The sponging paused. Joe could feel himself coming around, but the pain was getting worse. "If the bullets are still in him, he'll need a doc," Rusty said.

"Not much chance of that. With so much stock to round up in the morning, we won't be in Ogallala till late tomorrow at the soonest." Jesse's voice came from somewhere close. "He won't last long enough to—" The words ended in a sudden gasp. "Oh, my God!"

"What—?"

"Rusty, that's Joe Dollarhide!"

There was a beat of silence. "Couldn't be," Rusty said. "That kid got killed in the big stampede two years ago. Remember?"

"Sure. But we never found the body. The boss and I saw his horse, dead in a wash. I wanted to go down for a closer look, but Benteen needed to round up his cattle so we left. Lord, the kid could've been down there somewhere, still alive, and we just left him."

"Are you sure it's Joe?"

"Hell, yes. I remember that little scar on his chin and the way one ear kind of stuck out farther than the other one. He's grown some, but it's him. It's got to be." A strong hand gripped Joe's shoulder, shaking him, triggering jabs of hot pain. "Dollarhide! Can you hear me?"

Joe groaned. Summoning all his strength and will, he managed to open his eyes. What he saw, in the lantern light, was Jesse's shocked face staring down at him. "Hurts . . ." he muttered. "Hurts like hell . . ." His eyes closed again. He lay in a cloud of pain, struggling to piece together what his ears could hear.

"So what now, boss?" Rusty asked. "Don't forget Dollarhide was shot helping his buddies steal cattle."

Jesse exhaled. "I owe this man. I could've saved his life two years ago, and I rode away. If I'd gone down into that wash and found him, he wouldn't be where he is now. Patch him up as best you can. Load him in the chuckwagon and run him into Ogallala—it shouldn't take you more than two or three hours. If Dollarhide makes it there alive, leave him with a doctor and come back."

"And if he doesn't?"

"Leave the body with the sheriff and tell him we've got a couple more he can have."

"We'll need to unload the bedrolls for the men. And what about breakfast?"

"Anybody can make coffee," Jesse said. "We'll manage till you get back. I'll get the wagon ready while you wrap Dollarhide's wounds. And get some whiskey down him. He's going to need it."

"I'm already ahead of you." Rusty was shuffling items in what Joe remembered as the medical kit he carried on the chuck-wagon. The elderly cook raised his head and tipped a glass bottle to his lips. Whiskey. Joe swallowed all he could without choking. Its heat burned through his body, warming his flesh but dulling his thoughts.

"One more question." Propping Joe's upper body, Rusty pressed a wad of sheeting to his bleeding side and began to wrap it with long strips. "What do I say to the sheriff, or to anybody else, who asks me why a wounded cattle rustler would be worth getting to a doctor?"

Jesse's answer, when it came, was muted by distance. "Just tell them what I'm telling you. This man is one of ours."

CHAPTER EIGHT

JOE CLENCHED HIS JAW AGAINST THE PAIN THAT RIPPED THROUGH HIM with every jolt of the chuckwagon wheels over the rough prairie ground.

No talking. Not a word.

He repeated the message in his mind. *Stay silent.* If he couldn't speak, he wouldn't be questioned. If he couldn't be questioned, he wouldn't be forced to lie about who he was and how he'd been shot.

If he lived.

He lay on the thin blanket that had been used to lift him into the wagon bed. Beneath it there was nothing but hard boards. He could feel the blood seeping through the dressings Rusty had bound over his wounds. He'd probably bleed to death before they made it to Ogallala. But at least he wouldn't be alone. As the chuckwagon was getting ready to leave, two of the men had ridden up with the McCracken brothers' bodies slung behind their saddles. The rustlers had been wrapped in a canvas tarp and laid in the wagon bed next to Joe, to be dropped off at the sheriff's. If Joe ended up dead with them, it was no worse than he deserved. He'd thrown in his lot with the worthless pair. He was no better than they were.

Jesse Trumbo, with Rusty's help, had given him one last chance at a clean start. More than anything, Joe wanted to take that chance. But first he had to survive, and that alone would be a miracle.

Mercifully, as the miles wore on, he blacked out. The next thing Joe became aware of, the chuckwagon had stopped moving. He could hear the late-night sounds of a town—music and laughter from a saloon, the nicker of a horse, and the distant whistle of a train.

The chuckwagon creaked as Rusty moved across the seat. Joe could hear him talking to someone outside.

"I've got two dead rustlers to deliver to the sheriff and a gunshot cowboy that needs a doc. Can you help me out?"

"The sheriff lives two blocks from the other side of the tracks. There's a sign on the gate. You'll have to wake him up, but he's used to that." The speaker sounded young, maybe a kid sweeping up outside one of the saloons. "The doc's out of town—gone all week, I heard tell. But there's this lady. She doctors folks that can't pay cash. She helped my sis when her baby had the croup. Just follow this road to where the fields start. You'll see an old brown house with big trees around it. That's her place."

"Thank you, young man. Here's a little something for your trouble."

"Wow! Thanks, mister!" The boyish voice faded as he hurried away. Whatever Rusty had given the lad, it must've been generous.

Shifting his position on the open bench, Rusty leaned back over the wagon bed. "You still alive, Joe Dollarhide?"

Joe moaned through a red haze of pain.

"Hang on, then. Since those other two galoots ain't goin' nowhere, I'll deliver you first. Let's just hope the lady's at home and willin' to help you."

The jarring motion as the wagon started up again lanced fresh agony through Joe's body. The sticky wetness told him he was lying in his own blood and getting weaker by the minute. And Rusty was taking him not to a trained doctor, but to some woman who dosed her neighbors' rashes and coughs.

It was time he faced reality.

He was going to die.

*　*　*

Sarah had spent most of the night tossing and turning. After a long day of work, she'd fallen into bed, hoping to sleep. But that was when her worries had come flocking home to roost.

Only one medical school application had arrived in the mail. She'd filled it out and submitted it, but months had passed and she'd heard nothing back—not even a rejection letter. Meanwhile, Everett was pressuring her to wed him before he began his summer campaign. On top of that, the roof needed serious patching to stop the ruinous leaks, and her absentee landlord had left any repairs up to her. Ahab's hooves needed trimming and shoeing, and she barely had enough money to pay rent. Say yes to Everett, and all those other problems would vanish like magic. So why did she keep putting him off?

But she knew the answer to that question. Everett was a splendid catch by any woman's measure. But marrying him would mean giving up her dream.

It was well after midnight when she finally sank into a fitful sleep. She had just begun to dream when a hard rapping at the door jolted her awake.

Sweeping her hair out of her eyes, she swung her bare feet off the bed, stood, and flung Uncle Harlan's old woolen robe over her flannel nightgown. The knocking continued as she hurried to the door, pausing to knot the sash of the robe before releasing the latch.

The risen moon revealed a stocky, grizzled man, dressed in worn trail clothes, standing on the front porch. Behind him, parked at the front gate, stood what appeared to be a chuckwagon, with the canvas cover in place.

Before she could gather her wits, he spoke. "I'm looking for the lady who doctors folks. Is that you?"

"It is." Only then did she notice the bloodstains that spattered his clothes and the distressed look on his wrinkled face. "If this is a serious emergency, you'll probably want Dr. Phillips, in town. I can tell you how to—"

He cut her off. "The regular doc is off somewhere. I've got a wounded cowboy that had a run-in with some rustlers, and you're all the help I could find."

"How badly is he hurt? Did he get shot?"

The old man nodded. "There's at least one bullet in him, maybe two, and he's lost a lot of blood. If you can't help him, he'll die. Hell, maybe he'll die anyway, but it would be a damned shame. He's young—not much more than a boy. He's got a life to live if you can save him."

If you can save him. Anxiety formed a cold ball in the pit of Sarah's stomach. She could deliver babies and set broken limbs. But a critical wound was out of her depth. What if the man died due to her inexperience, when a real doctor could have saved him? But worrying would only waste time. As the old man had said, she was the only help available.

"Is he able to walk? Can you get him in here?" Sarah forced herself to speak calmly. She'd assisted Uncle Harlan with gunshot wounds, so she knew what was needed, but if a bullet was lodged deep, getting to it could be dangerous, even deadly.

"He can't even stand. He's barely alive. I've got him on a blanket. We can use that to carry him in. I can take his head and shoulders if you can lift his feet."

Sarah had left her shoes by the door. She thrust her feet into them. "Let's go," she said.

The spring night was chilly. Wind whipped the branches of the big cottonwood trees that surrounded the house as Sarah followed the old man out of the gate and around to the open back of the chuckwagon.

In the dark interior of the wagon bed, she could see the rangy figure of a man lying uncovered on a ragged blanket. Next to him lay a long bundle wrapped in a canvas tarpaulin. Something about it gave her the shivers. "What's that?" Sarah asked.

"That's the rustlers. Don't worry. They're past doin' any harm. I'll be droppin' them off with the sheriff." He lifted the end of the quilt and began tugging it back over the lowered tailgate. Sarah moved in to help him. The cowboy gasped and groaned as his body was dragged backward out of the wagon. Sarah kept his feet as level as possible, holding the end of the quilt as it supported him like a hammock.

Finding their way in the moonlight, they lugged him up the walk, through the front door, and into the kitchen. "Lay him out on the table," Sarah said. "That'll be the easiest place to work on him."

She'd cleared the table after supper, so there was no need to move anything. She would have chosen to lay out a clean sheet, but she didn't want to let go of the wounded cowboy to fetch it. Better to just lay him out on the blanket for now.

He sucked in his breath as they raised the quilt and lowered him onto the table. He had to be at least semi-conscious. But if he'd spoken a word or even opened his eyes, she hadn't noticed it. She wouldn't know how badly he was hurt until she could look at him under the light.

"I need to get rid of those two dead rustlers," said the old man, who'd introduced himself as Rusty. "If you can manage here, I'll go find the sheriff. When I get that taken care of, I'll stop back and see how he's doing."

Sarah took a moment to see him to the door. Rusty had said he'd stop back. Evidently, after that, he planned to return to his cattle drive and leave her to take care of this young cowboy alone.

But she'd have to worry about that later. Right now, she had a life to save.

A hook for suspending a lantern hung from a chain above the table. The unlit lantern sat on the counter. After lighting it, she climbed onto a chair and hung it by the handle. Light flooded the table below, illuminating the body of the man who lay there.

She took a moment to study him from above. He was young and tall, his rangy body still filling out. Above the bloodstained white bandage that wrapped his head, his dark hair clung damply to his scalp. A thin, scraggly beard hid his jawline. His eyes were closed.

An unaccustomed tenderness surged in her—maybe because he reminded her of a boy whose life had crossed hers for a brief time—a boy she might have loved if things had ended differently.

Maybe there was a girl waiting for this young man somewhere—a girl who loved him the way she'd almost loved Joe Dollarhide.

Heaven help her, she had to save him.

She climbed down from the chair and ran to fetch the things she needed—Uncle Harlan's medical bag, a box of wrappings, a clean sheet, and one of the long, white aprons the doctor had worn for surgery. Adding some wood to the coals in the stove, she coaxed them to a blaze, then set a shallow pan on the stove and dropped a scalpel and forceps in two different sizes into the water to boil.

Laying the robe aside, she tied back her hair, donned the apron over her nightgown, rolled up her sleeves, scrubbed her hands in a basin, and with a silent prayer, set to work.

First, she checked the head wound by lifting the edge of the bandage. It appeared to be a crease above the left ear. For now, the bloodstained wrap was holding. She could clean it and re-place the dressing later. The other injuries were more urgent.

"Can you hear me?" she asked, wishing she'd thought to ask Rusty the cowboy's name.

He didn't answer. His eyes remained closed, his breathing ragged. She continued speaking to him as if he could hear. "I'm going to cut back your shirt and underwear and then examine your wounds. It's bound to hurt some, but that can't be helped. I'll be as gentle as I can."

After cutting away his ruined shirt and the cotton undershirt beneath it, she used the larger forceps to peel back the blood-caked dressing on his shoulder. He'd been shot from behind. She could see where the bullet had exited just below the collarbone. He groaned as she rolled him partway onto his side to find the entrance wound above the shoulder blade. A lucky shot. Though the wound was still oozing, it would likely heal in time. Hands moving swiftly, she replaced the dressing on both sides to stanch the blood. The remaining wound, on the left side, two finger-breadths below the rib cage, was the critical one—the one that would kill him if she failed.

It had been a hard call, deciding whether to check the lesser wounds first, but this one was going to take time. She hadn't wanted anything else to go wrong before she was finished.

A quiver passed through him as she lifted away the blood-soaked dressing and saw the ugly hole, still bleeding like a well. Sarah stifled a gasp. If the bullet had struck a vital organ, he wouldn't have lived long enough to get here, she told herself. But he could still die from blood loss, or from infection or lead poisoning if she couldn't get the bullet out.

Unfolding the sheet, she laid it along his left side and worked it partway under him to cover the dirty blanket. In the medical kit was a knife with a leather sheath. Sarah removed the sheath, leaving the knife behind.

"Listen, if you can hear me," she said, "we've got to get that bullet out of you. I'm going to put something between your teeth to bite on when the pain gets bad." She leaned over him, opened his mouth slightly, and laid the knife sheath between his jaws. She'd half expected him to resist, but he accepted it. Maybe he really could hear her.

"All right. Wish me luck. Here goes." Taking the smaller and finer of the two forceps, she worked the tip into the wound and began to probe for the bullet.

Joe had been drifting in a red haze of pain, aware but not awake. The womanly voice drifted in and out of his hearing, soothing and strangely familiar. But he was too far below the surface to open his eyes, to speak, or even to move.

The leather between his teeth tasted salty and felt strange. He wasn't sure what it was for—the woman must've told him, but the words hadn't penetrated his foggy mind. He was testing the edge with his tongue when the pain struck, stabbing into him like a red-hot poker below the ribs. His teeth clamped on the leather. His body went rigid, every nerve and muscle quivering like a bow-string as the torture went on and on until, at last, a merciful darkness closed in.

* * *

Five agonizing minutes after she'd begun the probe, Sarah felt the solid bullet against the tip of the forceps. Clamping on to it, she eased it out of the wound and let it drop onto the table. She felt nauseous. Her legs quivered like jelly beneath her nightgown. Her body was soaked with sweat. She braced her arms against the table for a moment while her head cleared.

The young cowboy lay limp on the table, the leather knife sheath loose in his mouth. Sarah lifted it away and put it aside to be washed. For the first moment, she feared she'd killed him. Then she saw that he was breathing. When she checked his pulse, it felt a little steadier than before. But that didn't mean she'd saved him. He was still in danger from blood loss and infection.

Wetting a cloth in the boiled water, she cleaned around the wound, then applied a dressing. Wrapping his unconscious body was a challenge, but she managed to work the fabric strips beneath him and pull them tight to hold the dressing in place.

For the moment, it was all she could do. She covered him with a blanket, then stumbled into the sitting room area and sank into the rocker to rest. Getting him off the table would be the next challenge. There'd be no place to put him except her own bed, but she couldn't drag him there without opening up his wounds. She could only hope Rusty would keep his word and come back to help her.

She was beginning to worry when she heard the sound of horses outside. Moments later, she opened the door to his knock.

"How is he? Did you get the bullet out?" he asked, walking over to the table.

"I got it out, but he's in bad shape. He's going to need a lot of rest. How long can you stay?"

"Only a minute or two. I'm cookin' for a cattle drive, about fifteen miles out. The men can't work long unless I'm there with the chuckwagon to feed 'em."

"I hope you don't plan on taking him with you. He'd never survive the trip."

"No, I figured that much." He dug into his vest pocket and pulled out several folded bills. "Here," he said, thrusting them at Sarah. "This should help with his care. If it's not enough, I'll stop by again when the herd gets in, most likely after tomorrow. If you need more, just ask."

Sarah glanced at the money. What he'd given her was more than generous. It was extravagant. "I can't imagine I'll need this much," she said. "Are you sure you can spare it?"

The old man gave her a fleeting smile. "Don't worry," he said. "It isn't my money. It's Benteen Calder's, and he's got plenty more where that came from. Call it back pay."

Benteen Calder. The name surfaced in her memory as she laid the cash on the counter. What a small world it was.

"I need one more favor before you go. Your cowboy's passed out. I need help getting him off the table and into bed."

"Sure. Let's take his boots off first. His pants are pretty dirty, too. Don't worry, he'll have his drawers on underneath. I reckon, as a doctor, you've seen it all."

"You know I'm not a real doctor, don't you?" Sarah asked.

"I know. But bless you, lady, you sure should be."

After stripping the cowboy down to his socks and drawers, they managed to lift him with the blanket, carry him into Sarah's room, and slide him gently into her bed, leaving the blanket on the floor. He whimpered as they moved him but didn't open his eyes.

Sarah tucked the covers over him before they returned to the kitchen. She thought about trying to give him water, but he needed to be conscious to drink it. Otherwise, he'd only choke.

"I take it that's your bed where we put him," Rusty said. "He's liable to be there for a while. Where will you sleep?"

"Don't worry. I'll figure that out," Sarah said as the old man started for the front door. "Oh, I do have one more question."

"What's that?" He turned in the doorway.

"It would help to know his name. You never told me."

"Oh." He raised a grizzled eyebrow. "Sorry. I'm getting forgetful in my old age. It's Joe. Joe Dollarhide."

With that, he walked out the door, leaving Sarah in a state of bewildered shock.

She forced herself to clean up the mess in the kitchen before going back to look at her patient again. The soiled sheet and discarded bandages were bundled up and put out the back door to be burned the next day, along with the blood-soaked blanket he'd lain on in the chuckwagon. The kitchen table was wiped down, the surgical instruments washed and put away, and the apron put in a pan of cold water to soak out the stains.

As she worked, her thoughts spun, clashed, and tumbled. That summer day, two years ago, when Lorna Calder had come to tell her about Joe's death was etched like a scar in her memory.

Lorna had said that his body was never found. If the man in the other room was really Joe, he must've turned up alive later on. But if that was true, why hadn't he let her know? Why hadn't he come by, or at least written her a letter? If nothing else, Lorna, who knew how she'd felt about Joe, could have let her know he was all right.

The only explanation that made sense was that he hadn't cared enough to tell her.

She remembered all the times when she'd imagined the stampeding cattle trampling his body into dust, the nightmares, the tears. So much horror. So much sadness for the loss of his young life and the friendship that could never be.

And all this time Joe Dollarhide had been alive.

The hurt that welled in her was mixed with cold anger. If that was really Joe in her bed, he'd be waking up to some serious questions. No one, let alone a scruffy young cowboy, had the right to treat her so callously.

With the cleanup finished, she climbed onto the chair, lifted the glowing lantern off its hook above the table, and carried it into the bedroom.

Holding it above the bed, she gazed down at the man who lay there with his eyes closed, his chest rising and falling as he breathed. Time and maturity had changed him. He was taller, his features more balanced than she remembered. The bulky bandage around his head, which she'd decided to leave for now, was still in place, covering his forehead from hairline to eyebrows. That, and the scruffy beard he wore, had kept her from recognizing him at first. But seeing him clearly now, she could tell, beyond any doubt, that this was Joe. His mouth was just as she remembered. And half hidden by his beard, she could see the scar on his chin, where he'd taken that punch for her back in Dodge City.

She felt something soften inside her, the way a bud swells and loosens before bursting into bloom. But her resolve remained firm. This young cowboy had broken her heart. The least he owed her was an explanation. She would see that he lived to give her one.

The wall clock in the sitting room struck three—too early to start the day, and she was exhausted. But the house only had one bedroom, and hers was the only bed. Most of her patients were treated in their own homes. She'd made no provisions for keeping anyone overnight, and Joe was likely to be here for much longer than that.

Tomorrow she would fashion a bedroll to lay out on the floor. But tonight, she was exhausted, and she knew she'd get no rest sitting up in the rocker.

The rented house had come with some furniture, which included the sagging double bed, made for a married couple. Joe lay in the middle, taking up most of the space. But she could wrap herself in a spare quilt and lie along the edge, on top of the covers. Surely, with Joe injured and mostly unaware, there could be no impropriety in that. Besides, it would be a good idea to stay close by, in case he woke, confused and in pain.

The fire in the stove had burned down to coals, leaving a chill in the house. After taking the lantern back to the kitchen, Sarah put on the plaid robe and picked up the spare quilt she'd hung over the back of the rocker. After leaving her shoes next to the front door and extinguishing the lantern, she made her way back to the bedroom.

In the moonlight that shone faintly through the curtains, she could see Joe's body stretched out in the bed with his head on the pillow. There was just enough room for her along the edge.

Bundling the quilt around herself, she eased onto the narrow space. She lay on her side with her back toward him, comfortable enough as long as she didn't try to move. From behind her, she could hear each breath ending in a little snore—a hopeful sign. Real sleep was what his body needed.

The rhythm of his breathing blended with the rush of wind in the cottonwoods and the creaks and clicks of the old house settling with the cold. Sarah hadn't expected to sleep, but before long, she began to feel drowsy. With Joe's body warm beside her, she drifted in and out of sleep until finally, as the sky began to pale, she eased off the bed.

Joe was still asleep, his eyes closed, his breathing regular. When she brushed his pale, whiskered face with her fingertips, she felt no sign of fever. All to the good, but he wasn't out of danger. She would need to keep an eye on that deep wound to make sure it didn't fester. And she would need to get plenty of fluids down him to help his body replace the blood he'd lost.

As she gazed down at him, she felt a surge of tenderness. She willed it away. Joe's alleged death had cost her nearly two years of grief. He was going to have to answer for that.

Steeling her resolve, she gathered up her clothes and left the room to start her day.

Joe woke to a pain that felt as if a knife were being twisted into his left side. He groaned out loud as his eyes opened to a gray dawn in a room he'd never seen before. Morning light filtered through the thin curtains of a high, narrow window. An unaccustomed soft warmth cradled his body, its subtle fragrance stealing into his senses. He could almost believe he'd died and gone to heaven. But being dead couldn't possibly hurt this much—unless he'd gone to hell, as he probably deserved.

Fearing that a shift in position might make the pain worse, he lay still, searching his memory for any clue that might tell him where he was and how he'd come to be here.

His exploring hands found the bandages on his head and shoulder and the wrappings around his body that held the heavy dressing to his side. Some things were coming back now. He'd been shot by one of the Calder hands. Slinger and Clem were dead, and he would be, too, if Jesse Trumbo hadn't recognized him and shown him the miracle of mercy. He had a faint memory of Rusty binding his wounds, and then the agony of bouncing on hard boards in the back of a wagon . . .

Joe's memory was blurring once more. He barely had the strength to think, let alone raise his head and look around. He must have lost a lot of blood. That would explain his weakness. But it wouldn't explain where he was or how he'd come to be here.

He struggled to remember. There'd been some mention of a woman, then a woman's low voice, penetrating the fog of pain. She'd said she was going to hurt him, and she had. The last thing he remembered was biting on something she'd put in his mouth. After that, he must've blacked out.

Don't talk. Until now, silence had been his only protection. But how much longer would he need it? Was he a patient in this place? A guest? Or a prisoner?

He was still pondering the question when a familiar aroma crept into his senses from the next room. It was coffee, hot and fresh. If it was for him, he could use a cup. And it was time he met his rescuer.

Clasping the top of the metal bedframe above his head, he dragged himself backward and upward into a semi-sitting position with the pillow supporting his back. The pain in his side was so excruciating that he feared he was opening up the wound, but he'd had enough of lying helplessly on his back. As soon as he could stand and put on clothes, he meant to get out of here. But right now he needed some answers.

The bedroom door stood slightly ajar. Joe couldn't see through the opening, but he could hear the sound of approaching footsteps—light and quick, a woman's.

The door opened. Silhouetted by the light behind her, a petite woman with her hair twisted into a bun on her head stood on the threshold, holding a tray. With the morning light in his eyes, he couldn't make out her features, but there was something strangely familiar about the size and shape of her.

When she spoke, her tone was anything but friendly. "So you're awake. Good. After you drink this coffee, I've got some questions for you. And you'd better have some answers ready, Joe Dollarhide."

Joe's pulse lurched as she stepped out of the light, into the room, and he recognized her. Lord help him, it was Sarah!

CHAPTER NINE

THUNDERSTRUCK, JOE STARED AT HER. HE'D REMEMBERED SARAH AS a pretty, spirited girl. The Sarah walking toward him now, balancing a tray in her hands, was a beautiful woman who moved with an air of strength and confidence—a woman with the look of someone who'd struggled and survived.

What was she doing here—wherever *here* was? Where was her great-uncle, the doctor? Was he the one who'd treated the bullet wounds?

Joe's questions evaporated in the sheer joy of seeing her. Sarah, the angel who'd blessed his dreams, the girl he'd given up on ever finding again. She was here. She was real.

But she wasn't smiling.

As she bent close and placed the tray on his lap, Joe ached to reach out and touch her, if only to make sure he wasn't dreaming. But he checked the impulse when her stern glance warned him not to try.

Clearly, she wasn't ready to take up their friendship where they'd left it two years ago. After disappearing from her life for two years, he couldn't say he blamed her. How much did she know about him? What had Rusty told her?

On the tray, resting in a saucer, was a mug of steaming, black coffee. "It's hot, but drink it all," she said. "You need all the fluids you can get down. I've got soup on the stove. You'll want plenty of that when it's ready. Meanwhile, I'll bring you some water and fix you some breakfast."

"Thank you, Sarah." The words, which rasped from his parched throat, were the first he'd spoken since before he was shot.

"Just drink your coffee." He caught the moist glimmer in her eyes as she turned away and walked toward the door, her head high, her spine ramrod straight. At the last moment, she paused, turned back, moved a wooden chair to the side of the bed, and sat down. She took a deep breath, as if pulling herself together.

"Lorna Calder came to the house to tell me you'd been killed in a stampede," she said. "I cried myself to sleep that night, imagining the moment you'd died, thinking what an awful waste it was and how I would never know what we might have meant to each other.

"Now I find out you were alive the whole time." The wetness in her eyes had turned to fire. "And you never even had the decency to let me know. What was I supposed to think? What am I supposed to think now?"

The coffee, which he'd been sipping, had moistened his dry throat, making it easier for him to talk. But what could he say to her? How could he even begin to explain? He cleared his throat and tried.

"Before that stampede, the one you heard about, I was counting every day, every mile, that brought me closer to seeing you again. But afterward, when I was lying in that wash and Calder had given me up for dead and left me behind, it was all I could do to stay alive. I kept wanting to get back and find you, but the things that happened—things I had to do to survive—made that impossible. As time passed, I figured you'd probably moved on, maybe even married . . ."

Joe's voice trailed off. How could he tell her the rest of the story—being part of an outlaw gang, stealing stock with the McCracken brothers and then, after he'd escaped to live an honest life, going back to ride with them again? What would she think of him?

She frowned, her forehead forming a little furrow above her violet eyes. "But from what Rusty told me, I gathered you were back with the Calders. You could have sent me a letter, or even asked Lorna to let me know. Joe, I'm still in shock. I thought you were dead! I didn't even know you were alive until Rusty brought you here and told me your name." Her voice broke slightly. "After all this time, missing you and mourning you . . ."

Right then, he would have given anything to take her in his arms and hold her. But even if he'd been strong enough to do it, she might not have welcomed his embrace, especially if she'd known the truth about the past two years. Joe sensed that it was too soon to tell her. That would have to wait for the right time—if the right time ever came.

He finished the coffee, which had cooled by now. "There's more to the story," he said, hoping to change the subject. "But you'll have to wait till I'm feeling stronger to hear it. You said something about getting me some water."

"Of course." She took the mug and the tray, left the room, and returned moments later with a glass of water. Joe's pulse quickened when she walked back through the door. The sunlight of the new day, shining through the kitchen window, seemed to follow her into the room. This was her room and her bed, he realized, his gaze falling on the feminine touches—the ruffled curtains, the hairbrush and hand mirror on the dresser, the pretty, fringed shawl flung over a hook on the door. The light fragrance that had invaded his senses as he woke was hers.

"I didn't mean to take your bed," he said as she handed him the glass.

"There was no place else to put you."

"But how did you sleep? Do you live here alone? What happened to your uncle, the doctor?"

"He passed away last year. And yes, I do live here alone. And since you asked, I managed to sleep fine. Drink your water. Then I'll get you more. There's a chamber pot under the bed. Let me know when you need it. You might need help getting up."

Her offer startled him. He'd known from their first meeting that Sarah was a lady. But she'd mentioned his using the chamber pot without so much as a ladylike blush.

"Thanks, but I'm still pretty dry," he said, draining half the glass. The water was fresh and cold, and he could tell his body craved it. But if he emptied the glass she would leave again.

"When you're finished, I'll need to check the dressing on your wound," she said. "Are you in much pain?"

"Some. I'll be all right." The wound had hurt like blazes on waking, but he'd stopped thinking about the pain when Sarah walked into the room. "Was it you who patched me up after Rusty brought me here?"

"Yes—although getting that bullet out was the scariest thing I've ever done. I assisted Uncle Harlan for more than a year before he died. He taught me as much as he could—that's how I've made my living, helping poor folks who can't afford to pay Dr. Phillips." Her chin came up, giving him a glimpse of the stubborn determination he remembered. "I want to be a real doctor, Joe. I've already applied to one medical school. If they don't take me, I'll keep trying until I get in somewhere."

"You'd make a wonderful doctor, Sarah," Joe said. "But getting accepted can't be easy for a woman."

The ghost of a smile flickered on her lips. "Especially for a woman with no money," she said. "I was planning to sell Uncle Harlan's house to pay for school, but his estranged widow showed up and took it. That means I'll have to get a job to support myself through medical school. Maybe I can help in the laboratory, or even just scrub floors and empty bedpans. I'll do whatever it takes."

"I always knew you had the spunk and ambition to make something of your life." Joe felt the tension easing between them. They were talking like old friends now. But friends didn't hide the kind of secrets he was keeping from Sarah.

"I'll take that." She set the empty glass on the nightstand. "Now I need to check your wounds. Let's hope there's no sign of infection."

"And if there is?"

Her stunning eyes met his, then glanced away. "Let's just say we'll cross that bridge when we come to it."

Sarah opened the black leather medical bag that she'd brought into the room earlier. She wasn't worried about the shallow head wound, or the clean shot through the shoulder. But she was trou-

bled by the deep, bleeding wound in his side, which she'd exacer-
bated by having to dig for the bullet. Joe was young and strong.
Right now he didn't seem to have a fever. But that could change
at any time.

She felt his gaze on her as she laid out her instruments on a
clean towel. By the time she turned to face him, her pulse was racing. This was Joe. He was alive. He was here. Every fiber of her
being quivered with suppressed joy. But she knew better than to
let herself feel that joy. This man had broken her heart. She
couldn't afford to trust him. Not, at least, until she knew more
about the secrets he seemed to be hiding.

"First the head wound. Hold still." She leaned in close with the
scissors to cut away the bulky wrap around his head, which was
still in place. His hair smelled of woodsmoke and sweat and
horses. The aromas crept into her senses, creating a warm awareness. He'd been a boy the last time she was with him. He was a boy
no longer.

Taking care, she snipped through the wrapping and unwound
it from his head. The dressing above his ear stayed in place. Sarah
decided to leave it for another day or two. "Rusty did a good job,"
she said.

"He's had plenty of practice patching up cowboys. But he knew
better than to try and take that bullet out. You did a good job,
too, Sarah."

"Tell me that when you're healthy enough to walk out of here."
Sarah examined the shoulder wound, which was still oozing
blood where the bullet had entered. She replaced the dressings
with fresh ones and wrapped his shoulder again. Last night when
she'd cut away his clothes and dressed his wounds without knowing who he was, she'd had no reaction to their physical contact.
But this was different. This was Joe. He was awake and aware. So
was she.

Her palms felt the warmth and texture of his skin, and the hard
muscles beneath. Her hands lingered when there was no reason
to. Touching him was pure, raw pleasure.

As the heat crept into her face, she realized what was happening. Suddenly self-conscious, she lifted her hands away.

"Rusty left me plenty of cash," she said, filling the silence that had fallen between them. "I can ride into town and buy you something to wear. Except for the boots, your old clothes weren't worth saving. And I still have Uncle Harlan's clothes. You're about his size. If you don't mind dressing like a middle-aged doctor, you can wear them once you're out of bed."

"How soon can I get up?" he asked. "Can I try it today?"

"Not a good idea. You're so weak, you could pass out. The fall could open up your wound, and if you went down, I'm not sure I could get you up."

"I just feel guilty, taking your bed."

"Don't worry about it. My bed is the best place for you right now." Bending above him, she folded the covers back to check the wound in his side. "I'll need to unwrap it to change the dressing. It's bound to be tender. How's your tolerance for pain, cowboy?" She adopted a teasing tone, partly as a defense.

"I'm tough. I'll be fine. I can sit up all the way if you want."

"No, stay where you are. Just give me room to move."

Finding the end of the wrapping that held the dressing in place, she began unwinding it from around his body, a delicate task that involved reaching in close without putting pressure on his injuries.

As her cheek brushed the mat of dark hair on his chest, she heard—and felt—the sharp intake of his breath. "Did I hurt you?" she asked.

"No," he muttered. "I just—"

"Just what?"

"Never mind. Go ahead and do what you need to."

Joe swore silently as she leaned over him. The urges he'd felt when thinking and dreaming about Sarah were nothing compared to what he was feeling now. The subtle fragrance of her hair and skin crept through his senses. The touch of her hands on his bare skin, the accidental brush of a breast against his shoulder, and the nearness of those soft, ripe lips . . . Hellfire, she was driving him crazy.

Only the dangerous wound in his side—and the certainty that

he'd end up getting his face slapped—kept him from capturing her in his arms, pulling her down to him, and tasting the sweetness of her mouth.

He glanced down to make sure the quilt was covering him below the hips. To have her see what was happening to his body would be the ultimate embarrassment.

Anyway, what was he thinking? It wouldn't do to just grab her and force his mouth on hers, like some clumsy lout. If he ever got the chance to kiss Sarah, he wanted to do it right—with confidence and finesse, in a way that she'd like and remember—or even love.

And how in the devil was he supposed to figure that out? He'd kissed one girl—Betty Ann Flinders—before going on the cattle drive and then spending two years without a female in sight. As he remembered, Betty Ann had pretty much kissed him, and then she'd taken his hand and put it on her breast. He'd felt the nipple through the clinging fabric of her blouse, wet from the swimming hole.

He'd done his share of dreaming about Betty Ann, too. But something told him that wasn't the way things happened with a lady like Sarah.

A jolt of pain shattered the thought, and he realized that Sarah had just lifted away the dressing. She frowned as she studied the wound underneath.

"Bad?" He twisted his neck and tried, unsuccessfully, to see it. Maybe that was for the best.

"Bad enough," she said. "Although it could be worse. I don't see any sign of infection. But it's an ugly wound. I had to probe around for the bullet. Healing's going to take some time. I've got a poultice that might help."

"Well, I don't plan to spend that time taking up space in your bed." He tried to joke through the pain as she cleaned around the edges of the wound and applied a fresh dressing.

"For today, at least, you'll need to stay right here. We'll see how it looks tomorrow. If you're healing, you can maybe get up and sit in a chair. But we can't be too careful." She stood, gathering up the discarded wrappings and the medical bag. "Now, what would you say to a real breakfast?"

"Sarah, believe me, I didn't mean to put you out like this," he said.

"Don't be silly. You'd have died if no one had taken that bullet out of you. But I still haven't forgiven you for not letting me know you were alive."

"I understand, and I don't blame you," he said. "And yes, I'll take some breakfast if it's not too much bother."

"It's no bother at all. Oh—and just so you'll know, I may have patients come by. I'll leave your door open for now, but if anybody knocks, I'll close it for privacy."

She walked out, leaving the door open. Moments later, he could hear her rummaging in the kitchen. She couldn't have an easy life here, alone in this old house. A pretty woman like Sarah—why didn't she have a man around? Somebody to chop the wood, haul the water, and tend any animals she might be keeping out back?

Joe would have given anything to be that man. Instead, here he was, so helpless that he couldn't even risk getting out of her bed for fear of reopening his wound.

As he lay back into the pillow, cradled in the subtle fragrance of her bedding, new scents and sounds reached him through the open door—the aroma of frying bacon and eggs, and the long-forgotten smell of flapjacks, which he hadn't eaten since leaving his Texas home.

He was lying there, ravenous with anticipation, when there was an insistent knock at the front door of the house. Breakfast, it seemed, might have to wait.

As the knocking continued, Sarah moved the iron skillet to the back of the stove, quickly pulled the bedroom door shut, and hurried to answer. The timing was bad, but if someone needed her help, she could hardly leave a patient standing on the porch.

She opened the door. Standing on the threshold, with a brand-new buggy parked at the gate, was Everett.

"Aren't you going to invite me in, Sarah?" he asked when she hesitated.

"Oh, of course." She stepped aside for him to enter. "I was . . . just making breakfast."

"Actually, I came by because I've made an offer on a house and land across town, and I want to show it to you. But I don't mind giving you time to eat first." He glanced at the skillet on the stove and the pile of flapjacks on a plate in the open warmer. "Goodness, that's a lot of food for a little lady like you. Were you expecting company?"

Everett's arrival had created an awkward situation, but there was no reason to lie. "I'm nursing a patient," she said, "a young cowboy who was shot by cattle rustlers in the night. Most of this breakfast is for him. But there's plenty of food. You're certainly welcome to join us."

"A *cowboy*?" Everett's eyebrows rose disdainfully. "I don't see him anywhere. Is he hiding?"

"He's resting in the bedroom. I closed the door because I don't want to disturb him." Sarah glanced toward the door. When she'd swung it shut, the latch had failed to engage. It stood slightly ajar, open far enough for Joe to hear everything that was said.

"He's in your *bedroom*? In your *bed*?"

"He nearly died, Everett. I could hardly lay him on the floor."

"For heaven's sake, Sarah!" he exploded. "A pretty woman like you, here alone, with a man in your bed? Where's your common sense? Think about your reputation. If word got out about this, you could be ruined!"

"So, I'm supposed to care more about my precious reputation than I care about a man's life?" Sarah demanded.

"Listen to him, Sarah." The voice was Joe's. Sarah turned to see him standing in the open doorway, clad in bandages and blood-stained drawers. His face was pale. His left hand gripped the doorframe for support. "Your friend's right," he said. "I need to go now, before anybody else gets the wrong idea. Get me into some clothes, give me a little of the money Rusty left, and drop me off at some cheap hotel, where I can rest. I'll be fine."

"Don't be ridiculous," Sarah said. "If that wound becomes infected you could die. Get back into bed."

Paying her no attention, he fixed his gaze on Everett. "Joe Dollarhide's the name," he said, extending his hand. "And believe me, the last thing I want is to damage this lady's reputation. I'll be leaving as soon as I can get into some clothes and find a way out of here."

Ignoring Joe's hand, as if he were unworthy of notice, Everett turned to Sarah. "I was anxious to show you the house I was buying," he said. "I wanted you to see it as a suitable home for raising our family and entertaining our guests. Instead, I walk in here to find you with a man in your bed."

"For heaven's sake, Everett, it wasn't—"

"No, just listen. I know your intentions were pure, my dear. So I'm willing to overlook your indiscretion if you'll get rid of him now. You told me you saved your great-uncle's clothes. Get him some, and I'll take him into town myself. I know just the place—a boardinghouse that won't cost much."

"No." Sarah met his gaze with steel. "He could die without care. He's staying here, for a few more days at least. And you"—she turned to Joe—"get back into that bed before you fall and make everything worse."

Joe remained where he was. Sarah understood that he was clinging to his stubborn pride. Only that, and his tight grip on the doorframe, kept him from sliding to the floor.

Everett sighed. "All right, Sarah. You've won this round. But I want him gone as soon as he's able to leave. And for God's sake, keep him out of sight. You know how gossip can spread in this town."

With a sudden move that took Sarah by surprise, he caught her waist, whipped her against him, and captured her mouth in a forceful, dominating kiss. Too stunned to resist, she froze in his arms. There was no tenderness, or even affection, in his embrace. He was showing her that he was in charge—and showing Joe that she was his property.

By the time she'd regained her wits, he'd let her go. She

stepped away from him, quivering with fury. Creating a scene would only make things worse. She just wanted him gone.

He planted a hand at the small of her back. "She's mine, Dollarhide, and don't you forget it. If you so much as lay a finger on her, so help me, you'll live to regret it. I'll make you curse the day you were born."

"Just go, Everett," she said in a small, tight voice.

"All right. But this isn't over. I won't be satisfied until this piece of trail trash is gone." He turned and strode out the front door, letting it bang shut behind him.

Sarah's knees quivered beneath her. Summoning her self-control, she crossed the room to where Joe stood, still supporting himself in the bedroom doorway.

"Let's get you back where you belong," she said, taking his arm and setting her weight to steady him. This time he didn't have the strength to resist. He let her guide him back through the door and into bed.

"I'm sorry you had to see that." She eased him back onto the pillows and pulled up the quilt to cover him. Joe felt a jab of pain as he adjusted his position. The effort of walking to the door and standing on his feet to face the man named Everett had cost him dearly. His side wound was a knot of excruciating pain.

"I'm sorry, too," he said. "I never wanted to cause trouble for you, Sarah. I need to leave before I cause more."

"No, you don't." She sat down next to the bed. A heart-melting smile teased her lips. "It wasn't me you caused trouble for, Joe. It was only Everett. As long as I'm not doing anything wrong, I don't give a dang what people think. I don't plan to stay in Ogallala forever. If I get accepted by a medical school, I'll be gone in a flash, and I'll never look back."

"I got the impression that Everett had other plans for you."

"His plans, not mine. He wants to go into politics. It wouldn't do for him to have a tarnished woman at his side, would it?"

The undertone of bitterness in her voice wasn't lost on Joe. "Do you want to marry him?" Even asking the question was painful.

"I want to become a doctor," she said. "If I can do that, I won't likely marry at all."

"And if you can't? If medical school doesn't happen? What then? Would you give in and marry the man?"

"Everett's been good to me, and he's been very patient. I've thought about it. But there've been times like today, when he's shown me the side he's kept hidden—arrogant, judgmental, and controlling. You saw how he treated both of us. I'd have to be desperate to say yes to him."

She blinked away a tear, giving Joe a glimpse of how near to desperate she'd become. She was young, poor, and alone, living for a dream that might never come true.

If only he could give her that dream. Given the chance, he would gladly marry her himself and work to support her schooling. But the sad truth was, he had nothing to offer except love— and the love of a penniless young cowboy would be as worthless as dust.

More tears were welling in her eyes, spilling over to flow down her cheeks. She dabbed them away with a furious swipe of her hand. "I'm sorry," she muttered. "It's been so long since I've had somebody I could talk to." The tears kept coming. "Forgive me. I—I'm making such a fool of myself."

"Everybody has the right to be a fool sometimes, Sarah." As Joe spoke, he did something he'd never done before. Turning slightly toward her, he pulled her down to rest her head on his chest. She could have resisted, but she came willingly, her tears wetting his bare skin. He could feel her trembling as his hand stroked her hair.

"It's all right, girl," he murmured. "You don't always have to be brave and strong."

If Joe could have frozen a moment in time, it would have been this one, with Sarah in his arms, her hair silky soft against his throat, and her sweet fragrance creeping into his senses. The urge to kiss her was an ache inside him, but he knew that trying would likely spoil the fragile moment. For now, just holding her would have to be enough.

Far too soon, she lifted her head and pulled away. Her tears were dry, her cheeks flushed. "Heavens, you must be hungry," she said, jumping up and smoothing her skirt. "I'll get your breakfast."

After she'd rushed out of the room, Joe lay still, listening to the sweet sounds of her rummaging in the kitchen and enjoying the aromas in the air as she warmed up the food. He wouldn't mind staying here awhile, he thought. He could help her with the chores, help her fix up the old house, maybe even get a job in town to help out with money.

No, that idea was nothing more than a fantasy. Once his wound was safely on the mend, concern for her reputation and Everett's displeasure would force him to be on his way.

Even if Sarah's circumstances were different, Joe had plans of his own. As soon as he was able, he'd be off for Montana to pursue his own dream—the dream that the stampede had cut short. And he wouldn't rest until Benteen Calder had paid for leaving him to die in that wash.

Maybe once he'd made something of himself, he could come back for Sarah. But he couldn't expect her to be here. And he certainly couldn't ask her to wait. Fate had brought them back together for this short time only. All he could do was savor every moment before he had to leave her.

CHAPTER TEN

*T*HREE MORNINGS LATER, RUSTY STOPPED BY THE HOUSE. SARAH ANswered the door to find the old man standing on the porch. The chuckwagon was parked outside the gate, with a buckskin horse tethered to the tailgate.

"Come on in." Sarah was delighted to see him. "Breakfast is almost ready. You're welcome to join us."

"That's a right kind offer, and I do believe I'll take you up on it." Rusty glanced around the room. "Where's our patient? Don't tell me the boy didn't make it!"

"Oh, he made it all right," Sarah said. "He's out back tending to my mule and feeding the chickens. I told him he wasn't strong enough to help with chores, but he insisted."

"So he's healin' up all right?"

"He's done amazingly well. The dressing's off his head, and his shoulder wound is almost ready to uncover. But the wound in his side is going to take more time. An old woman who came by a while back gave me a dried plant she'd used as a poultice for wounds. She said she learned about it from her mother, who was half-Pawnee. I was a little hesitant to try it, but it's worked wonders."

"I brought his horse," Rusty said. "That's it tied behind the wagon. I've got the saddle and bridle and his other gear, too. He won't be up to ridin' for a spell, but he'll need it when he's ready to leave. I'm hopin' you'll let me put the horse out back for now."

"Of course. You'll see a shed with a corral next to it. Joe can show you where to put the horse and tack. And maybe you can make sure he isn't overdoing. I worry that he might open up that wound again. I'll call you when breakfast is ready."

He turned to step out the front door again, then paused. "Is the cash holding out? Have you got enough to last?"

"There's plenty, thank you. And please thank Mr. Calder."

"I just might do that, if I choose to tell him about it." Rusty headed outside to get Joe's horse.

Joe was forking hay into the mule's feeder. He could feel the lingering weakness and the strain on his body as he worked, but being out in the fresh air, doing something useful, was better than any medicine. He'd heard the sound of horses out front but, guessing that Everett might be paying Sarah a visit, he'd kept his head down and continued working.

"Hey, Joe!" He glanced up at the sound of a familiar voice. Rusty was coming around the house, leading the buckskin gelding that had been left with the remuda after Joe had been shot and taken to town.

"Rusty! What a surprise. And you brought Flint. I was afraid I'd never see that horse again."

"Your gear's in the wagon. I'll bring it around before I go." Rusty handed Joe the lead rope. "That horse is a good 'un. A couple of the boys rode him and wanted to keep him in the remuda with the other rustlers' horses. I had a devil of a time makin' up an excuse to take him away."

"He's Kiowa broke," Joe said, letting the horse into the corral. "An old man who'd lived with the Kiowa taught me how to do it. But that's a long story. Thanks for coming by—and for dropping me here. Sarah saved my life. And she's been taking good care of me."

"She's a peach. And prettier than a Texas sunrise. You could do a lot worse than her, Joe Dollarhide."

"I know. But Sarah's got other plans—and so have I. Since you're here, I'm guessing the herd's made it to Ogallala."

"That's right. We've been camped on the plain, resting, for the past couple of days. We'll be movin' out first thing tomorrow. So far nobody knows about you bein' alive but me and Jesse. The men didn't see your face, not even the man who shot you. As far as they're concerned, you died with your rustler pals. But I need to ask. What do you want us to tell Benteen?"

"Nothing yet. I'll be heading to Montana myself, and I'd kind of like to surprise him. Don't worry. When I tell my story, I won't mention what you and Jesse did for me. The last thing you deserve is to get in trouble with the boss."

Rusty spat a stream of tobacco juice onto the ground. "I wouldn't mind hearing your story myself—the real version, not the one you'd tell Benteen."

"It's a long one." Joe hesitated. He'd have no problem telling Rusty how he was rescued by the McCrackens, and how he finally escaped to find a place with Elijah. But how could he justify going back with the outlaws just to get revenge on Benteen Calder? Rusty was loyal to his boss. That part of the story wouldn't set well. But considering what the old man had done for him, Joe knew that he deserved to hear the truth—the whole truth.

Joe was about to begin when Sarah appeared at the back door to call them to breakfast. Joe breathed a secret sigh of relief.

"How much does she know?" Rusty whispered as they walked back toward the house.

"Not much more than what you told her when you brought me here."

"Fine, I'll keep your secret," Rusty said. "Sooner or later, you'll have to come to terms with what you did. But I guess that'll have to be on your own conscience."

They sat down to a hearty breakfast, with Rusty and Sarah making small talk, about life on the trail and her hopes of becoming a doctor. Joe ate in silence, glancing from one to the other. He owed his life to these good people. Didn't he owe them the truth, as well?

But he knew he wasn't ready to tell them. He wasn't ready to face the disgust in Sarah's eyes or the disappointment on Rusty's face when he confessed that it had been his own choice to help the rustlers steal Benteen Calder's cattle.

When the meal was over, Rusty excused himself and went out to the buggy to get Joe's saddle and the other gear he'd brought. Joe went out with him, to help.

"I can take that," he said as Rusty lifted the saddle out of the wagon.

"Not on your life. You don't want to open up that wound. You can take the lighter things."

After gathering up the bridle and blanket, the canteen, and a few other odds and ends, Joe followed Rusty around the house to the shed, where they stowed his gear in an out-of-the-way corner.

Rusty turned to face him. "Will I see you in Montana—that is, if you don't get into more trouble on the way?"

"That's the plan," Joe said. "Believe me, I've had enough trouble to last the rest of my life."

"To find the ranch, just follow the cattle trails. If you get lost, there'll be plenty of folks you can ask. They all know the Calder place. It's the biggest spread in the territory."

Of course, it would be, Joe thought. Benteen Calder was ruthlessly ambitious. Nothing less than the biggest ranch would do for him. But Joe wasn't sure he was ready to show up there as a saddle bum with nothing to call his own but his horse and gear.

"There's a little town nearby," Rusty continued. "Not much more than a bump in the road. It's called Blue Moon. You can get a drink there and buy some supplies."

"Thanks, I'll remember that," Joe said.

"Your pistol's in one of the saddlebags. It's still loaded. You might want to keep it someplace handy. And one more thing before I go." Rusty fixed Joe with his stern gaze. "I've noticed how Sarah looks at you. I may be an old man, but I haven't forgotten the signs that a woman's in love."

"*What?*" Joe felt as if he'd been punched. "But she's already got a man coming around. He's older and rich. She even lets him kiss her. She couldn't be in love with me."

"Then you're blind, or not as smart as I used to think you were. But here's why I'm telling you this. Sarah's a fine, tenderhearted girl. If you don't do right by her—if you break her heart, then you're worse than a cattle thief. If you can't give her what she needs, be a man and get out of her life as soon as you're fit to go. Understand?"

But what if I love her, too? Joe knew better than to speak those words aloud. "I understand," he said.

"Then I'll leave you with that. I hope to see you in Montana. If not, I wish you well, Joe Dollarhide." Rusty extended a trail-roughened hand. Joe shook it.

"Thanks for everything. I owe you, Rusty."

"Well, if you do, you can repay me by not wasting the second chance you've been given."

With that, Rusty turned away and headed around the house and down the walk to the chuckwagon. Joe listened to him drive away. Then he went back inside, where Sarah was clearing the table, preparing to wash the breakfast dishes. She looked beautiful with her cheeks flushed from the heat of the stove and tendrils of golden brown hair framing her face.

Was the old man right? Did she really love him?

"Can I help you clean up?" he offered.

She smiled and shook her head. "No need. It won't take me long. Get some rest, Joe. That's an order. You need to heal, not work."

Giving in, he settled in the rocking chair, from which he could enjoy watching her. In the corner he could see the rolled-up bundle of quilts she'd laid out in front of the warm stove for her bed at night. It was time he traded sleeping places with her. Sarah was stubborn, but he would insist. He'd slept in her bed long enough. And he was tired of being coddled.

He remembered holding her while she cried, her shoulders trembling, her hot tears wet against the skin of his bare chest. As he watched her moving about in the kitchen, hips swaying gracefully beneath her skirt, the desire to hold her again and pillage her mouth with kisses burned like a branding fire. If she loved him, she would let him do it, he thought. She might even welcome it.

Everett Hamilton, who'd dropped by almost every day to check on her, had threatened him with violence if he so much as touched her. But Joe had already crossed that line. And there were times, like now, when he didn't care if Everett beat him to death, as long as he could hold Sarah in his arms.

But then he remembered Rusty's wise words.

If you break her heart, then you're worse than a cattle thief. If you can't give her what she needs, be a man and get out of her life as soon as you're fit to go.

Those words gave him pause. Sarah wasn't a plaything, to be enjoyed and cast aside. She deserved a man who could offer her a lifetime of love and security, a man who would be there to provide for her and her future children. A man like Everett Hamilton—or maybe someone else who had yet to happen along. Someone better than Everett and much better than a penniless, rootless ex-cattle rustler named Joe Dollarhide.

With a sigh, Joe laid his fantasies to rest. Sarah had saved his life. He would thank her by being her friend, without pushing the boundaries of that friendship.

Then, as soon as he was able to sit a horse without pain, he would saddle up and ride away, taking his hopeless love with him—the love she would never know.

Over the next few days, Joe's condition improved dramatically. Sarah was amazed when she checked the dressings to find the shoulder wound healed and the side wound almost closed, the flesh pink and healthy, with no sign of infection. She replaced the bulky dressing with a patch of gauze and a few pieces from her precious store of surgical tape. Maybe it was the old woman's poultice that had helped him heal—or maybe it was only Joe's strong, young body that had brought him this far.

Whatever it was, she was grateful, even if it meant that he would be leaving her soon. She was doing her best to accept that reality. Once he was healed, there'd be nothing to hold him here—not even her.

By now he was doing the outside chores. Over the past few days he'd repaired the sagging fence around the corral and shored up the run-down chicken coop to keep the hens safe from marauding foxes and coyotes. Working together, with her steadying the ladder, handing him tools and materials, and holding her breath, they'd even managed to patch the leaks in the roof.

She'd cautioned him against riding. As far as she knew, he hadn't tried to mount his horse. But even that was bound to happen soon. Once he was comfortable in the saddle, he would be gone.

A few nights ago, he'd insisted that she take back her bed and leave the bedroll to him. Now he was spending his nights on the floor, waking early to dress, start the coffee, and go outside to do chores before she woke to cook breakfast. They'd fallen into a routine that she enjoyed, and she sensed that he enjoyed it, too. But she knew better than to think it could last.

Two nights ago, needing a drink of water, she'd gotten up, pattered barefoot into the kitchen, and looked down at Joe where he lay next to the stove. For a long moment, she'd stood gazing at his sleeping face. The yearnings that welled in her almost brought tears as she resisted the urge to bend down, kiss his virile mouth, and invite him back to bed with her. Sarah might be a virgin, but she was no innocent. She'd delivered babies and discussed the most intimate matters with her female patients. She knew what was likely to happen—and right then she'd wanted it. She'd ached for it. With him.

But they were sensible people, she and Joe. Nothing was going to happen. They would part as friends and go their separate ways—maybe exchange a letter or two, then nothing more.

Joe was still wearing Uncle Harlan's clothes—trousers of fine gray worsted, linen shirts, and a knitted vest, with the underwear and stockings that went underneath. The clothes fit him, but they didn't suit him, and they wouldn't do for the trail. Before he left, he was going to need some clothes of his own.

After Rusty's last visit, Sarah had discovered another stash of bills he'd tucked under the sourdough crock on the counter. There would be plenty of money to buy what she needed, with enough left over to give Joe when he left. Since she needed other supplies as well, it was time for a trip to the general store in town.

She'd spent most of the morning seeing patients, but the afternoon was free, the spring weather clear and warm. Joe was busy replacing the loose boards on the back porch, but he took the time to hitch Ahab to her two-wheeled cart. After telling him she'd be back in a couple of hours, Sarah tied on her straw bonnet, drove out the gate, and headed south toward the main part of town.

She hadn't been away from the house and yard since well before Joe's arrival. It was a pleasure to see the changes spring had brought. The prairie, dotted with scattered homesteads, was green with new grass. Meadowlarks caroled their songs from fence posts. Dandelions, white-top, and tiny purple flowers with no name bloomed along the roadsides where the water from spring rains had pooled.

Ogallala had never been a large town. But with the coming of the Union Pacific Railroad, it had become a hub for rail travelers going west and cattle drives going north or stopping to fatten their herds on rich prairie grass before shipping them off on the train.

The heart of the town was Railroad Street, which ran along the tracks. Stores, banks, business offices, a hotel with a restaurant, a schoolhouse, and most of the town's private homes were built north of the tracks. On the south side, saloons, gambling houses, dance halls, and brothels did a raucous business day and night. The town was quiet during the fall and winter. But once the cattle drives started arriving in the spring, the goings-on would put even Dodge City to shame. Brawls, gunfights, robberies, and even murders were common, and the town jail was never empty.

Luckily for Sarah, her house was north of Ogallala. There was no need for her to pass through the wild, dangerous world south of the tracks. She was able to drive into town, leave her mule and cart at the hitching rail on a side street, and follow the boardwalk along busy Railroad Street.

The boardwalk was crowded today, with townspeople taking advantage of the good weather to do their shopping. As Sarah walked down the block toward the general store, with her empty shopping basket, she smiled and nodded at people she knew. Some had been her patients. Others she remembered from working with Uncle Harlan.

By the time she reached the general store, she'd begun to notice something strange. As she approached groups of people on her way, a hush seemed to fall over their conversations. They averted their eyes as she passed or, if they greeted her, their expressions and voices seemed strained.

But maybe that was only her imagination. She shrugged off her unease as she walked into the store.

She'd made a list of the things she needed for Joe. After waiting a few minutes for help, she was able to give the list to a young clerk, who hurried off to find the items—two pairs of denim pants, two shirts—one plaid flannel and one blue chambray—a leather belt, a Stetson hat, and three sets of underwear and socks. The prices would add up, but thanks to Rusty—or perhaps she should thank Benteen Calder—she had the money to pay.

While she waited for the clerk, she browsed for the other items she needed and put them in her basket—sewing thread and a packet of needles, flour and sugar, soap, matches, coffee, and a little tin of raisins for some cookies she was planning to make.

The store was crowded with other shoppers, mostly strangers. Sarah kept to herself, her attention focused on the items she was choosing. She didn't see the well-dressed, middle-aged woman who'd stepped in front of her until they'd almost collided.

"My dear Sarah." Only after the woman had spoken her name did Sarah recognize her. Her name was Margaret Lacy. Her husband was Everett's business partner. Sarah had met her briefly, at dinner in the hotel, when she'd gone there with Everett.

"I was hoping to run into you, my dear—not literally, of course." Her laugh sounded forced. "But I do need to have a word with you. Come with me. There's no one in the dressing room."

The skirt of her burgundy silk dress, worn with a matching

jacket, rustled as she led Sarah to the rear of the store. Her hat, adorned with a teal blue ostrich plume, perched atop upswept red hair that was fading to gray at the roots. She was an imposing woman, tall, with strong features and penetrating eyes. Pulled along behind her, Sarah sensed that she was about to be taken to the woodshed. Her heart sank as she realized what it must be about— and why people appeared to be acting strangely toward her.

At the rear of the store was a closet-sized room with a calico curtain hung over the doorway. Inside, a cheap mirror was mounted on the wall. The only furniture was a single wooden chair.

"Sit down, my dear," Margaret said, pointing to the chair.

"Thank you, but I'll stand," Sarah said. "I can't imagine this will take long."

"Very well. But you should thank me, Sarah. Everyone else is talking behind your back. At least I have the decency to talk with you face-to-face." Margaret frowned. "I don't have to tell you what this is about, do I?"

Sarah shook her head. "Probably not. But tell me anyway."

"All right." Margaret's tongue clicked disparagingly. "It's about that *man*, the one who's living with you. I'm afraid you've created quite a scandal, my dear. Poor Everett is beside himself with worry for your reputation."

Sarah didn't reply. She should have known something like this was coming. The surprising thing was how little she cared.

"Well?" Margaret's tongue clicked again. "What have you got to say for yourself?"

Sarah lifted her chin, meeting the woman's sharp gaze. "First of all, he isn't *living* with me. He's my patient. He was brought to me in the middle of the night with a dangerous gunshot wound. I removed the bullet and kept him there so I could take care of him."

"But couldn't he have gone to Dr. Phillips?"

"Dr. Phillips was out of town."

"Well, Everett told me he offered to take the man to a boardinghouse. But you wouldn't hear of it."

"I know the kind of boardinghouse he meant. No one there would have cared for my patient's wound. If it had become infected or started bleeding again, he would have died."

"Maybe so, my dear. But your house isn't exactly a hospital. I happen to know there's only one bedroom—and one bed!"

"I know what you're implying," Sarah said. "But it wasn't a problem to make an extra bed on the floor. Nothing is going on between us. As soon as he's well enough to ride, he'll be leaving for Montana."

Margaret sighed. "You're a decent, well-meaning young woman. I know that, Sarah. If you say you're innocent, I believe you. But don't you see? It's all about appearances! Looking as if you're doing something wrong is almost as bad as actually doing it. Everett is going into politics. He could be governor someday. How can you expect him to marry you if your reputation is in tatters?"

Sarah's simmering anger spilled over. "I think I've explained myself enough," she said. "If anyone asks you about me, you can tell them I said to mind their own business. Now, if you'll excuse me, I think my purchases are ready."

"I've tried to warn you, Sarah. If you don't do something to set this straight, you won't have a friend left in this town."

Margaret's words rang in Sarah's ears as she strode to the front of the store. The clothes she'd requested were piled on the counter. She added the items to her basket. While she counted out her cash, the clerk wrapped everything but the hat in brown paper and gave her a receipt.

"If you don't mind waiting, I can have somebody help you carry it out," the clerk offered.

"Thank you, but I'll be fine." Sarah took the bundle, the hat and her basket, and left the store. With her arms loaded, she walked back down the boardwalk. This time she understood the whispers and the sudden silences as she passed. She'd told herself she didn't care. But the hurt was there. How could people judge her for a simple act of kindness—one that had been nothing more than that?

But as she piled her purchases in the cart and drove back toward home, she knew that she was deceiving herself. Her feelings for Joe had grown into something far from simple and far beyond compassion.

* * *

By the time the plodding mule pulled the cart through the yard gate, the late-afternoon sun hung low above the prairie. Joe was waiting to unhitch Ahab, let him into the corral, and put the cart away.

Sarah had taken her purchases into the house. She unwrapped the bundled clothes and placed them, with the hat, on the table for Joe to discover when he came in.

He shook his head when he saw everything laid out. "This is too much, Sarah. I can't imagine how much these things cost, and I don't have a damned nickel to repay you."

"You can thank Rusty. He's the one who left the money," Sarah said, handing him what was left over. "This is yours. He said you could call it back pay."

"We'll split it." He counted out the bills and returned half to her. "I still remember when you bought me lunch in Dodge City. I always wanted to find you again and treat you to a nice dinner. Do you know of a good restaurant?"

Sarah thought of the gossip she'd faced in town. "Another time," she said. "I'm afraid we've already caused enough of a stir."

"Then we'll have to make sure that we find another time," he said. "Oh—I almost forgot. The postman came by while you were gone. He left something in your mailbox. It's still there. I didn't take it out because I thought it might be personal."

"Oh!" Sarah's pulse catapulted. *Calm down,* she told herself. *It's probably nothing. Some kind of notice from the landlord, or Lenore demanding something else of Uncle Harlan's. Even if it is from the medical school, it's probably a rejection.*

"I can get it for you," Joe said, but Sarah barely heard him as she flew out the door and down the front walk to the roadside mailbox.

The thin envelope was from the Bennett Medical College of Chicago, the only school that had sent her an application. Sarah carried it back to the house in shaking hands, feeling the slight weight of it—there wouldn't be more than a page or two inside, she guessed. It wouldn't take much paper to say no.

Joe took one look at her face and guessed what she had. "You heard from the medical school. What did they say?"

"I don't know." Sarah's heart was pounding against her ribs. "I'm scared to open it. You take it." She thrust the envelope into his hands. "Open it and read it to me."

"If you say so . . ." he muttered, working a finger under the flap of the envelope. "Let's hope it's good news."

"Just read it," Sarah said.

There were two pages in the envelope. Joe took a moment to smooth out the folds, then began to read.

> *"Dear Miss Foxworth,*
> *While we wouldn't usually consider a female applicant for admission, we feel that your experience as an assistant to Dr. Blake would make you a highly suitable candidate. Therefore, it is my pleasure to notify you that you have been accepted for the first semester, beginning September 6 of this year . . ."*

Joe dropped the papers on the table. "I think I've read enough. They want you, Sarah! You're going to be a real doctor!"

"Oh!" Sarah was beside herself. "Oh, I can't believe it! It's like a dream come true!" Impulsively, she flung her arms around his neck and kissed him on the mouth.

Joe's body stiffened in surprise. Then his arms went around her, molding her against him, his lips desperately hungry, as if he'd waited his whole life to kiss her. Sarah responded with a whimper as need swept through her like a prairie fire. Her fingers tangled in his hair, pulling him down to her, deepening the kiss, and the next one, and the next one.

The letter from the medical school lay on the table, forgotten for the moment as they opened the floodgates of all they'd been holding back—hands seeking to touch, to hold; lips searching, whispering wild words; hearts pumping the heat of desire through their eager young bodies.

Lost in each other, they failed to hear the opening of the front door and the creak of a footstep until it was too late. Suddenly aware, they broke apart to face Everett Hamilton, standing in the open doorway.

No explanation could have made a difference. Speechless for the moment, they simply looked at him.

Everett cleared his throat and spoke. "How could you be so foolish, Sarah, falling for this trail bum who'll never be worth a dime? You could've had a great future with me—a home, a family, a successful husband. Now—"

"That's enough, Everett." Sarah stepped forward to confront him. "I'm going to have a great future without you. I'll be going to medical school. I'm going to be a doctor. Feel free to look elsewhere for a wife. You should have no trouble finding one."

Everett's face was a rictus of self-restraint. "Good-bye, Sarah." He turned and took a step out the door, then spun back, his fury fixed on Joe. "I warned you not to touch her, Dollarhide," he said, spitting out the words. "Mark my words, you're not going to get away with this. I intend to see that you pay."

CHAPTER ELEVEN

JOE LAY ON HIS BEDROLL, LISTENING TO THE STEADY TICK OF THE WALL clock that hung next to the door. By now it was well after midnight, but he couldn't have slept even if he'd wanted to.

The dying coals glowed like red eyes through the mica panes in the stove's firebox. Outside, the spring night was chilly, lit by a waning gibbous moon. Dressed in the clothes that Sarah had brought home, Joe listened in the darkness. Everett Hamilton's parting words, he sensed, had been more than an empty threat. The man had pride and power. If he wanted to punish a rival, he had the means to do it—almost certainly without soiling his own hands.

Through the blanket, Joe felt the solid lump of the heavy .44 pistol that Clem had given him for the raid on the Calder herd. It was loaded, but Joe had never fired it. He could only hope he wouldn't need to fire it tonight.

Turning onto his side, he felt the tenderness where his wound had closed. Yesterday he'd removed the dressing for good. The spot was still sore, but no longer a worry.

The door to Sarah's bedroom stood ajar. Was it an invitation? But he couldn't let himself think about that. The memory of holding her, kissing her, would have to be enough to last him for the rest of his life. He was a danger to her reputation and to her safety. It was time for him to leave.

Tension had hung between them after Everett had stalked out

to his buggy and driven away. Joe had hugged her, assuring her that everything would be all right. "We'll talk later, when we've both had a chance to calm down," he'd told her. Then he'd left her to read her letter while he went out to finish his work on the back porch.

Over supper they'd made small talk about her plans for school, avoiding the reality that hung over them—the need for him to go. But Sarah was a perceptive woman. Joe had the feeling that she already knew. He had always meant to tell her the story of his own past and the truth about how he'd come to be wounded. But maybe it was for the best that the right time had never presented itself. Once he was gone it wouldn't matter.

Sarah would be all right, Joe told himself. Her dream was within reach now. It was time for him to go and make good on his own dream.

The creak of the front gate jerked him to full alert. Someone was outside. As he closed his hand around the pistol and pushed to his feet, something struck the door with a rattling sound, as if someone had tossed a handful of pebbles against the wood. It was easy enough to guess the plan. When he went outside to investigate, he would be jumped by Everett Hamilton's thugs, sent to beat him senseless, or maybe worse. If he didn't come out, they would break in.

"Joe, what is it?" Sarah had emerged from the bedroom. She stood trembling in her white nightgown, her eyes wide with fear.

"Go back in your room and close the door, Sarah," Joe said. "Make sure the windows are locked and keep low. I'll take care of this."

"But what if—"

"Don't argue, damn it. Just *go*!"

As her door clicked shut behind him, he thumbed back the hammer to cock the pistol, walked to the front door, and opened it a few inches.

The shadowed yard was quiet with no sign of movement. But somebody was out there, probably pressed against the side of the house, waiting for him to step off the porch and start down the walk so they could jump him from behind.

Did they mean to kill him? Not likely, Joe reasoned. Everett had threatened to make him curse the day he was born. He couldn't do that if he were dead. And with Everett going into politics, a murder charge, even a hired murder, wouldn't look good.

More than likely the weapon—or weapons—would be clubs or knives. If they got to him before he could use the gun, he'd be out of luck. Joe was a good shot. He'd had plenty of practice on the farm, target shooting, killing deer, grouse, and rabbits for food, and bringing down coyotes and other vermin that would attack the animals. But even in the cattle raids with the McCrackens, he had never fired at another human being.

When the time came, he couldn't afford to hesitate. For now, his best chance was to keep his back protected and wait for the attack.

The doorway was recessed about sixteen inches from the front of the house. He slipped through the door and eased it shut behind him, mostly for Sarah's safety. Then, standing on the doorstep with the pistol cocked, he kept perfectly still.

Seconds crept by. Joe could feel the tossed pebbles through his boot soles as he waited, his taut muscles tightening into knots. Sooner or later, whoever was out there would show themselves. When they did, he would have to be ready.

As time crawled past, doubts began to gnaw at him. What if the intruder had lured him outside only to break in some other way and harm Sarah? But no, he'd heard nothing from inside the house. The best plan was to stay where he was and wait.

The moonlight cast shadows on the ground. One of the shadows moved, taking shape before Joe's eyes. A man—a huge man, armed with a long, stout club. He'd been waiting against the side of the house, right where Joe had expected him to be.

The thug stepped into the moonlight and turned to face the door. Seeing Joe, a startled look crossed his brutish face. He lunged, swinging the stick.

With the pistol aimed at the biggest part of him, Joe pulled the trigger. There was a sickening click as the gun misfired.

By now the man was almost on top of him. Acting on reflex, Joe pulled back the hammer again. As the club glanced off his head, he pulled the trigger. The deafening roar of the large caliber gun filled the night. The big man reeled backward, dropping the club and clutching his arm. Cocking the pistol with one hand and seizing the club with the other, Joe swung at his attacker. Bone crunched as the club hit the man's face. Cursing, the man wheeled, and fled out the gate. As Joe slumped on the porch, heart pounding, breath rasping, he heard the sound of a horse, galloping away.

He took a moment to recover, then pushed to his feet, opened the door, and stepped inside the house. Sarah was standing a few paces from the door, still in her nightgown, her hands clutching the iron stove poker.

Joe closed the door and locked it behind him, then laid the club and the pistol on the kitchen counter. "It's all right, Sarah," he said. "I wounded the man. He's gone. I can't imagine he'll be coming back."

The poker clattered to the floor as she flung herself into his arms. "I was so scared," she murmured. "When I heard that shot, I didn't know what to think. . . ."

She was trembling. He held her close, feeling her naked curves beneath the fabric of her nightgown. "I told you to stay in your bedroom," he said. "But I should've known you wouldn't."

"You know me." Her arms tightened around him. "Sometimes I think you're the only person who does."

He kissed her upturned face, her forehead, her eyelids, her cheeks, and her ripe, silky mouth. Her lips parted. The first tentative flick of her tongue lit a fire in him. He responded in kind, tasting her, thrusting into the moist warmth, as he imagined a different thrusting, a different moist heat. His body was rock hard, ready for her, the urge so powerful that he knew he couldn't make himself stop what was happening—nor did he want to. Neither, it seemed, did Sarah.

She moaned, stretching on tiptoe to mold her body to his. His hands traced her womanly curves through the nightgown, the smooth arch of her back, the firm, round moons of her buttocks. With a boldness that took his breath away, he raised the hem of the nightgown and touched her bare skin. How could anything on God's earth be so soft? She whimpered as he stroked her back, his fingertips stealing around to skim the edge of one breast.

Should he tell her she could stop him if she wanted? Or did that no longer matter. "Sarah—"

She touched a finger to his lips. "Don't talk, Joe," she said. "Words will just complicate things."

She fumbled with his shirt buttons, but her hands were shaking. Was this her first time, too? But that didn't matter, and he wasn't about to ask. All he knew was that he wanted her. And he wanted this to be as right for her as it was for him.

Somehow, with his arousal jutting, he made it out of his shirt, pants, and boots and into the bedroom. She slipped into bed and held out her arms to him. Dropping his drawers in the darkness, he moved in beside her and gathered her close. She was still wearing her nightgown, but it came off easily. Naked and trembling, she lay in his arms. She was so beautiful, so perfect. Guided by instinct and desire, he cradled her breasts, stroking and kissing them.

Her breathing quickened. A moan of pleasure stirred in her throat. Then, as if she'd caught fire, she began exploring and caressing his skin. She'd touched him while caring for his wounds, but never before like this, tender and curious, stroking his chest, tracing the line of hair down his belly, then, suddenly, hesitating.

"Don't be afraid, Sarah. Touch me." His voice emerged as a husky growl. Gently, he guided her. As her fingers closed around him, he nearly exploded in her hand. With a rough chuckle, he pulled her hand away and kissed it.

"Yes," she whispered, saying everything in a single word.

Unable to wait any longer, he shifted and moved between her legs. She opened to him like a flower, all slick, petal-soft folds. As he thrust into that warm, honeyed wetness, he felt a slight resistance. She gave a little cry as something gave way, then clasped his buttocks and pulled him deep inside her, holding him a long moment before need drove them to move.

There were no words for the feel of loving her, pushing deep while she met each thrust. He felt his release mounting, surging. Just when he couldn't hold back any longer, she gave a gasp. "Oh . . ." she whispered. "It's so . . ."

He shattered, his senses soaring like rocket bursts. Then he drifted back to Earth and lay spent in her arms, feeling more contented than he'd ever been in his life.

And knowing that their time together had to be over.

She nestled close, pressing her face against his chest. "I can't stay, Sarah," he said. "My being here puts you in danger as well as me."

"You don't have to tell me. I know. Just hold me a little longer."

"Here, then." He spooned her against him, cradling her like a child. Without her asking, the words began to flow. He told her all the things he'd been holding back—the stampede and the fall, the surge of hope when Benteen Calder had almost found him, and the sense of betrayal when he'd ridden away; then his struggle to survive, his rescue by the McCrackens, his time with Elijah and the horses; and finally, his near-fatal decision to raid the Calder herd, and the act of mercy that had given him a new life.

After he'd finished, she was still for a moment. Then she turned in his arms and kissed him. "Thank you for being honest," she said. "I knew you were holding things back from me. But nothing you've said or done could change the way I feel about you. I do have one question."

"Ask me anything. There's nothing I haven't told you."

"Just this. Have you forgiven Benteen Calder?"

"No. Not yet."

"Will you?"

"Not until he knows what he did to me—and not until he pays for it."

"Then I wish you the best, Joe." She sat up, covering herself with the sheet. "Now it's time for you to go. If you can get clear of town before first light, you'll have less chance of being trailed."

He sat up and swung his legs to the floor. His clothes had fallen in a trail from the front room to the bedside. In the moonlit darkness, he found his drawers and pulled them on. When he stood and turned around, Sarah was out of bed, clad in her nightgown once more. She reached for her robe, which hung from a hook on the wall, and put it on.

"Can I make you some coffee?" she asked as if he were going off on some simple errand.

"I'd better not take the time," he said, fearing that if he stayed any longer, he wouldn't have the strength to leave her.

"At least, take some food," she said, stuffing biscuits, cheese, and a few small apples into an empty flour sack. "There may not be much to eat where you're going."

"Thanks." He finished dressing and took the bag. Knowing he'd have to leave soon, he'd already organized his gear outside and filled the canteen with water.

The pistol lay on the counter where he'd left it last night. "I want you to keep this," he said. "I can't imagine Everett wanting to hurt you, but somebody else might get ideas about a pretty woman living out here alone."

"You'll need it on the trail," she said.

"I'll get another one. Can you shoot?"

"Yes. What I don't know about this gun, I can learn." She sounded doubtful, but there was no time to teach her. Maybe just having the gun would be a deterrent. She'd talked about going to Chicago to find some work before the start of medical school in September. This might be a good time for her to leave. But that would have to be her decision.

She stepped into her shoes, walked outside with him, and stood watching while he saddled his horse and loaded his gear, including a bedroll that held his spare clothes. Before mounting up, he turned to her. "I owe you my life, and more. Will you be all right?"

She smiled up at him, the moonlight soft on her face. "I'm a big girl. I'll be fine. And in case you're wondering, I'm not sorry—not for anything. Godspeed, Joe."

"You're going to be a wonderful doctor, Sarah." He gave her a quick, hard hug and swung into the saddle. At the gate he looked back one last time, to see her standing where he'd left her, her beautiful face in shadow. He would never stop loving her. But the best thing he could do for her was ride away and never come back.

With a wave of farewell, he nudged the horse to a brisk trot and headed up the road, bound for the vast, open grasslands of Montana.

Two months later

Mounted on his buckskin horse, Joe gazed out over the Montana prairie. As far as the eye could see the land was a waving sea of grass, summer green and high enough to tickle a cow's belly. Broken with buttes, ravines, and coulees, it stretched all the way to the horizon, where the sky began—a sky so endlessly wide and blue, that it overwhelmed belief.

In the near distance, below the knoll that overlooked the grassy plain, longhorn cattle by the hundreds grazed and fattened after the long, arduous march from Texas. It was Joe's job to make sure none of the new arrivals strayed from the herd or fell into the hands of cattle thieves.

If cows could think like humans, these animals would probably imagine they'd stumbled into paradise. The idle thought brought a smile to Joe's lips. He was enjoying his own run of good luck. Two days out of Ogallala, he'd caught up with a shorthanded cattle drive and signed on as a drover. The rest of the way to Montana, through the Platte River Valley, into Wyoming, north out of Cheyenne, and into Montana, he'd had work, plenty of food, and the promise of a fair payout at the end of the trail.

Blaise Ransom, the owner and trail boss, had been moving a herd of eight hundred head to the Montana acreage he'd staked out. His ranch was modest in size, but he had big plans for it. Those plans included breaking wild mustangs to stock his operation, and eventually breed and sell to others. After learning about Joe's experience with wild horses, Ransom had hired him on at the drive's end, as a ranch hand and horse-breaker.

Square-built, redheaded, and plainspoken, Ransom was blessed with a tough, practical wife and two half-grown boys. Joe liked and respected him, but he didn't plan on sticking around forever.

He was still determined to do two things—first, to start a ranch of his own; second, to get satisfaction for the wrong Benteen Calder had done him.

But that satisfaction wouldn't come from stealing Benteen's cattle or burning his barn. Joe had learned from his mistakes, and he knew better. Besting Benteen Calder would have to be done legally—and that was going to take time, maybe even years. Meanwhile, he was saving every cent he earned, learning how to run a ranch, and keeping an ear to the ground for any available free land or a better job opportunity.

So far, he'd been lucky. But he couldn't depend on luck to get him what he wanted. For that he would need to make solid plans and push them, just as Benteen had.

The Ransom spread was an hour beyond Blue Moon and more than two hours from the border of the Calder ranch. Joe had kept his distance, waiting for the right time. He didn't want to confront Benteen or face his old friends until he'd made something of himself. That was going to take some time.

On the far side of the knoll lay the family's sturdy log house, the rough bunkhouse, and a complex of sheds and corrals. Joe could hear the ring of hammers from the barn that Ransom and his sons hoped to have finished before winter set in. From his vantage point, he could see that a black buggy with a team of matched bays had pulled up in front of the house. Interesting, he mused. The Ransoms didn't get much company out this way—especially the kind of visitors who could afford a rig like that one.

Hearing a shout from that direction, Joe glanced over his shoulder. Slim Perkins, one of the ranch's three cowhands, was galloping his horse up the slope toward him. Turning, Joe rode down to meet him partway.

"The boss wants you back at the house, pronto, Dollarhide," Slim said.

"Any notion why?" Joe asked. "I'm not in trouble, am I?"

"No sign of that. He's got some fancy visitors. I reckon he wants to let 'em watch how you break horses. Go on. I'll keep an eye on the cows."

Joe rode back toward the ranch house. Just last week, Blaise

Ransom had bought a half-dozen wild mustangs from a trader. He was hoping to break and sell them for some extra cash. Maybe his guest was a prospective buyer.

Elijah had taught Joe the Kiowa method of training a special horse, which took time and patience. But Joe had also learned a faster method. Still based on gentleness and trust, it could produce a number of dependable mounts within a few days.

These new mustangs would be a challenge. They were sound and healthy, but after being chased, roped, and driven for miles, they were scared and full of fight. They'd had a taste of how humans treated them, and they didn't want any more of it. Joe had spent a little time with them, but they had a long way to go. Today the best he could hope for was to put on a good show for the boss's visitors.

He dismounted alongside the ranch house, tethered his horse, and walked around front to find Blaise waiting on the porch with a well-dressed, middle-aged man and a girl who appeared to be about seventeen. Joe's gaze was drawn to the girl. She was strikingly pretty, with fiery curls, porcelain skin shaded by a broad-brimmed hat, and stunning green eyes. She was dressed in a white blouse and a tan riding skirt with a wide belt that accentuated her curvy, tiny-waisted figure. As if fully aware that Joe was admiring her, she gave him a dazzling smile. Remembering his manners, he took off his hat.

"This is my neighbor, Mr. Loren Hollister," Blaise said, making the introductions. "He owns that big spread to the north of here. He's interested in your method of horse-breaking, so I offered him a demonstration."

"Dollarhide." Hollister, who'd evidently been told Joe's name, extended a hand. Dressed in new denims and an expensive-looking leather jacket, he was a small man, lean and distinguished looking, with a well-trimmed mustache and iron gray hair. His handshake was firm and confident. Joe had seen his house from the wagon road. Built of logs, like most of the homes in these parts, it was raised on a stone foundation with second-floor dormers, a shingled roof, and a tall stone chimney at one end. Seeing it, Joe had vowed silently that someday he would have a house just as grand.

The girl nudged Hollister's arm, as if to remind him that she deserved an introduction, too.

"Oh—and this is my daughter, Amelia," he said. "When I told her I was going to see a man who tamed wild horses, she insisted on coming along."

"I'll try not to disappoint you, Amelia," Joe said.

"I'm sure you won't." Her disarming smile made his chest swell a little.

The six mustangs—four mares and two geldings that had been castrated by the trader—were in a corral, separated by a gate from the round pen where training was done. Choosing a buckskin mare, Joe mounted up and used his horse to cut her away from the others and herd her into the training pen. Then, dismounting and leaving his own horse by the fence, he walked to the center of the pen on foot and stood perfectly still.

Horses are curious animals. He heard Elijah's voice, speaking in his head. *Give them enough time to feel safe, and after a while they'll start to wonder about you. Give them more time, and they'll decide to investigate.*

Blaise, Hollister, and Amelia stood outside the log fence, watching. Joe had cautioned them to be quiet. The other mustangs watched from the corral. Even watching was part of their training.

For now, the mare was keeping her distance, snorting and dancing nervously. Joe opened his hand to reveal a small carrot. Elijah had taught him a song in the Kiowa language. Singing softly, he held his hand flat, with the carrot on his palm.

Seconds passed, then minutes. The mare was calm now, but still not coming any closer. Joe stayed in place as if he'd sprouted roots. More time passed. Ears pricking, nostrils flaring, the mare extended her neck and inched forward. This was a dangerous time. She was still a wild animal, big and powerful. If she spooked, she could kick or bite him, even kill him. At this point, the trust had to be as much on his side as on hers.

Joe waited, still singing, as she edged closer. With a sudden move, she snatched the carrot from his hand and danced away, still cautious but less fearful than before. The next time would be easier.

Making sure the mare was at a safe distance, Joe walked back to the fence. "Seen enough?" he asked Hollister.

"For now," Hollister said. "But I'd like to see more when I've got time. And I've got a lot of questions."

"Lunch is almost ready," Blaise said. "My wife's set extra places. You join us too, Joe. You can answer Mr. Hollister's questions while we eat."

As they walked back toward the house, Joe paused to wash his hands at the outside pump. Amelia stopped beside him. "What you did with that mare was amazing," she said, her eyes shining. "How did you learn to do that?"

"It's a long story," Joe said. "I'll tell you sometime if you want to hear it."

"I'd love to hear your story." She fell into step beside him.

"That's good," Joe said, "because I'd really like to hear your story, too."

Lunch was homemade vegetable beef soup and fresh buttered bread—a plain meal, but Florence Ransom was a good cook and did her best as a hostess. She'd used her nice dishes, set a bouquet of wildflowers on the table, and fed her two boys on the back porch so they wouldn't distract the adults.

It was Loren Hollister who controlled the conversation. Most of his questions were directed at Joe. "I like your approach to breaking horses. But doesn't it take a long time?"

"Just a few days. Maybe a week to do a good job," Joe said. "And I can train several horses at a time. The idea is they learn from each other as well as from me. I know you can jump on a wild horse's back and break it in a few hours. But then you've got a horse that doesn't trust you, let alone like you—a horse that can only be controlled by the threat of pain."

Joe could hear Elijah's voice in his head as he spoke. "The idea is this. Horses are herd animals. In the wild, the strongest stallion

leads and makes the decisions for his band. They follow him because they know he'll do what's best for his family. What you aim
to do, as a rider, is to take the place of that stallion, so that you
and the horse become a band of two. If you do it right, the horse
will trust you and want to follow your lead."

"It sounds as if you need to train the rider as well as the horse."
It was Amelia who spoke up.

"That's the ideal way—especially if a man wants a horse to be
his lifetime companion. But I can train horses to be ridden by
anybody who knows better than to use force with them."

"And if a rider does force one of your horses?"

"Then, after a few times, the horse unlearns what he's been taught
and becomes like any horse that's been broken the usual way."

"That's fascinating," Amelia said. "I would very much like to
have a horse that you've trained."

"I'd like to train one for you. But that would be up to your father," Joe said.

"Oh, please, Daddy!" Amelia turned to her father, begging in a
plaintive, little-girl voice. "You know how much I've wanted a
horse of my very own!"

"We'll talk about that later." Hollister gave her a dismissive frown.
"Dollarhide, I hear you worked for the Calder outfit."

Joe had been admiring Amelia, but the Calder name jolted
him to full attention. "That's right. I came up from Texas with
them a couple of years ago. But I got hurt in a stampede between
Dodge and Ogallala and they had to go on without me." It was the
half truth he'd settled on as a ready explanation. "Do you know
Benteen Calder? Is he a friend of yours?"

Hollister raised an eyebrow. "Do I know him? Yes. Is he a
friend? No, I can't say that he is. Grabbing all that land for himself, blocking the rest of us from getting our fair share. And now
he's building a mansion on his ranch that would put the White
House in Washington to shame. The sonofabitch thinks he's king
of Montana. I'd love an excuse to take him down a few pegs."

Joe could feel his blood racing. "Well, that would be fine with
me," he said. "After that stampede, when my horse went down,

Benteen Calder rode off and left me for dead. All he cared about was rounding up his damned cattle. Ever since then, I've been hoping to find a way to make him pay."

Hollister smiled. "Well, Joe Dollarhide, I'd say that you and I have something in common."

Sarah finished hanging the last bedsheet on the clotheslines she'd strung between the big cottonwood trees. She'd been at the tubs and washboard all morning. Now, while the long lines of laundry dried in the summer sun, she'd have time for a meal and a rest before welcoming any patients who stopped by. Later in the day, she'd take the clean laundry off the lines, fold it, iron the things that required it, and deliver everything by mule cart first thing tomorrow.

Taking in wash was a hard way to earn money, but she needed cash to pay for the move to Chicago and her medical training. The money Rusty had given her was already set aside in the bank. But it wasn't enough. Since she had only meager skills as a cook or seamstress, and no one would hire her for a temporary job, doing laundry had been her only respectable option.

A wooden clothespin slipped out of her hand and dropped to the ground. Bending to pick it up, she felt a slight wave of dizziness. But by the time she'd finished pinning up the sheet, it had gone away. She was only hungry, Sarah told herself. She'd had nothing but coffee and a dry biscuit this morning, and that had been hours ago.

The blackened copper wash boiler sat on its iron stand over the coals of the small fire. She would give the soapy water time to cool before she emptied it and scrubbed it for tomorrow. The lye soap cracked and roughened her hands. Some cream or lotion would help that problem, but such luxuries cost money—money that she was going to need for more important things.

In the kitchen, she took a pot of lentil and onion soup off the back burner of the stove, made sure it was still warm, and poured some into a bowl. She knew that she needed to eat, but the brown color and earthy smell did nothing for her appetite. Setting the bowl on the table, she sank onto a chair, forcing herself to swallow every spoonful. She felt exhausted and longed for a day of rest. But the dirty laundry just kept coming.

This time wouldn't last forever, she reminded herself. Weeks from now, if she kept saving her money, she would be on her way to a brand-new life.

By now, she'd read the pages from the medical school so many times that she knew the text by heart. The first page was her notice of acceptance. The second page was a list of things she should expect—and things that would be expected of her.

The medical course consisted of two sixteen-week semesters—thirty-two weeks of lectures and exams in all, involving no hands-on experience, but she already had that. Less than a year from now, she would be a licensed physician.

On her part, she was expected to attend all lectures, pay her fees in a timely manner, remain unmarried, and indulge in no immoral conduct that could tarnish her reputation or that of the school.

Only the question of payment worried her. She would need to get night or weekend work—hopefully some kind of nursing position—so she could attend classes on weekdays. Aside from that . . .

The soup seemed to turn rancid in her stomach. She doubled over as the first wave of nausea struck her. Toppling her chair in her haste, she plunged toward the back door and stumbled down the porch steps. She made it just in time to retch up everything she'd eaten.

Wiping her mouth on her damp sleeve, she sank onto the steps and buried her face in her hands. She had to face it—the reality she'd been denying for weeks, even when her menses hadn't come.

She was never going to be a doctor.

She was not going to marry Everett or any other man.

She was all alone.

And she was going to be a mother.

CHAPTER TWELVE

JOE HADN'T KNOWN FOR SURE WHEN, OR EVEN WHETHER, HOLLISTER would contact him again. The man had seemed interested, both in his horse-training skills and in sharing their common enmity toward Benteen Calder. But as the weeks passed with no word, Joe had dismissed the idea of an alliance.

The real reason Hollister had stayed away, he suspected, was to keep his daughter from getting too friendly with a rootless cowboy. Joe was fine with that. Amelia was a stunner, but she was out of his class. And staying on her father's good side was more important than romancing a pretty girl.

Now it was autumn. The grass that carpeted the plains and foothills had faded to the pale hue of ripened wheat. In the high meadows and on the slopes of the distant mountains, tapestry patterns of bright gold aspen and splashes of fiery maple contrasted with the dark, velvety green of pines. The peaks were already dusted with snow. Migrating birds crossed the sky. Buck deer, bull elk, and mountain rams battled for the right to pass their bloodlines on to the next generation.

On the ranches, it was fall roundup—a time to gather the cattle and bring them to winter pasture. For a small operation like Blaise Ransom's, with all hands helping, including Blaise's two sons, the roundup was over in a few days. The barn was finished just in time and stocked with hay. Montana winters could be deadly, but the hope was, as always, that this one would be mild enough for the cows to survive.

The six mustangs trained by Joe had sold for a good profit, in which Joe had shared. Blaise was already talking about getting more wild horses in the spring, but Joe could feel the itch to move on. The Ransoms were fine people. They'd treated him, well. But aside from the money he'd saved, Joe was no closer to getting his own land than when he'd arrived. Things weren't moving fast enough to suit him.

Lying in his bunk at night, his thoughts often drifted to Sarah—her beauty, her tenderness, and her passion. By now, she would be in Chicago, studying to become a doctor. Life being what it was, he would probably never see her again. But he would never forget her. As his first love, she would always hold a place in his heart.

On a chilly day, ablaze with autumn color, Joe was riding herd on the Ransom cattle, keeping an eye out for marauding Cheyenne and Lakota that still left the reservation to steal an occasional beef, when he saw two riders approaching. As they came closer, he recognized them. One was his boss. The other was Loren Hollister.

They pulled up alongside him. After a brief greeting, Hollister got right to the business that had brought him here. "I've got a new horse in my corral, a stallion," he said. "Some Lakota showed up with it. They wanted to trade it for a couple of steers. I asked them where they got it. They didn't understand or pretended not to. They probably stole it. It had rope burns around its neck and was wild as hell. Looked like it had been through some rough handling."

"So I'm guessing you gave them the two steers," Joe said. "Otherwise you wouldn't be here."

"I did. They said that if I didn't trade, they'd kill the horse and eat it. I couldn't let that happen. You'll understand when you see it. They left it in the corral, and I pitched over some hay for it. But when I tried to get close, the bastard damn near killed me. I'd like you to take a look and let me know if you can work with him."

"Hollister's already cleared it with me," Blaise said. "If you decide to take the horse on, you'll be staying in his bunkhouse.

He'll be paying your wages, plus a bonus if you do the job. You can come back here when you're done."

"So are you interested?" Hollister asked.

"Sure," Joe said. "But I'll need to see the horse before I give you my final answer. I can't work miracles. If he's really a killer, you'll be better off putting him down."

"I understand," Hollister said. "Get your gear. You can always bring it back."

Loren Hollister had been one of the early settlers in the area. He'd arrived with money to buy land. But the lion's share of the land he'd wanted had been taken by Benteen Calder, including some parcels with Hollister's pending claims. Calder had filed on land for himself, his wife, his cowboys, and his friends and combined them all into one huge spread.

It was a blasted kingdom, Hollister had told Joe on the ride to his ranch. And now Calder was building a castle where he could be king. Nothing he'd done had been illegal, but it had been damned underhanded, and Hollister was determined to get revenge. It was just a question of when and how.

Joe had listened and sympathized. Neither of them had mentioned working together to punish Benteen Calder, but the idea had hung unspoken between them. *Give it time,* Joe told himself.

Hollister's house, although made of logs, was well-built and impressive in size, with a big barn and a network of sheds, pens, and corrals behind it. "Are you ready to see the stallion?" Hollister asked as they paused to open the gate. "We can have drinks first if you want."

"Thanks, but let's do it now." Still mounted, Joe followed Hollister around the house and back toward a corral behind the barn, in the far corner of the complex. The stallion had clearly heard them coming. His piercing war cry raised the hair on the back of Joe's neck. A dim memory stirred. Even before he saw the animal, he sensed that the stallion would be a blue roan—and it was.

He studied it from a safe distance as it snorted and threatened.

No, it couldn't be the horse he'd seen in Kansas. Wild horses had their range, and they kept to it. The stallion he remembered would never have traveled this far. And there were subtle differences in the markings—the ears seemed darker. And there was that small white spot on the right front foot—surely he would have remembered that. No way was this the stallion he'd seen before. Still, it was as if the hand of fate had brought the animal here—maybe as a gift, or more likely a challenge.

"Well, what do you think?" Hollister asked.

Joe didn't reply. He was studying the stallion, sensing more pain and fear in him than rage. He gave a slow nod.

"I'll get somebody to put your horse away and take your gear to the bunkhouse," Hollister said. "You can start anytime."

"I'll start now," Joe said.

For the first few days, Joe did little more than stand outside the corral fence, watching the stallion, talking and singing to him. The horse was a splendid animal, elegant of line and proportion, as if he might have some Arabian blood in his ancestry. Joe and Hollister had agreed that he shouldn't be gelded, even though it might calm him. He might never be gentle enough to ride safely. But as a stud, bred to the right mares, such a horse could produce a line of great foals.

The stallion viewed Joe, and every other human, as an enemy. The deep rope burn around his neck and other marks on his body were enough to explain the reason why. When he felt threatened, he would charge the fence, snorting and shrieking. When this happened, Joe would remain calm and in place, still singing. After many attempts to drive the hated man away, the stallion began to accept his presence. It was a first step. But winning this abused horse's trust, if it could be done at all, was going to take time.

"Why do you sing to him?" Amelia had come up to the fence to stand beside Joe. Joe let her stay. This wasn't the first time she'd shown up. He was still a little worried about her father, but he enjoyed her company. She was as friendly and curious as she was pretty.

"It's not just for him," Joe said, thinking it might be time for a break. "I sing to keep myself calm. If I feel any fear, the horse will know, and he'll try to take advantage. Horses aren't just big, dumb brutes. They're smart—smarter than we are in some ways."

She gave him a dimpled smile. "You're an interesting man, Joe Dollarhide. I've never met anybody quite like you."

"I'm just a trail bum with dirt behind my ears. And I've got a feeling your dad wouldn't like it if he knew you were spending time out here with me."

"My dad doesn't care how I spend my time. He's too busy taking care of his precious ranch and figuring out ways to make more money."

"Where's your mother?" Joe asked. "Sorry, I shouldn't have asked such a personal question."

"No, it's all right. My mother—Evelyn, as she likes me to call her—is in St. Louis with her latest husband. My parents parted ways when I was still in diapers. My dad went off to make money, and I stayed with my mother and her parents."

"But you're here now. How long have you lived in Montana?"

"Only for a few months. It's a long story. You don't really want to hear it. Anyway, my dad hasn't had much experience being a father. He pays more attention to his stupid old cows than he does to me." Amelia brushed a speck of hay off her skirt. Every move she made was a study in prettiness, a graceful little gesture.

"Those stupid old cows, as you call them, are his livelihood. The money from selling them pays for the food you eat and the clothes you wear."

They were strolling away from the horse pens now, in the direction of the barn and the house. She walked a little ahead of him, tossing her auburn curls as she spoke.

"But it's so boring here, Joe—I may call you Joe, mayn't I? Don't you agree?"

"I'm never bored here. Most of the time I'm either working or eating or sleeping."

"That may be fine for you," she said. "But in St. Louis I could go shopping, or eat in a nice restaurant, or dress up and go to the theater at night. There's nothing here. Daddy won't even take me into Miles City or Deadwood."

"Believe me, Amelia, you don't want to go to those cow towns. No lady is safe on the streets there. And there's nothing to do unless you like to drink and gamble."

"I could always learn to drink and gamble. Maybe I'd even be good at it—win me a pile of money." She gave him a teasing look. "This morning I found something in the barn. Do you want me to show it to you?"

"Sure." Maybe one of the long-legged dogs that hung around the ranch had had pups, Joe thought. Or maybe she'd found a nest of baby chicks in the straw.

They were nearing the barn, a roomy structure with a hayloft in the top. "Come on!" she said, laughing as she grabbed his hand and pulled him in through the open doorway.

After the bright sunlight, the barn seemed as dark as a cave inside. As Joe's eyes adjusted, he could see the long row of box stalls for the horses, the tool rack for the pitchforks and shovels, the wheelbarrows for hay and manure, the door to the tack room, and the ladder leading up to the loft. There was no one else in the barn.

"So what was it you wanted to show me?" Joe asked.

She guided him into an empty stall. Only then did she let go of his hand. "Close your eyes," she said. "Don't open them until I count to three. That's it . . ."

Joe stood with his eyes closed. He was beginning to feel foolish, but he'd come this far. He'd go along with her game for now.

"Ready?" she teased. "Here we go. One . . . two . . ." Joe could feel her standing close to him. He could smell the gardenia scent of her hair. "Three," she whispered as her satiny mouth closed on his. Her arms went around his neck, pulling him down to her.

His pulse slammed as their lips clung. Molten heat shot through his body as his arms jerked her close. The voice of caution screamed that this was a bad idea, but with liquid fire pulsing through his veins, he wasn't listening. He didn't love her, but the reaction of pure, physical lust was overpowering.

For a moment he gave in to it. Then like a drowning man, he began to struggle. This was trouble. Big trouble. He had to end it now.

Summoning every ounce of strength, he thrust her away from him. "We can't do this, Amelia. Not unless you want to get me fired. Go back to the house—and stay away from me. I've got work to do. I don't need your kind of distraction."

She stood facing him, her trembling lips swollen from his kiss. "*You bastard!*" Her hand flew up and slapped his face hard. Then, spinning away, she raced out of the barn.

Catching his breath, he watched her go. He'd tried to stay out of trouble, but it was already too late. Amelia would go straight to her father, who would believe everything she told him, whether it was true or not. And after that, Joe told himself, he'd be packing his bags—if Hollister didn't shoot him first.

Expecting to be fired any minute, he went back and began working with the horse again. Earlier, he'd asked for, and been given, a few carrots from the root cellar. Protected by the sturdy fence, he laid a carrot on his open hand and thrust his arm through the rails. It was a risky move. The big blue roan could easily break his arm with a lunge or cripple his hand with a powerful bite. But maybe he'd been too cautious with the stallion. Maybe it was time to raise the stakes.

Holding his arm steady, he began to sing again. He could have worn a leather glove, but that would have defeated the purpose of what he was doing. He wanted the horse to understand that the hand, with its human smell and feel, was a good thing.

As he sang, the stallion's ears pricked. The sensitive nostrils quivered as the horse took a step forward, hesitated, then took a few more steps, neck stretching; then he snorted and danced away. As a wild animal, he'd probably never tasted a carrot.

Carefully pulling back his arm, Joe reached under the bottom rail and laid the carrot on the ground, inside the pen. Then he walked away to do other work, leaving the horse to discover it for himself.

When he came back to the pen, after eating supper in the bunkhouse, the carrot was gone. At the sight of him, outside the fence, the stallion pricked its ears, as if expecting another treat. Leaning on the fence, Joe chuckled. "No more carrots for you tonight, boy. Wait until tomorrow. Then we'll see what you can do to earn another one."

He lingered by the fence, enjoying the chill of the twilight air, the smell of pine on the breeze, and the sounds of awakening night. Maybe there'd be no tomorrow here for him. Maybe by breakfast time, he'd be on the road with his gear, fired on the word of a willful beauty. Amelia's blistering kiss had nearly scorched his boot soles. But at the price of his future here, it had been a bad bargain.

"Well, at least he's not trying to kill us. That's progress." Loren Hollister's voice, coming from just behind his shoulder, made Joe flinch. If the ax was about to fall, it would happen now.

"He's doing better," Joe said. "But it's taking time."

"Like most good things," Hollister said. "I know I haven't been around much, but I've kept an eye on you. You're doing a good job."

Joe swallowed. Maybe he'd be all right. "I try, sir," he said. "If you plan to ride him yourself, you might want to come around more. We'll want him to know whose horse he is."

"Good idea. And I haven't forgotten that bonus I offered if you train him."

"About that," Joe said. "What I really want, instead of a bonus, is your help getting my own land. I don't mean for you to pay for it. Just show me how to find the best parcel out there and file on it as a homestead. If Calder can do it, so can I, but I need to know the rules—when to follow them and when to break them."

Hollister chuckled. "Smart move. I can tell you what to do. You have to understand that most of the good land around here is already taken. But there should be some left in the foothills and the canyons, or even a parcel that's been abandoned by folks who gave up and left. We can talk about it later, after you've got that horse under control. But that isn't why I'm here. What I really want to talk to you about is my daughter."

Joe's heart sank. He braced himself for a tirade. "Whatever she told you—"

"What she told me doesn't matter," Hollister said. "I know you're a respectful man who wouldn't take undue advantage of a girl. But since the juices are already flowing, there are some things you need to know about Amelia.

"She may have told you that her mother, Evelyn, and I divorced when she was a baby. I'm afraid she didn't have the best upbringing, watching her mother go through men. This past summer, Evelyn sent her to live with me because the girl was out of control—staying out till all hours with the worst sort of people, sneaking out of the house, ruining her reputation. Even here, I worry about her. In her own way, she's as wild as that stallion."

"I understand, sir," Joe said. "You don't have to worry about me. I'm here to work, not fool around. I'll steer clear of her."

"That's not what I'm asking. You're young. You're decent. And you're as much of a gentleman as a cowboy can be. Sure as sunup, Amelia's going to throw herself at some man. I'd rather it be you than some sonofabitch who's going to mistreat her—drink, chase women, abuse her, spend all her money, and most likely leave her pregnant."

Joe stared at him, feeling as if he'd just been whacked with a side of beef. "Are you saying you want me to *encourage* her?"

"That's exactly what I'm saying. The only way I can see to save Amelia from ruining her own life is to pair her with a good man—and I've seen enough of you, and heard enough from Blaise Ransom, to know that a good man is what you are. If it turns out that you want to marry her, I'd most likely say yes. If not, you could at least be her friend and try to show her a little fun." Hollister paused, fixing Joe with a piercing gaze. "So, do you need time to think about it?"

Joe struggled to recover his wits. "I'd have to talk to Blaise. I told him I'd be back there after I trained the stallion."

Hollister laid a hand on Joe's shoulder. "Don't worry about it. I already talked to him. It's been settled."

Once the big blue roan discovered carrots, his training moved ahead. Within a few days, Joe was able to feed him from inside the pen, although he had yet to stroke the stallion with his hands. For a horse that had been abused and was still fearful, this next step would have to be approached with caution and sensitivity.

Amelia was back once more, standing by the fence, laughing and flirting. Did she know about her father's conversation with Joe? Probably not, Joe surmised. She loved breaking rules and hated being manipulated. Telling her the truth would have sent her fleeing in the other direction.

The other cowboys in the bunkhouse had begun to notice how much attention she paid Joe. If they teased him, it was out of envy. Any one of them would've given his boots and saddle for the chance to hold her hand and enjoy the sunshine of her dimpled smile.

Leaving the stallion, Joe climbed over the fence and joined her. "You've done wonders with that horse, Joe," she said. "But I was thinking, he needs a name. Don't you agree?"

"Good idea," he said. "Do you have a name in mind?"

"I was thinking we could call him Dusk, because of his color. Do you like that?"

"I think it's perfect. But you should ask your father. After all, the stallion is his."

"Daddy won't care. But I'll ask him anyway—after you and I get back from Blue Moon."

"You want to go to Blue Moon?" Joe had put off going to the town, or anyplace else where he might run into people from the Calder ranch. But he knew he couldn't avoid the place forever.

"Don't look like such a dunce," Amelia teased. "I need some things from the store, and it's a nice, sunny day for a ride. Daddy already told me I could have you drive me."

"Fine," Joe said. "It could get chilly on the way. Go get something warm to wear. I'll hitch up the buggy."

As he wheeled the buggy out of the shed, laid out the harness, and led the glossy matched bays out of their stalls, Joe's thoughts were moving and shifting like a river in a spring flood. For the past few days he'd puzzled over Hollister's offer. Why him, a poor young cowboy? And what was the man thinking? Hollister was no fool. He wouldn't do anything without a reason.

Then last night, lying in his bunk, a memory had surfaced— the day Zeke Taylor had invited him into Dodge City, and the discovery that he'd been chosen to go only because Zeke wanted to be the one in charge.

Hollister's motives were the same—just on a larger scale. Match his willful daughter to a young man he could control, someone who would do what he was told and never be a threat to his power.

And there was more. Joe had looked into the homestead laws that dictated who could file for the 160-acre land parcels. A married man over eighteen could get twice as much land by filing for himself and his wife. If Hollister married off his daughter to a young man who wouldn't oppose him, he could add 320 acres to his own holdings.

With that sudden epiphany had come anger, followed by an icy determination. Loren Hollister wasn't the only one who could play power games, Joe had vowed. He would watch and learn from the man, but his only loyalty would be to himself.

As he honed the rules of the game, he would keep his own counsel, trust no man or woman, and use any means he could to get and keep what was rightfully his.

That's exactly what Benteen Calder would have done. Joe would follow his example until he could beat Calder at his own game.

By the time Joe had the team hitched to the buggy, Amelia had come outside wrapped in a woolen shawl and carrying her shopping basket. Minutes later they'd pulled out of the yard and were following the worn wheel ruts that passed for a road between the outlying ranches and the ramshackle community of Blue Moon, which, in the last couple of years, had sprouted from the prairie like a crop of wild mushrooms on a rotting log.

The town had taken root when an enterprising man named Fat Frank Fitzsimmons had lost a wagon wheel on the prairie and decided to set up a saloon. Blue Moon now boasted a general store with a bar in the back, a blacksmith's shop, and two cabins for the Fitzsimmons family. It wasn't much, but as more families moved into the area, the place was bound to grow. New buildings—maybe a restaurant or even a real saloon, were already going up. Hammers rang out on the autumn air as workers hurried to cover the frames with planking before winter set in.

Joe felt a prickle of wariness as he helped Amelia down from the buggy and walked with her to open and hold the door of the general store. There was no telling who was going to be inside, but he'd better have his story ready in case he met anyone from the Calder place.

Strolling ahead of him, in a manner calculated to catch the eye of any man within range, Amelia glanced back with a toss of her pretty head. "No need to follow me around, Joe," she said. "I know what I need and where to find it. You can entertain yourself until I've finished shopping."

She disappeared, leaving Joe to look around. The store was a cozy place, warmed by a potbellied stove and crammed to the rafters with everything from canned food and tools to clothes, cooking and sewing supplies, ammunition, riding gear, tobacco, blocks of rock salt, and even candies in pretty glass jars on the counter. A plain woman, trailed by two small children, was filling her basket. She and Amelia were the only customers in sight.

Walled off by a curtain in the back was the makeshift bar where whiskey was sold. Joe had never been much of a drinker, but it would be something to do while Amelia shopped.

As Joe moved toward the rear of the store, he heard a familiar voice behind him. "Joe Dollarhide! As I live and breathe!"

"Rusty!" Joe was genuinely glad to see the old man. Rusty could also tell him a lot about the Calders, but Joe knew better than to appear too curious. "Come on back. I'll buy you a drink," he said.

"Thanks. Just a beer for me," Rusty said as they passed through the opening in the curtain. The bar was quiet at this hour. They ordered beers and sat down on two wooden crates in a corner.

"So you finally made it here," Rusty said. "The last time I saw you was at Sarah's. I know what I told you about not breaking her heart. But I still can't believe you left her. If I'd had a woman like that one . . ." His voice trailed off. He shook his grizzled head.

"I didn't break her heart," Joe said. "She got her acceptance to medical school. Sarah's off in Chicago learning to be a doctor."

"Hell, she could probably teach those doctor classes. But I guess she needs the damn fool piece of paper that makes it legal. So what about you? I was hopin' you might show up at the Calder place."

"Too much water under the bridge," Joe said. "I found a job with a cattle drive on the way here. Blaise Ransom was the boss. He kept me on after the drive to break horses. Do you know him?"

"Heard of him. Good man, from what folks say. Sounds like you done all right for yourself."

"I did even better. I'm working for one of the big outfits now—Loren Hollister's ranch. I drove his daughter into town today."

"You mean that pretty little bit that's flittin' around here like she's at a fancy dress ball?" Rusty put down his unfinished beer. He looked as if he might be about to spit in the glass. "I can't tell you how to live your life, Joe. But you watch yourself with Hollister. At least you can trust a snake to rattle before he strikes. But Hollister's done a lot of dirt and made a lot of enemies—including Benteen. What's worse, he's hand-in-glove with Judd Boston, the dirty skunk that grabbed Benteen's family ranch back in Texas. I don't need to tell you any more about him."

"Don't worry, I'm watching my back," Joe said. "What about you?"

"Me, I'm just gettin' old," Rusty said. "I'm makin' one more drive for Benteen in the spring. I figure it's the last one I've got in me. Then it'll be the rockin' chair on the front porch."

"And the Calders? How much does Benteen know about me?"

"Not much. Jesse and me swore not to tell how we come to find you. As far as Benteen and the boys know, we just happened into you in Ogallala. So they know you survived, but that's about all. You can tell them whatever the hell you want to. Just don't go makin' us wish we'd never saved you and lied about it. Understand?"

"I understand." Joe cleared his throat. "I hear Benteen's building a new house."

"That he is. And the place is going to make us all proud. Lorna's been livin' in that cabin long enough—her and them two little boys they got now. She deserves to live like the queen she is. You know we'd all welcome you back, don't you?"

"I know," Joe said. "But like I say, it's water under the bridge."

"Joe, I'm finished. We can leave now." Amelia stood in the gap at the side of the curtain, her basket filled.

Joe stood. "Guess I'd better get going. Good to see you, Rusty."

"I'll tell the boys you said hello." Rusty shook his head as Joe took the basket Amelia handed him and followed her out.

As they drove home, with the sun warm overhead, Amelia slipped off her shawl. "What a lovely day it's turned out to be. It's a shame I didn't have the cook pack us a lunch. We could stop and have ourselves a picnic. Maybe next time."

"Next time might be too cold," Joe said.

She gave him a saucy look. "Oh, pooh! You're such a sourpuss! Sometimes I wonder why I bother with you. Maybe it's because I really, really like you."

"Well, at least we can stop for a few minutes." They'd reached the highest part of the rough wagon road, a level stretch with a sweeping view of the grassy plain and the distant, snow-capped peaks beyond. Joe pulled the team to a halt and applied the brake to the buggy wheel.

"If I seem like a sourpuss, as you call me, Amelia, it's because I have serious plans, and I spend a lot of time thinking about them."

"What kind of plans?" She shifted closer to him as a chilly breeze ruffled the prairie grass.

"Take a look," he said with a sweeping gesture toward the scene before them. "I'm not always going to be a poor cowboy. Someday I plan to own a spread bigger than everything you see here, with cattle and horses and a house as grand as Benteen Calder's. And when I get it, I'll need a woman to share it and raise a family with me."

She was silent for a moment, her hands clasping and unclasping in her lap. At last she spoke. "I like that plan, Joe," she said.

"Good. I like it, too." He pulled her to him and kissed her, deep and hard and long.

CHAPTER THIRTEEN

Ogallala, nine months later

SITTING UP IN BED, SARAH FINISHED NURSING HER SON AND LIFTED him against her shoulder. She held him tenderly, feeling the warm weight of his head against her neck and savoring the sweet baby smell of his skin as she patted his small, strong back.

After a moment, he rewarded her with a lusty belch, so loud in the silent bedroom that it made her laugh. When she lowered him to her lap, he looked up at her with Joe's blue eyes and gave her a baby version of Joe's smile. Hair as dark as his father's curled over his forehead. No one who had seen Joe could have a moment's doubt who had sired this little boy.

Sarah had given birth alone, three months ago, with a spring thunderstorm battering the old house. Luckily, the birth had been an easy one. She'd known what to expect and what to do. When she'd cradled her baby in her arms for the first time, the love that surged through her had been so powerful that she'd broken down and wept.

She'd named him Blake, in honor of her great-uncle, and given him her own last name, since she had no legal right to Joe's. But his middle name was Joseph, in acknowledgment of his parentage. Blake Joseph Foxworth. It was a good name. She liked the sound of it.

With early-morning sunlight slanting through the curtains, Sarah laid her baby in the bureau drawer that served as a makeshift cradle and hurriedly dressed for the day. She was still seeing patients, although not so many as before. And, ruined woman though she was, there were still a few customers for her laundry service. But her everyday life was a constant struggle for enough food, enough money, and all the things a baby needed.

"If you don't do something to set this straight, you won't have a friend left in this town."

Margaret Lacy's words, spoken that day in the dressing room of the general store, still came back to haunt Sarah. True to the lady's prediction, the so-called "decent" folk of Ogallala had turned their backs on her as soon as her pregnancy began to show. People had stopped greeting her on the street. Everett had married another woman. But even with an attractive, charming wife by his side, he'd still lost the election for county commissioner.

Only the poor families she'd helped, and the few women who'd been in her situation, remained her friends. They'd brought her food and items like clothing and diapers for the baby. Sarah had been grateful, but there was so much more she was going to need before young Blake was grown. She had to find a way to give her son a better life than this one.

The baby had fallen asleep in his drawer, which she'd left on the bed. Sarah used the free time to tidy the house and fix a simple breakfast of coffee and toasted bread. She was about to go out back to fill the wash boiler and make the fire underneath when she heard the sound of horses, followed by a knock at the front door.

She unlocked the door and opened it. Standing on the front porch was Rusty.

"What a surprise!" She hugged the old man, even though she hadn't done it the last time he was here. "Come in, Rusty. Let me fix you some breakfast."

"No need." He looked older, but his smile was the same. "I ate this morning when I cooked for the crew. We're camped with the herd, a few miles out of town. I had to come in for supplies." His gaze narrowed below his grizzled eyebrows. "I didn't expect to find you here, but I thought it wouldn't hurt to check. I'm glad to see you, girl."

"And I'm glad to see you. Here, have a seat." She ushered him to the rocking chair, while she sat on the footstool, facing him. She could tell that he was studying her, noticing how she'd changed—her bosom straining the buttons of her dress, her face showing a few lines of worry and weariness.

"You say you're with a cattle drive. Are you still working for the Calders?" she asked.

"Yup. But I told Benteen this would be my last time. I'm gettin' old. Ready to park the chuckwagon and take it easy. And before you have to ask, no, Joe's not with us. He's workin' for another outfit in Montana. Doin' right well for himself." Rusty frowned. "But last time I talked to him, he told me you were goin' to doctor school in Chicago. What are you doing back here? Did you finish already?"

Sarah had known the question was coming. The only answer she could give was the truth. "I didn't even start," she said, remembering the day she'd crumpled the acceptance letter, stuffed it into the stove, and watched it burst into flame. "I . . . couldn't."

"You couldn't? But why, Sarah? If you'd needed money—"

"No. I'd been working and saving. It wasn't that."

"Then what? What happened?"

"Rather than tell you, let me show you." Rising, she walked into the bedroom and returned a moment later, carrying the drawer with her sleeping son in it. She set the drawer on the footstool where Rusty could see inside. "This happened," she said.

As Rusty gazed down, in a mixture of wonder and shock, the baby opened his eyes, smiled, and gurgled at him. "Oh, Lordy," the old man muttered. "If I'd known what that rascal was up to, I'd have horsewhipped him. How the hell could he do this to you, and then leave you here alone?"

Sarah gave him a fleeting smile. "You can't put all the blame on Joe. What happened was as much my fault as his. And when he left, I was still planning to go to medical school."

"So he doesn't know about the baby?"

"How could he know? I had no way to reach him."

"I could take him a message. Is that what you want?"

The baby had begun to fuss. Sarah lifted him into her arms. "I don't know. Until you walked in, I thought I'd heard the last of Joe. Now . . ." Torn, she shook her head. "I don't know what to say. He deserves to know he has a son, but it would complicate things for both of us. I need to think about it."

Rusty rose from the rocker. His pale eyes, bloodshot from years of trail dust, seemed to hold a secret sadness.

"Before you make up your mind, there's one thing you need to know—something I haven't told you."

"What's that?" Worry seized her. "Is Joe all right?"

"Yes. But here's the thing, and I'm sorry as hell to be the one to tell you."

"Just say it."

Rusty cleared his throat. "Joe is married, Sarah."

Sarah clutched her baby as the words sank in, sharp and bitter, changing her forever. Something hardened inside her.

"Don't tell him about my baby," she said. "Don't you tell anybody—ever."

Dressed for riding, Joe paused next to the bed, gazing down at his sleeping wife. With her glorious auburn hair spread on the pillow, and her lashes lying like silken fringe against her cheeks, she looked like a beautiful doll—or perhaps like the child she was. Pampered and indulged for the full seventeen years of her life, what else could he have expected of her?

Joe had proposed to Amelia in the fall and married her six months ago in a simple ceremony at the Hollister home. Amelia, who'd dreamed of a lavish church wedding, had cried through her vows. She had wanted to get married in St. Louis, with her friends as bridesmaids, followed by a honeymoon in New York, or at least Denver. But given the long, expensive journey and dangerous weather conditions, it couldn't be done in the winter; and spring was roundup time, when Joe and her father couldn't be spared.

They'd spent their wedding night at the McQueen House in Miles City. Despite more weeping from the bride, they'd managed to consummate the marriage. After two more nights that had gone somewhat better, they'd returned to the big ranch house and moved into an upstairs bedroom. The next day, Joe had returned to work on the ranch.

Joe knew that Amelia had expected more of marriage than this—being left alone most days while her husband worked. He knew that he owed her more attention. But his head was full of ambitions that he was determined to carry out. He would never settle for just being Loren Hollister's son-in-law. He had plans for a ranch of his own.

When it came to claiming land under the Homestead Act, Joe had known better than to wait for his father-in-law's promised help. Something told him that any parcel he wanted to file on would be claimed by Loren Hollister, as part of what the older man called the family empire. In other words, Hollister would be doing what Benteen Calder had done—having friends and employees file on 160-acre parcels that would then become part of his own bigger ranch.

Joe wanted none of that. He was determined to have an empire he could claim for himself. In the years ahead, when Loren passed away, with Amelia and her future children as his only heirs, that would be the time to combine all the land into one big spread.

Bending over the bed, he brushed a kiss onto her forehead. She made a little purring sound, stirred, and settled back into sleep. He would be good to her, Joe vowed. He would shelter her, protect her, and see that she and their children wanted for nothing. In time, he could only hope that he would grow to love her in something like the warm, passionate way he'd loved Sarah.

Without taking time for breakfast, he crossed the yard to the stable. The pen that had held the blue roan stallion was empty now. A few months ago, when Joe was elsewhere, a friend of Loren's, a man named Loman Janes, had decided to ride the horse. When the stallion balked at his rough handling, Janes had taken a whip to him. Joe had come home to find Dusk standing with his head down and his coat streaked with blood. Late that night, when the ranch was asleep, Joe had broken down the fence and arranged an escape. No one had seen the stallion since.

In the stable, he saddled his buckskin and rode out of the ranch gate. Now that he was family instead of hired help, Joe enjoyed not having to report to the foreman or even to Loren. He could go wherever his business took him.

Today his business was taking him to the bank in Miles City. Over the past weeks, with the spring roundup and calving season over, Joe, who'd studied the maps, had taken to riding out alone, exploring the land parcels that were still available for homesteading.

As Loren had told him, most of the good grazing pasture was already taken. But there was acreage to be had in the patches of hilly land that rose above the prairie. One of these intrigued Joe more than any of the others. The terrain wasn't ideal for cattle. The land was steep and hilly, the soil rocky, the grass spare, the winters colder and snowier than on the plain. But there was shelter in the canyons and water from a swift-flowing creek. The slopes were forested with pines, which could be cut and sold for lumber or used to build a home on a level plateau with a sweeping view of the land below. Here and there, narrow box canyons cut into the hills, perfect for capturing and holding the wild horses he planned to break. When Joe had spotted the tracks of unshod horses on the plain nearby, he had known that this was the place he wanted.

The parcel's location, an easy ride from the Hollister ranch, made it an even better choice. Joe could work on building a home and leave Amelia at the ranch until it was finished. As a married man, he could claim 160 acres for himself and another 160 acres for his wife—a total of 320 acres. Under the Timber Culture Act of 1873, it might be possible to get even more land if he contracted to keep forty acres of it planted in trees for the next ten years.

He hadn't told Loren or Amelia about his plans. They would

no doubt argue for keeping him on the ranch and for keeping any land he claimed in the family. That was why he wanted to file the claim first. Only then would he give them the news and brace himself for the storm that was bound to follow.

With dreams and ideas churning in his head, he followed the wagon road across the grassland to Miles City to file for his land. The Homestead Act of 1862 had been passed by Congress to encourage the settlement of the West. Settlers could get title to a parcel of land by filing a claim, then living on the property and making improvements for five years. An alternative plan, called commuting, gave title after six months and payment of $1.25 an acre. Joe had hoped to use the commuting option, but it might make more sense to invest all the money he earned in improvements—such as a sawmill powered by the creek, along with a wagon and a team of draft horses for hauling lumber.

By the time he reached Miles City, the sun had risen well above the horizon. The bustling cow town had begun as a small trading post. Over the years, it had grown to fill the needs of the cattlemen and landowners. At this hour, shops and saloons, restaurants and legal offices were all doing a brisk trade. There was even a newspaper office and a fine hotel next to the bank.

Joe tied up his horse, went straight to the bank, and waited in line for the land office clerk. When his turn came, he produced his marriage certificate and paid the filing fee for each of the parcels and registered his claims. The clerk suggested that he put an announcement in the newspaper as well, so that neighboring ranchers would know the land was taken.

He strode out of the bank feeling a little taller than when he'd gone in. He was no longer a simple cowboy. He was a man with his own land.

The visit to the newspaper office took only a few minutes. After that, Joe's business in Miles City was finished. He was about to mount up and head out of town when he realized he was ravenously hungry. He'd skipped breakfast to get an early start this morning; and in the excitement of filing on his land, eating had been the last thing on his mind. But now his hunger had reawakened. He remembered the fine food in the restaurant at the McQueen House, where he and Amelia had spent their brief honeymoon. Why not celebrate his new status with a good meal?

The breakfast crowd had cleared, and it was early for lunch, so there were plenty of empty tables. The headwaiter showed Joe to a sunny corner, where he ordered steak and eggs with potatoes, toast, and coffee.

He was sipping his coffee and waiting for his meal when he heard a deep voice at his shoulder.

"May I join you, Joe Dollarhide?"

Startled, Joe glanced up. Standing next to him, with a coffee cup in his hand, was Benteen Calder.

"Sure. Have a seat." Joe was surprised, but he willed himself not to show it. He'd known that sooner or later he would run into his old boss. The timing was as good as any. He could only wish he'd been better prepared. He'd spent years thinking of the things he would say to Calder when they met. But now they had fled his mind.

Calder pulled out the chair on the opposite side of the table and sat down. He had aged some—the creases deeper around his eyes, a touch of gray at the temples—but he was still a man who exuded power.

He took a sip of his coffee. "Lorna and I were happy to hear you'd survived the stampede," he said. "What happened to you?"

"When I went over the edge of that wash, my dead horse pinned me against a big tree stump. You and Jesse were right above me. I could hear you talking. But you couldn't hear me. If you'd let Jesse go down and investigate, he'd have found me. But you had cattle to round up." Joe felt his anger building. "Cattle—when you could've saved a man with a few extra minutes of searching."

"I see." Calder's face was impassive. The sonofabitch didn't even care enough to say he was sorry.

"By the time I dug myself out from under that horse, you and the herd were long gone," Joe said. "I damn near died again on the prairie. But I was found, and I did whatever it took to survive."

"Rusty said he ran into you in Ogallala. You could've joined up with the herd again and come back here. We'd have welcomed you."

Not if Rusty had told you the truth.

"By then I had other plans," Joe said.

"So I heard. You signed on with Loren Hollister and married his daughter. I might've warned you about the man, but since you're family now, it's probably too late for that."

"Hollister may be my father-in-law, but he doesn't own me," Joe said. "I'm my own man. And I haven't forgotten how you walked away and left me for dead. I don't want you to forget it, either."

"I'll keep that in mind." Calder finished his coffee and stood. "I see the waiter's bringing your meal, so I'll be on my way. I'll tell Lorna that I saw you. She'll be glad to hear you're doing well."

"Give her my best. She was always good to me," Joe said. But by then Benteen Calder had walked out of hearing.

He ate his steak and eggs, his spirits somewhat dampened after the encounter with the man he'd come to think of as his archenemy. Joe had held his own with his former boss, but not by much. Calder had walked away unintimidated.

Joe paid for the meal, left the restaurant, and mounted his horse for the ride home. He wasn't looking forward to the fight he'd be facing at home, when he told his father-in-law about the land he'd acquired. But he had no regrets. He'd found the place to build his dream, and nothing was going to stop him.

CHAPTER FOURTEEN

JOE HAD RIDDEN ABOUT HALFWAY HOME WHEN AN IRRESISTIBLE URGE pulled him aside. The last time he'd seen the forested hills, claiming them had been only a dream. Now they were his to build on and use as he chose. He wanted to see them—to run the soil through his fingers, to stand in the shade of his trees, and to drink clear water from his stream. And he wanted to do it now, before the realities of how much work lay ahead of him sank in.

An hour of riding took him to his land. By the time he rode his horse to the level area where he planned to build a house, he was already making a list in his head. First, he was going to need access to his claim. That would mean getting permission to cross someone else's land, and it might not come cheap. He would have to plan for that. And the house—it made sense to build a cabin first, to satisfy the terms of the claim. After that, he could expand the cabin into the house he wanted. And he would need corrals, shelter for horses, and storage for hay. He couldn't expect to get it all done himself. He would need to hire some help.

Thinking of the labor and money it would take to make this land pay was almost enough to make Joe lose heart. But when he marked the boundaries of the spot where his future house would stand and gazed out over the sweeping landscape below, he knew he'd made the right choice. With time and hard work, he would build a future here.

By the time he rode through the gate of the Hollister ranch, the sun was going down. Joe was braced for a battle with his father-in-law, but as he neared the house, he saw that Loren had company. Two elegant-looking buggies, drawn by matched black horses, were tied to the hitching rail in the front yard.

After handing his horse off to the stable boy, he climbed the front steps. He was weary after the long day, and the last thing he felt like was company for dinner, but he knew Loren would insist on his presence.

As he mounted the porch, Amelia, looking like a porcelain doll in a peach-hued gown trimmed with lace, came flying out of the front door. "Where have you been all day?" she sputtered. "You ride off without telling me where you're going. I worry all day. Now we have company, and you're not even dressed for dinner! Daddy's very annoyed. Hurry. Get changed while they're still having drinks."

Dress for dinner? Joe skirted the parlor without being seen and hurried up the stairs. Where he'd grown up, folks ate dinner in the clothes they'd worn all day. And they called it supper. These fancy customs were still new to him. But this was no time to displease his wife and father-in-law.

After washing up, he put on a clean white shirt and the brown suit he'd worn for his wedding and made it back downstairs just as the host and guests were sitting down to dinner. Amelia nodded toward an empty chair. Joe took it and sat down.

The spotless tablecloth was set with the china he'd only seen in the glass-fronted cabinet. Each plate was flanked by a folded napkin, a knife, two spoons, and three forks. *Three damn forks. What was he supposed to do with them?* Luckily, Amelia had seated him directly across from her. He knew enough to watch her and follow her manners.

As the cook served up the roast beef, stewed vegetables, and fresh rolls, Joe glanced around the table at the guests. He recognized Loman Janes, the bastard who'd ruined the roan stallion. Next to him was his employer Judd Boston, who owned a bank in Miles City and a ranch not far from here.

Joe had met both of them before when they'd visited Loren.

He remembered how Rusty had warned him that they were not to be trusted. Considering the way Loman Janes had abused the stallion, Joe was inclined to believe the wise old man. But if the two of them were enemies of Benteen Calder, they might yet prove useful.

The third man—husky, with coarse features and a thick neck, looked vaguely familiar. It took a moment for Joe to remember that he'd once seen him arguing with Calder in Texas, at the beginning of the cattle drive. Bull, the man was aptly called. Bull Giles.

The fourth guest, a woman, was seated next to Loren on the right. Joe had to force himself not to stare at her. She was far from young—probably older than his mother. But she was the most stunningly elegant creature he'd ever laid eyes on.

Her black dress, which Joe assumed to be silk, was expensively detailed and tailored to her slender figure. Her upswept hair was silver blond, her face showing some age but framed over exquisite bones.

Loren had introduced her as Lady Crawford. It appeared that she and Giles, who served as her driver and bodyguard, would be spending the night here at the ranch before returning to Miles City tomorrow. This dinner was, of course, in her honor.

Amelia was all smiles and flutters over the glamorous guest. Clearly, she was the one who'd planned the table setting and dictated formal dress. Joe enjoyed seeing her so happy.

So why was she glaring at him across the table, as if he'd just committed some grievous social error? Meeting her gaze, he raised a questioning eyebrow. In silent reply, she jabbed a finger in the direction of her neck. That was when Joe realized he'd forgotten to put on a necktie.

There was nothing to do about it now. But he would surely have to answer for it later—and maybe for other transgressions, as well.

Lady Crawford gave Amelia a smile and spoke over the low buzz of conversation. "I must compliment you as a hostess, my dear. The table is perfect, and you look lovely. I hope your husband appreciates what a lucky man he is."

"I suspect my husband would appreciate me more if I had four hooves and a mane." Amelia smiled as she spoke, but Joe couldn't miss the annoyance in her green eyes.

Lady Crawford had the grace to look amused. "Yes, I understand your husband has a gift for working with horses." She turned her attention to Joe. "Isn't that so, Mr. Dollarhide?"

"I wouldn't call it a gift," Joe said. "Let's just say I've had more experience with horses than I have with women."

Amelia's look shot daggers at her husband. Lady Crawford, appearing not to notice, smiled. Joe caught the glimmer of keen intelligence in her mysterious dark eyes. "I'd like to hear more about your work when we have time to talk," she said. "After dinner, perhaps."

"Of course." Her show of interest surprised and intrigued Joe. But maybe she was only making pleasantries.

"So," she continued, "do you have ambitions to be a cattleman?"

"Maybe later," Joe said. "But I mean to get my start breaking wild horses and selling them. With so many ranches starting up, the market for well-broken horses is good. And I can sell them cheaper than the Texas horses that come up with the cattle drives. If that changes, there are other ways to make money. Take lumbering, for example. There's already a big demand for wood."

Joe glanced toward his father-in-law, who sat at the head of the table. The color had deepened in Loren's face, a sign that an explosion was building. But the man would hold his tongue in front of his guests—which was why this might be the best time for Joe to break his news.

"It sounds as if you've already done a great deal of planning," Lady Crawford said.

"I've done more than plan." Joe hesitated, then plunged ahead. "Today I filed claim to 320 acres of hill country, with trees and a creek and box canyons for keeping horses. All I need to do is get access, build pens and gates, along with a hay shed and a cabin, and I'll be ready."

"But what about the horses?" Lady Crawford asked. "Where will you find them?"

"They're out there. I've seen their tracks near my land. The ranchers will be glad to get rid of them. They eat the grass and crowd the cattle. The stallions even lure tame mares and geldings into joining their bands."

Joe glanced at his father-in-law. Loren's mouth was pressed into a thin, hard line. His face had gone crimson. He was like a boiling pot with a tight lid, barely holding back his fury for the sake of his guests.

Amelia had gone white. Her forced smile remained in place, but her emerald eyes blazed with indignation.

Lady Crawford's knowing expression remained unchanged. She almost appeared to be enjoying the drama.

Judd Boston's gruff voice broke the silence. "Well, fine. But we didn't come here to talk about horses. We came to talk about Benteen Calder and how to get our hands on some of that land he grabbed. Hell, he's got twice as much as he needs, while the rest of us are hurting for enough pasture to run our cattle."

"I thought you were going to file on those two parcels that Calder was about to lose because he hadn't made any improvements," Loren said.

Boston swore, then glanced over at Amelia with a muttered apology. "I was. But he went into the bank, paid the cash, and commuted them. Somebody must've tipped him off. I'd sure as hell like to know who it was."

Joe happened to look at Lady Crawford, seeing her in profile. She hadn't spoken or stirred, but he noticed a slight twitch at the corner of her mouth, as if she were holding back a smile. There was more to this woman, he sensed, than a classic face and an elegant manner.

"So now what do we do?" Loman Janes asked. "How do we get back at Calder and get more land?"

Loren cleared his throat. "I had a plan for my son-in-law to file on a parcel of grazing land that the owner was going to quit. But now it seems that Joe, here, has shot me in the back. I fear I'm out of ideas, gentlemen."

"I've been thinking on it," Judd Boston said. "Calder's rich in land and cattle, but that's where his money is. And he's spent a lot on that mansion he's building to shame us all. The man's got to be strapped for cash."

"I hear you," Loren said. "If we can figure out a way to set his finances back, he'll be forced to sell some land. But how do we make that happen?"

"That's my job," Loman Janes said. "I've got a few ideas up my sleeve. Give me some time. I know how to make a man hurt. And there's nobody I'd rather hurt than Benteen Calder."

Joe had listened to the conversation in silence. He ought to be happy for any chance to repay Calder for leaving him in that wash, he told himself. But after the incident with the stallion, he had nothing but contempt for Loman Janes. Any scheme the man devised was bound to be cruel and dirty. The memory of trying to steal Calder's cattle was fresh in his mind. He wanted no part of this. When he got his revenge on Benteen Calder, it would be clean and legal.

The cook brought in blueberry pie with whipped cream for dessert. After that, Loren and the three other men went into the study for drinks and cigars. Joe was not invited. He was tempted to disappear, but that would be the coward's way out.

After Boston and Loman left, and after Giles and Lady Crawford retired to their rooms, it would be time for Joe to face his wife and father-in-law and own up to what he'd done.

Whatever happened, he sensed, things would never be the same between them again.

Joe faced his father-in-law in the study, the two of them separated by the width of the heavy walnut desk. Joe had expected to see Amelia here, too. But after their guests had retired, she'd gone upstairs to the bedroom without a word.

Loren Hollister was a small man—a half head shorter than Joe. Standing face-to-face might have put him at a disadvantage. But seated behind the imposing desk, in his leather banker's chair, he appeared powerful and in charge.

"Do you think I let you marry my daughter so you could betray our family?" he demanded in an icy voice. "First you ask me to help you find some good land. Then you turn around and do a damn fool thing like this. What the hell have you got to say for yourself, Joe Dollarhide?"

"I know why you encouraged me to marry Amelia." Joe spoke boldly. "You wanted a man you could use to build your own holdings—a man who could claim more land for your ranch. A man you could control. But I have my own dream, my own plans. And they don't include adding to your property, working your cattle, and waiting years for you to die so I can take over."

Joe had known his words would make Loren even angrier. He could already see the color rising in the man's face and see his fists clenching on the surface of the desk. For the first time Joe found himself wondering if his father-in-law was capable of killing him.

He forced himself to ignore that concern. He wanted to make his intentions absolutely clear—to get the truth out once and for all.

With visible effort, Loren brought himself under control. "What about Amelia?" he asked. "Did you even talk to your wife about this before you filed on an extra parcel for her?"

"There was no need for that. As her husband, it was my decision. I plan to raise our family on that land—in a home as fine as this one. I've already chosen the site for the house and marked it off. Of course, I'll need to put up a cabin first, to meet the terms of the claim."

"You stupid, mule-assed fool!" Loren had sprung to his feet behind the desk. He was shouting now. "You could have worked with me, for the good of the ranch and your future family. Now, instead, you do this. Do you have any idea how much work and expense you'll be taking on—and believe me I'm not putting one red cent toward helping you. That land isn't even fit for cattle. What'll you do with it when you get tired of chasing wild horses? Raise sheep?"

"Now there's a thought." Joe couldn't resist saying it. Cattlemen hated sheep.

"I'll give you six months before you lose it all and come crawling back to me, if Amelia hasn't thrown you out by then," Loren snarled. "Now get the hell out of here and leave me alone. God, I need a drink."

Joe left him, relieved that the confrontation was over for now. But the clash had left him drained, and he had yet to face Amelia.

Needing some air to clear his head, he wandered out onto the porch and stood leaning on the rail. The darkness was alive with the sounds of the summer night—the whine of insects, the far-away howl of a coyote, the shifting and lowing of cattle, and the rustling breeze in the long grass. A waning crescent moon hung low over the horizon.

What if his father-in-law was right? For a grassland claim to pay, all you needed was a herd of cows and a cabin. But his wooded, rocky hill claim, beautiful as it was, would demand a mountain of work and more money than he could even imagine. Had he made a mistake? Had he taken on too much?

But he couldn't allow himself to think like that. He had to believe in himself and in the gut feeling that had prompted him to claim the challenging land.

"I was hoping I'd find you out here." Lady Crawford's velvety voice startled him for an instant. Still in her dinner clothes, she moved to stand beside him at the rail. "I was impressed with your plans for your claim," she said. "It appears you're not satisfied with being an ordinary cattleman—or simply being Loren Hollister's son-in-law. I like you for that."

Joe forced a chuckle. "Right now you seem to be the only person who does."

"Actually, I have a confession to make," she said. "I came here tonight because I'd heard about your work with horses. I wanted to meet you. So far, you haven't disappointed me."

"Is there something I can do for you?" Joe asked.

"Maybe I can do something for both of us," she said. "I'll get right to the point. What I have is a business proposition. If you can come up with enough good horses, I have connections with a buyer in Canada—don't ask me to divulge any names—who'll take all you can supply and pay good money for them."

"I'm certainly interested," Joe said. "But I've only just filed claim on my land. The horses are out there, but if you need a lot of them, and soon, that's a problem."

"I understand," she said. "We can work out the time and numbers later. But hear me out. What I'm offering you is a partnership. I'll lend you start-up money for the operation—pens, gates, feed, and pay for some experienced help. In return, when the horses are sold, we split the profits. How does that sound?"

"Almost too good to be true," Joe said. "But what happens if you stake me and I can't deliver?"

"Then you'd have to pay me back, of course, any way you could. But I feel comfortable making the offer. I have a similar arrangement with another partner. So far it seems to be working out fine. But he's only providing my buyer with beef cattle. There's a good market for horses as well."

"Can you tell me who he is, this other partner of yours?" Joe asked.

Lady Crawford shook her elegant head. "I'm sorry, but our agreement is confidential—as my agreement with you would be. Not even Loren would be aware of it."

"And my wife?"

A knowing look crossed her face. "That would depend on where her loyalties lie. For now, assuming we have a deal, you might want to keep it to yourself. If word were to get out, it would spread like wildfire. Everyone who has livestock to sell would want to do what we're doing. Do you understand what a disaster that would be?"

"I do."

"And do we have a deal?"

"If we can really make this work, we do."

"Fine. I'll be at the McQueen House in Miles City for the next ten days. Meet me there when you're able to get away. We can draw up the contract and go to the bank. All right?" She smiled and extended her hand.

"All right." Joe had never exchanged a handshake with a woman before. Her strong fingers were slender with prominent joints. Her skin was like fine glove leather.

"I'm looking forward to making money with you, Joe," she said. "You may call me Elaine."

Buoyed by Elaine's offer of a partnership, Joe went into the house and mounted the stairs. But with each upward step, his spirits deflated and sank. Facing Loren had been trying enough. Facing Amelia would be downright painful.

Sharing his news with her would be out of the question. She'd go straight to her father with it. Not that he blamed her. In the short time they'd been married, he'd treated her like a child, never confiding in her or even trusting her. Unfortunately, that wasn't about to change.

Their bedroom was at the end of the upstairs hallway. The door was closed. When he tried to open it, he found it locked.

"Amelia?" He rapped gently. "Open the door, Amelia. We need to talk."

He waited in tense silence. Just when he was about to knock again, the latch clicked and the door opened a few inches. Angry and injured, Amelia stood looking at him. Her eyes were red, her face streaked with tears.

"All right," she said. "Let's talk."

"Are you going to make me stand out here? We've got company in the house, you know."

The door opened just wide enough for Joe to step inside. He closed it behind him. By then she'd moved across the room. Her dress was rumpled, as if she'd flung herself, weeping, onto the bed.

"Aren't you going to say you're sorry?" she demanded.

"I'm sorry for hurting you and making you angry. But not for what I did. We're going to be fine, Amelia. I've got plans to make that land pay."

"And what about me? Is that why you married me, Joe—and why my father let you—so you could claim land as a married man and get twice as much? I thought you loved me. But I'm no more to you, or to my father, than one of those cows out there. You used me—both of you."

"Amelia, it's not like that," Joe began. But in a way she was right. Loren had encouraged the marriage because it would tie

Joe to the ranch and allow him to get double the land by filing for himself and his wife. And now, though he hadn't planned it, Joe had used the marriage for a similar purpose.

"Wait till I show you the land," he said, changing the subject. "It'll be a beautiful place to raise our family once I get the house built—a fine house, as big as this one, with a view you'd have to see to believe."

"And what am I supposed to do while you're building that house? Live in a one-room cabin, chopping wood, skinning rabbits, and scrubbing clothes on a washboard, with no hired help?"

A cabin was good enough for Lorna Calder. And look what she's getting now.

The thought crossed Joe's mind, but he knew better than to say it aloud. He'd wanted a wife like Lorna, who was as tough and capable as she was lovely. What he'd gotten was a pretty little toy.

"You're nothing but a dreamer, Joe," she said. "We could stay here. We could live in this house. You could work with Daddy, and when he died, all this would be ours. Isn't that enough for you?"

"It might be, if I were a different man."

"Then maybe I should have married a different man."

"Maybe you should have," Joe said. "But this is who I am. I want to build something of my own. If you don't like it, you can always pack up and go back to St. Louis."

The words were out, and it was too late to take them back. Had they passed a point of no return in their marriage? Was this the beginning of the end? Silent now, Joe waited for her to speak.

With a sigh, Amelia sank onto the edge of the bed. "I can't go back to St. Louis, or anywhere else, Joe," she said. "I'm going to have a baby."

CHAPTER FIFTEEN

Four years later

THE JULY DAY HAD BEEN HOT AND SULTRY, BUT A CHANGE WAS IN THE air. In the west, clouds billowed over the horizon. A breeze, smelling of dust and rain, rippled the ripening wheat fields. In the distance, a flock of blackbirds rose and scattered.

With the help of Blake, her four-year-old son, Sarah opened the windows of the stifling house. After moving the rocker out to the vine-covered front porch, she sat down to savor the coolness and watch the storm come in. Her hands reached for the knitting bag she'd hung over one arm of the chair. She wasn't an accomplished knitter. But she hoped to finish the sweater she was making for Blake before cold weather arrived in the fall.

Blake came outside and sat on the top step, near Sarah's feet. Humdinger, the big, yellow mutt they'd rescued as a puppy two years ago, settled next to his young master. The dog was devoted to Blake and protective of Sarah. Gentle as he was, he also looked menacing enough to scare off intruders.

Blake reached up and scratched the dog's ears. Joe's son was a good boy, bright, compassionate, and eager to learn. Sarah could no longer imagine her life without him. Studying him now, she thought of Joe and how alike the two of them were. But Joe probably had children of his own by now. He would never know this wonderful son he had given her.

"Mama, what are clouds made of?" Blake was curious about everything, always asking questions.

"You know how steam looks when it comes out of the kettle on a cold morning? That's what a cloud is made of."

"They look soft, like you could bounce on them."

Sarah smiled, her fingers plying the knitting needles. "If you tried to bounce on a cloud, you would fall right through, all the way to the ground."

Sarah loved teaching her son—and she'd discovered that she loved teaching other children as well. Her tarnished reputation would never allow her to teach in a school. But she had found other ways—or they had found her.

Two years ago, she'd answered a knock. Instead of the patient she'd expected, she'd opened the door to a worried-looking couple standing on her porch. They'd looked familiar. But she couldn't place them until she'd noticed the woman's red hair. They were the parents of Ezra, the young boy who'd greeted her at the train station years ago—the boy who loved books.

Ezra's health had taken a downturn, they'd told her. The doctor had ordered him to stay home and rest, which meant that he couldn't go to school. Since they were hoping to prepare him for college, he was going to need a tutor to keep him up on his schoolwork. Ezra had insisted that Sarah—and only Sarah—be the one to teach him.

The family had paid Sarah fairly and allowed her to bring Blake when she went to their home. By the time Ezra was strong enough to go back to school—a matter of months—he was well ahead of his classmates in all subjects. As word got around, other parents, who had ambitions for their sons and daughters, were willing to overlook Sarah's reputation and pay for her services as a part-time tutor.

The money didn't amount to much. But it allowed her to stop taking in laundry and make some improvements on the old house. She'd been lucky, Sarah told herself. But now, looking at her son, she realized that she was going to need more than luck.

Blake was growing up fast, and she couldn't keep him to herself forever. Soon he'd be old enough to go to school and be around other children.

And children could be brutal.

There was a horrible word, a cruel word, for children born to unmarried mothers. Blake had never been called a bastard. But it was bound to happen. Not just once, but again and again until the harsh truth threatened to destroy him.

There was only one way to keep that from happening—move away and start over someplace else where she could pass as a widow. But where could she go? How could she move, resettle, and survive with barely enough money to live on as it was?

The clouds had darkened. Blown by the rising wind, they were moving in fast. Lightning danced above the distant fields.

As the first drops began to fall, Blake and the dog moved up under the shelter of the porch. Sarah was about to take the chair and go back inside when a familiar buggy, with the top raised, pulled up to the gate.

"It's the postman! He's stopping here!" Blake jumped up and raced down the sidewalk, with the dog at his heels.

The postman leaned out of his buggy and handed the boy an envelope. "Here you are, young man," he said. "Give this to your mother."

Clucking to the horse, he turned the buggy around and headed back toward town, racing the storm.

Sarah took the envelope from her son. She didn't get much mail. But she and Rusty had stayed in touch since his return to Montana—not close touch, just letters exchanged once or twice a year. Maybe this letter was from him.

But no—her name and address on the envelope were written in a graceful hand that Sarah had never seen before.

The rain was coming down hard now. Before opening the letter, she shooed Blake and the dog back into the house and followed them with the chair. Inside, she latched the screen door, worked a finger beneath the envelope flap and sat down to read the letter.

My dear Sarah,

It's been a long time since we spoke. I don't know if you'll even remember me. But I've thought of you often. Rusty has told me a little about your situation—enough that I feel emboldened to contact you and make you an offer.

Here in this part of Montana, there are children growing up without any education except what they can learn from their parents. I and other women in the community have banded together to get a school built and find a teacher.

The school, in the town of Blue Moon, will be finished this fall. But we are still in need of a teacher. Rusty tells me you've been successful in helping and motivating students. Since I've met you and know you to be well educated and of good character, we would like to offer you the position, which would include a salary, a small, furnished house, and the use of a horse and buggy.

Sarah's eyes blurred with tears. It would be the answer to her prayers—a salaried job and a place to live, somewhere far from Ogallala. But how could she accept, given her circumstances? She wiped her eyes and read the next page of the long letter.

Before you make a decision, please forgive me for getting personal. I know about your son—and no, Rusty didn't betray your secret. I simply guessed. I would be happy to introduce you to the community as a widow. Only Rusty and I would know the truth.

If you decide to accept our offer—and I truly hope you will— please let me know as soon as possible. I will send train fare from Ogallala to Miles City for you, your son, and the dog that Rusty says you have. I will look forward to meeting you there and taking you to your new home.

Yours truly,

Lorna Calder

Sarah read the letter again, then again, until the trembling of her hands blurred the pages. A new start. A new life for her and her son. This had to be the answer. How could she not accept Lorna Calder's generous offer?

But there was one question Lorna had left unanswered—a question Sarah knew she had no right to ask.

Where was Joe in all this?

Joe was dreaming again—the old dream of the wild horses, led by the blue roan stallion. They galloped over a rise and into his vision, swirling past him like a mirage. As they swung away, the stallion turned toward him, reared, and was gone.

He opened his eyes to darkness. Alone in his wide bed, he lay still, remembering. The dream hadn't visited him in years, but it always seemed to come when his life was about to change— almost as a sign, or as a warning.

Or maybe the dream was only that—an illusion, rising from the depths of his imagination.

Seen through the curtainless window, the stars were beginning to fade. Swinging his feet to the floor, Joe stood, pulled on his robe, and padded barefoot into the kitchen to make coffee.

A few minutes later, with the cup warming his palms, he walked out onto the broad, covered porch and stood at the rail, watching the day begin. The wooded slopes of his land stretched below him, and beyond that the rolling prairie, the road, and the distant town of Blue Moon, which from here was little more than a dark smudge against the pale landscape. This was his world, the kingdom he'd forged and fought for. Once, he'd believed it would be enough. But every day he lived told him he'd been wrong.

As a young cowpuncher, Joe had dreamed of having his own brand—the outline of a hide with a dollar sign on it. Now it was his, custom made by the blacksmith in Blue Moon, and stamped on everything from horses to cattle to lumber.

The horse-breaking venture with Elaine, Lady Crawford, had been profitable beyond his wildest dreams. Over two years' time, the work, with the help of the cowboys he'd trained, had furnished the Canadian government with more than a thousand horses for the army, the North-West Mounted Police, and the ranches lying north of the border.

Only when their business had concluded and the profits were

settled had Elaine confided that her other partner, selling cattle to the same buyer, had been Benteen Calder. Joe had been surprised, but as long as the money was good, he'd had no cause to complain.

With the profit from the horses, he'd bought wagons and equipment, hired loggers, and begun harvesting trees from his land. Lumber for buildings, fences, and bridges was in high demand, especially after the arrival of the railroad in Miles City. With a direct rail line to ship cattle to the stockyards and slaughterhouses of Chicago, the whole area was booming.

When he'd realized he couldn't harvest enough trees to meet that demand, he'd sent wagons west to the mountain country, to buy and bring back load after load of cut pine logs. Using power from the creek, he'd put up a sawmill to cut the logs into boards. Towns were being built with Dollarhide lumber.

The money from the lumber business had gone to buy grazing land and stock it with the new Western cattle that were beefier than the tough, leggy longhorns.

Along with everything else, Joe had also finished his house, which was everything he'd promised Amelia it would be.

But except for the retired cowboy who served as part-time cook and housekeeper, he lived in it alone. Amelia had dug in her dainty heels and refused to move to this beautiful but lonely spot. She lived at her father's house, with their three-year-old son, Mason. It wasn't what Joe had wanted. He missed his boy every day. But their arrangement was Amelia's choice. Their marriage remained in place, bound by Mason and the entanglements of money and property.

Now all that remained was getting *more*. More land. More cash. More livestock. Even his determination to best Benteen Calder had been put aside after a terrible tragedy—instigated by Judd Boston and Loman Janes—had caused the death of Benteen and Lorna's younger son.

Boston, Janes, and their cohorts had paid with their lives. But as a father himself, Joe could imagine the anguish that the Calders must be feeling. He would get even with his former boss one day. But for now, waiting was the only decent thing to do.

After finishing his coffee, he dressed for the day, went out to the stable, and saddled Flint, the aging buckskin who was still his favorite horse. He needed to check things at the sawmill, meet with his foreman, and later, pay a call at the Hollister ranch. The visit was bound to be awkward, but there was no other way to see his son.

As he rode downhill, into the sunrise, he found himself thinking of Sarah, and how different things might've been if he could have married her. But he'd been young at the time, with nothing to offer, and she'd been set on following her own plan. Now their youthful passion was nothing but a cherished memory. Sarah had moved on to become a doctor, and he had achieved almost everything he'd hoped for—everything except what he'd lost when he left her.

The train rolled into Miles City and pulled up to the station. Weary from the long trip, the passengers climbed down the steps and onto the platform. With one hand gripping her son and the other clasping the carpetbag that held their meager possessions, Sarah waited for Humdinger to be led out of the baggage car. The dog jumped to the ground, shook his coat, and lifted his leg on a wheel of the train.

"Are we here, Mama?" Blake took in the crowds of scurrying people.

"We are here." Sarah's gaze searched the platform, hoping to see a friendly face. She'd tried to imagine how she would manage if no one was here to meet the train. But she needn't have worried. Lorna was hurrying toward her, through the crowd, followed by Rusty, doing his best to keep up with her.

"Welcome, Sarah!" Lorna enfolded her in a warm hug. She was as beautiful as Sarah remembered, but in a more mature way. Sarah knew, from Rusty's letters, that she'd borne two sons and lost the younger one when he'd caught a bullet in a gunfight. Sorrow was written in the creases around her eyes, but today she was smiling.

"And who's this handsome young man?" She bent low to greet Blake.

"I'm Blake. Pleased to meet you, ma'am," he answered as Sarah had coached him on the way here.

"And is this your dog?"

"Uh-huh. His name's Humdinger, but we call him Hummy for short."

Then Sarah was greeting her old friend Rusty. He, too, had aged. But his blue eyes were as lively as ever.

"There are facilities in the station house if you need them," Lorna said. "I know you'll be hungry, too. We've got sandwiches and cookies in the buggy."

"Thank you so much—for everything," Sarah said, clasping Lorna's hands. "You can't imagine how much your kindness means to me."

After Sarah and Blake had cleaned up, they climbed into the buggy, with Rusty driving up front. Blake shared a sandwich with the dog, wolfed down two oatmeal cookies, and promptly fell asleep with his dark head in Sarah's lap.

Lorna smiled down at him. "Such a handsome boy," she said. "He looks just like his father. How much does he know?"

"Only that his father had to go away and work. I'll tell him more when he's older. Meanwhile, I hope you'll keep our secret safe."

"Of course I will," Lorna said. "And since I know you're concerned, I can tell you that your chances of running into Joe are slim. He lives a few miles south of here, and he rarely comes into Blue Moon. But you'll need to be prepared, in case it happens."

"Yes, I know." But it wouldn't matter, Sarah told herself, even though her pulse had quickened at the mention of Joe's name. Joe had a family of his own now. What had happened between them was long since over.

"How is he doing?" she couldn't resist asking.

"Oh, very well. He's one of the wealthiest men in the county now. Land, lumber, horses, and cattle. Joe has made them all pay. His wife is heir to a big ranch, too. They have a little boy who'll probably inherit it all one day—oh!" Lorna covered her mouth with her fingertips. "I'm sorry. That was very insensitive of me. Please forgive me."

"No, it's fine," Sarah said. "After all, it's true. Blake may not be the heir to a fortune, but I can help him grow up to be a fine man. In this world, that's what really counts." Sarah paused to regroup. "Now, why don't you tell me about the school?"

Joe rode through the gate of the Hollister ranch. As he reached the house, he saw Amelia waiting alone on the porch. He could tell that she'd taken extra pains to look pretty—maybe to remind him of what he was missing. The green ribbon in her hair enhanced the sparkle in her eyes, and her flower-sprigged dress hugged a waist that was almost as small as it had been before the birth of their son.

Joe dismounted and looped the horse's reins over the hitching rail. "Where's Mason?" he asked.

"He's in the house with Daddy. You can see him, but I want to talk to you first." She took a seat on the porch swing, leaving room for him to join her. Joe mounted the steps and sat down, bracing himself for whatever she planned to say. Whatever it was, something told him he wasn't going to like it.

"Is everything all right, Amelia?" he asked, leaving an opening for her.

"Nobody's sick, or dying, if that's what you're asking." She pouted prettily. "But I've been thinking about last winter and how miserable it was, all that snow and cold—and no place to go. I thought I was going to die of boredom."

Joe knew what was coming next. And knew he wasn't going to like it. Amelia could go wherever the hell she pleased, but he'd be damned if he'd let her take Mason.

"I got a letter from my mother in St. Louis," she said. "Things didn't work out with her husband. She's all alone, and she wants to see her grandson. She's invited me to come and stay with her over the winter."

Joe sighed. "We've been down this road before, Amelia. Mason is my son. If you want to go to St. Louis, fine. Go. But the boy stays with me."

"How can I do that? He's only three. He needs his mother. And you don't have time to take care of him. You're always working."

"I could make time. But fine. If you don't like the idea of my taking him, you can stay here."

Her expression hardened. "I don't need your permission, you know. I could just take Mason and leave. Once we were on the train, you wouldn't be able to stop us."

"Do that, and the marriage is over," Joe said. "And I'll get my son back if I have to break into your mother's house and take him by force."

Once again they were at a standoff. It might have escalated into a fight, with Amelia railing and Joe remaining stone-faced. But just then the front door opened, and a small figure came racing across the porch.

"Daddy!"

Joe sprang out of the swing and bent low in time to catch the little boy in his arms. Standing, he lifted his son high. Mason squealed with laughter. He was a beautiful child with his mother's green eyes and reddish glints in his dark, curly hair.

"Did you come to see me, Daddy?" he asked as Joe lowered him to shoulder level.

"I did. Just you."

"Did you bring me something?"

"Not this time. But if it's all right with your mother, I can take you for a ride on my horse. You'll have to ask her, though."

"Please, can he take me, Mama?" The boy's look would have melted stone. "I really, really want to go for a ride."

Amelia threw up her hands. "All right, Joe. I won't be forced to play the villain. You can take him. But don't be gone too long. We mustn't miss his naptime."

"Come on, son." Joe carried the boy out to his horse, boosted him onto the saddle behind the horn and, freeing the reins, mounted up behind him. Nudging the gentle gelding to a walk, he headed down the drive to the gate and onto the road.

"Can we go to your house, Daddy?" Mason loved being at Joe's house, with its large, mostly empty rooms to explore and its wide porch where he could run and play with stick horses fashioned from cut willows.

"Not today," Joe said. "Your mother wants you back in time for your nap."

"I don't need naps. I'm a big boy."

"Tell that to your mother."

"Can we go get a peppermint stick?"

Joe hesitated. The general store in Blue Moon was farther than he'd planned to go. But why not? It took so little to make his son happy. And Amelia could wait. "Want to trot?" he asked. He felt the boy's head nod.

Holding the small body securely with one hand, Joe kicked the horse to an easy trot. Bouncing in the saddle, Mason shrieked and giggled with delight.

They were within sight of the town when Joe looked ahead and saw a buggy with a two-horse team approaching them on the road. Slowing the horse to a walk once more, he moved far to the right, giving the rig plenty of room to pass.

As the buggy drew closer, Joe recognized it as the one belonging to the Calders. The driver was Rusty. Sitting next to him was a big, yellow dog. Two women sat in the back—Lorna and probably one of her friends. At least Benteen wasn't with them to darken his mood.

Moving off the road, he stopped and waited. As a neighbor, it behooved him to at least be sociable and say hello.

Rusty had seen him. Joe expected him to slow down, but he kept going at the same pace. Now they were almost even. Rusty gave him a nod of greeting as the rig passed. Lorna did the same as Joe tipped his hat.

The woman with Lorna was wearing a straw bonnet. She kept her gaze downcast, her hands covering something in her lap— something Joe couldn't see. At the last second, as the buggy was passing, she raised her head. He caught the flash of violet eyes in an unforgettable face. Then she was gone.

His racing pulse told him the truth. It was Sarah.

Looking back, he watched the buggy turn off the road toward the newly built school with its small, adjoining house. What was she doing here? None of what he'd just seen made any sense.

Sarah had gone off to medical school. What was she doing in Blue Moon?

But this was no time to follow her and find out. He had Mason with him, and it was clear that the people in the buggy hadn't wanted her to be recognized.

He was determined to find out more. Maybe his eyes had been playing tricks on him. But what if he'd really just seen Sarah? What if she was really here? What could he do about it?

There was only one answer to that question.

Nothing.

By the time the buggy stopped in front of the log schoolhouse, Sarah was trembling. Lorna reached over and clasped her hand. "It's all right, Sarah," she said. "I doubt if he even recognized you. See, he didn't follow us. He's gone now."

Sarah shook her head. She'd done her best to prepare herself. But seeing Joe with his little boy had hit her like a bullet to the heart. "Maybe this was a mistake," she said. "I should have known better than to come here."

"Nonsense," Lorna soothed. "Everything will work out fine. You'll see. Right now we're going to show you the school and your new little home. Then we'll be driving you back to my place to have dinner and meet my husband. You can stay the night, and we'll bring you back to get settled in the morning. Everything will look brighter then."

Blake stirred and sat up, looking around at the grassy landscape and the two neat log buildings with a shed out back.

"Are we home now, Mama?" he asked.

Sarah forced herself to smile. "Yes, dear, I do believe we are."

Joe sat on the porch of his house, drinking a beer and watching the sunset fade above the distant prairie. The summer night was warm, the breeze fragrant with the scent of pine. From the pond he'd made by widening the creek bed, frogs filled the darkness with their songs.

He rolled a cigarette from the pouch and papers in his shirt pocket, then changed his mind and dropped the unlit cigarette onto the deck.

He had taken Mason home after the visit to the store, then left Amelia, still complaining, to go about his business for the rest of the day. Through it all, one thought had played over and over like a song in his mind.

Sarah.

They'd been so young—little more than children—when they'd made love, but he'd never forgotten the sweetness of it. Now they were older, and the urge to have her again was a burning ache inside him. But that was wrong, all wrong. He was married to Amelia. What could he do? Make Sarah his mistress? She deserved better than that. She deserved better than anything he could possibly give her.

Restless, he rose, walked to the rail, and stood looking down at the winding road that led up the slope. His eyes caught a moving flicker of light—a lantern. A rider was coming up the road.

Peering through the twilight, he waited. A white head and stocky body came into view. The rider, mounted on a mule, was Rusty. Joe hurried down the steps to greet the old man, take the lantern, and help him dismount. "What are you doing out at this hour, Rusty?" he asked. "Is something wrong?"

"Nothing like that. Just need to clear the air with you." Rusty climbed the stairs to the porch with effort. Joe lent him an arm, helped him to a chair, and set the lantern next to him.

"Can I warm up some stew? Maybe get you a beer?"

"Never mind that. I just need to talk."

"You've come a long way just to talk."

"Sit down, boy. It's about Sarah. I know you saw her today. And she saw you."

"Fine, you've got my attention." Joe pulled a chair up close to the old man and sat down. "What's she doing here? I thought she'd gone off to become a doctor."

"It's a long story. I've come to tell it to you so you won't go nosing around and bothering her. She didn't come to see you, Joe. She already knew you had a family."

"So tell me the whole story. Did she go to medical school?"

"She couldn't. It turns out you left her in a family way."

The impact of the words hit Joe like a gut punch. He groaned out loud, almost doubling over with the emotional pain. Sarah, pregnant, alone, and then with a baby to support. Lord, why hadn't she let him know? But he already knew the answer to that question. He'd left her with no way to reach him. And he hadn't tried to contact her. After she'd learned that he was married, no doubt she'd given up.

"She's had a pretty rough time of it," Rusty said. "Folks in Ogallala pretty much turned their backs on her. When Lorna needed a teacher for the new school, I suggested Sarah. Lorna thought it was a great idea. So here she is."

"But . . . the baby. What about the baby?"

"She's got a fine boy. He looks a lot like you, but you've got no claim on him. She gave him her last name, not yours. As far as the town's concerned, she's a widow. The only ones that know the truth are Lorna, me, and now you. And you'd better make damned sure it stays that way."

"But if I could just see my son—"

"Your son? Did you take care of him or contribute a dime of your precious money? Did you stand by his mother and help raise him? You're no father to that boy, Joe. I'm tellin' you to leave him alone. And leave Sarah alone. You broke her heart once. She doesn't need you doin' it again and neither does her boy. Stay away from them. Hear?"

Joe rose, feeling as if a heavy weight had been laid on his shoulders. "I hear you, Rusty. And I understand."

"Then I'll be on my way." Rusty pushed to his feet. "It's past my bedtime."

"You're welcome to bunk here tonight," Joe said. "I'll even see that you get some breakfast. Or I'd be glad to saddle up and ride with you."

"That's all right. My old mule knows the way home. He could probably tuck me into bed if he had to. I'll be fine."

Joe helped him down the dark steps, steadied him while he

mounted his mule, and handed him the lantern. "Sarah's lucky to have you for a friend, Rusty," he said.

"And if you're her friend, Joe Dollarhide, you'll leave her alone. She doesn't need your kind of heartbreak."

With those parting words, Rusty nudged his mule to a walk and headed down the winding road. Joe stood watching as the light from the bobbing lantern vanished into the darkness. Rusty was right, he told himself. The kindest thing he could do for Sarah was to stay away from her.

But how could he turn his back on the only woman he'd ever truly loved—and on his son?

CHAPTER SIXTEEN

SARAH HAD LOVED THE NEW HOUSE ON SIGHT. BUILT SOLIDLY OF logs and attached to the school by a covered passageway, it was smaller than her old rental home in Ogallala, but there was a coziness about the place that she felt at once. The cookstove in the kitchen would warm the house in the coldest weather. The windows, cut high for privacy, could be opened to let in fresh air. There was a bedroom with a bed and dresser, and a loft, accessed by a ladder, that could be used for storage and to provide a place for a growing boy to sleep. A well and a privy out back would serve both the house and the school.

The attached single classroom had a potbellied stove, a desk for the teacher, a chalkboard on the wall, a bookshelf, and coat hooks next to the door. Two long plank tables, one low, and one higher, with benches, served as makeshift desks, until real desks could be purchased. Slates and readers were coming and would be here by the time school started in September.

Sarah had been prepared to move in and start unpacking on the spot. But at Lorna's insistence, she and Blake had gone back to the elegant Calder home, shared dinner with the family, and slept in the guest bedroom. After hearing of Benteen Calder from Joe, Sarah had been uneasy about meeting him. But Benteen had put her at ease and had proven to be a gracious host. If he knew anything about her past connection to Joe, he'd shown no sign of it.

Their son Webb, a couple of years older than Blake, was to be one of Sarah's pupils at the school. He struck her as bright but restless, the kind of student who was apt to become bored in the classroom. Keeping him interested would be a challenge—her challenge, she reminded herself.

Sarah had welcomed the distraction of a good meal and pleasant conversation. She'd welcomed anything that might blur the image lingering in her mind—Joe on his horse, with his beautiful young son in his arms. But that night, lying awake in the spacious bed, that image had come back to haunt her. Her eyes had met his for only an instant. But she'd recognized him at once, and she was certain he'd recognized her.

But that wasn't the problem. She'd come here knowing Joe had a family. She could accept that, and even deal with meeting him if she had to. It was Blake she was worried about—her tenderhearted son who was at an age to start asking questions about his father. What could she tell him? How could she keep him from being hurt if—or more likely when—he learned the truth?

Maybe coming here had been a mistake.

The next morning, Lorna drove Sarah, Blake, and the dog to their new home. Sarah had been promised access to a horse and small buggy. The buggy was in the shed behind the house, along with a washtub, scrub board, a few tools, and other useful things. The use of a horse had yet to be arranged. Meanwhile, the weather was warm, and the general store was an easy walk, little more than a quarter mile from the school, just past the saloon.

While Blake romped with the dog outside, Sarah unpacked their things and did her best to settle into the new place. The cupboards had already been stocked with the basics—flour and other baking ingredients, oatmeal, eggs, a slab of bacon, and even a loaf of fresh bread, and a jar of cookies. There were dishes and utensils, soap and towels, as well as linens and warm quilts for the bed. Someone—most likely Lorna—had taken great pains to see that she and Blake would have what they needed. The thought brought tears to Sarah's eyes. She couldn't remember anyone ever having made her feel so welcome.

Blake, who'd always shared his mother's room, was elated over having his own space in the loft. Standing partway up the ladder, Sarah made him a bed next to the wall, making sure he wouldn't tumble off the edge in his sleep. "Can Hummy sleep up here with me?" he asked.

"Humdinger is too big for the ladder," Sarah said. "He'll have to sleep downstairs. Maybe before it gets cold outside, we can even build him a doghouse."

Sarah had her son practice climbing up and down the ladder to make sure he could do it without falling. Then she let him take a couple of cookies and his favorite picture book and settle down in his new spot. "I'm going to look at the schoolroom next door," she said. "If you need me, you'll know where to find me."

Leaving the dog behind, she went out the side door, walked through the passageway, and entered the classroom—*her* classroom. A tingle of anticipation slid through her as she imagined her students walking in through the front door, greeting her with smiles, and sitting at the tables, ready to learn.

Lorna had told her to expect about twelve pupils, most of them young, but some already in their teens. For the older ones, she'd shipped three boxes of books ahead of her arrival. They included her own treasured collection as well as books on science, history, and mathematics that she'd salvaged from Uncle Harlan's house. She'd also collected some books for younger children. If she could instill her own love of reading in her students, that would be the most valuable gift she could impart to them.

The boxes were already here. Someone had piled them next to her desk. Now would be as good a time as any to unpack them and arrange them on the shelves.

She'd emptied the first box and had just started on the second when she heard the sound of a footstep and a familiar voice behind her.

"Hello, Sarah."

Her breath caught. Heart slamming, she turned. Joe had come in through the front door and was standing behind her—taller and broader than she remembered, his face fully a man's now, sharp-chiseled and determined but with the same warm blue eyes.

Conflicting emotions flooded her, but strongest of all was the need to protect her son.

She stood up to face him. The first words out of her mouth were "You can't be here."

"I know." He remained where she was, making no effort to come closer. "Rusty already read me the riot act and told me to leave you alone. But just this once I had to see you. And I had to see our son. Just this once, and I'll never trouble you again."

"No!" She kept her voice low, fearing it might carry through the open passageway. "I won't let you see him. I won't let him be confused or hurt. I won't damage your family or open myself to the scandal I left behind in Ogallala. As far as you're concerned, we're strangers. I'm a widow, and he's my son. Mine and no one else's."

"Sarah, I swear I didn't know," he said. "I thought you'd gone off to school. Rusty didn't say anything about it to me."

"It wouldn't have mattered if he had. By the time Rusty found out about the baby, you were married."

"But I would've done something—sent you money at least."

"I wouldn't have accepted your charity." Sarah's voice was cold. "Now go away. Go home to your family, and don't come back."

There was a beat of dead silence in the room. Then a small voice piped into the stillness. "Mama, I heard somebody. Who's this man?"

Blake, with the dog at his side, was standing in the entrance to the passageway.

Joe turned, taking his time, perhaps trying not to startle his son. The resemblance between the two was stunning. Joe would notice it at once. But Blake, who rarely bothered to look at himself in a mirror, might not. Sarah held her breath, waiting, as if her world were about to shatter.

Blake stepped forward, his hand extended as his mother had taught him. "Hello, mister," he said. "My name is Blake. Pleased to meet you."

Sarah's knees went limp beneath her skirt. She had never been prouder of her son than at this moment.

Joe bent to accept the handshake. When he spoke, his voice shook slightly. "Pleased to meet you, too, Blake. My name is Mr. Joe Dollarhide. Is that your dog?"

"Uh-huh. His name's Humdinger because that's the kind of dog he is."

"Well, he certainly is a humdinger." Joe scratched the big mutt's ears, then straightened. "I just came by to welcome the new teacher. Now I need to go. It was a pleasure meeting you both. And Humdinger, too."

His eyes met Sarah's. Her mouth formed the words *Just go.*

Without another word, Joe turned around and left by the front door. As the sounds of his horse faded, Sarah sank onto a chair. Her heart was pounding so loudly that she could barely hear Blake's question.

"Mama, who was that man?"

She forced herself to speak. "Just a curious neighbor. I don't think we'll be seeing much of him. Come on, let's get Humdinger's leash and walk down to the store. Maybe they'll know where we can buy some milk."

Joe rode back up the wagon road, still reeling from his encounter with Sarah and her son—*his* son, stamped in his image, bright and well-mannered, and so appealing that as soon as the boy spoke, Joe had felt his heart begin to melt.

He loved Mason, his perfect little boy. But his love for the son he barely knew burned just as fiercely. And Sarah—she was all woman now, strong and beautiful, protecting her son like a lioness. Lord, how he wanted her.

Rusty had been right.

He had to leave them alone. Otherwise, the love he felt would burn him alive, and them with it—to say nothing of what it would do to Amelia and Mason.

He was coming up on the trail that turned off the wagon road and ended at his hilltop home. If he kept on the main road for another three miles, he would end up at the Hollister ranch. He'd spent time with Mason only yesterday. But his world had turned upside down since then. Maybe being with his family would remind him of his commitment to them, and his duty to make the right choices.

Seeing Mason was always a joy. But he didn't look forward to another argument with Amelia—especially if she pressed him about allowing her to take their son to St. Louis for the winter.

But what if I were to let her? The forbidden thought whispered in his mind. *It would leave me free to see Sarah, free to know my other son.*

No! He forced the idea away. Allowing such a thing to happen would only lead to heartache, shame, and guilt. Now, more than ever, it was important that his wife and Mason stay here in Montana.

As he rode through the front gate and approached the house, he sensed that something wasn't right. Mason was on the porch alone—something that wasn't usually allowed. There was no sign of Amelia or anyone else outside, but the front door was standing partway open.

"Daddy!" Mason ran down the front steps, sounding more distressed than happy. Stopping the horse, Joe dismounted and picked up his son. His eyes were red, his small cheeks wet with tears.

"What is it, Mason? What's the matter?" Carrying the boy next to his shoulder, Joe led his horse to the hitching rail and looped the reins.

"It's Grandpa," Mason whimpered. "He fell down. Mama can't get him up."

Instantly worried, Joe set the boy on the porch swing. "Stay right here while I go inside and help. Promise?"

"Promise." Mason wiped his nose with his sleeve.

"That's a big boy. I'll come back as soon as I can." Joe raced through the open front door and into the house.

In the study, he found Loren sprawled on the Turkish carpet. He was struggling to get up, but something was wrong. His speech was garbled, and his facial features had a lopsided appearance.

Amelia knelt beside him, pulling at his hands and stroking his face. "I tried to get him to a chair, but I couldn't move him," she said. "I don't know what's the matter." She sounded scared, but she wasn't weeping.

Joe knelt beside her, murmuring words of support to his father-in-law as he studied the stricken face. Loren was conscious but visibly confused and frightened. As he struggled to form words, a thread of spittle trailed from the corner of his mouth.

"It looks like a stroke." Joe worked his hands under Loren's shoulders, and, with Amelia's help, got him into an armchair. Loren wasn't a big man, but he was dead weight. "We'll need to get him to the doctor in Miles City."

"How much can the doctor do?" Amelia brushed the hair back from her father's face. Joe had expected her to be fluttery and helpless, but she was surprisingly calm.

"I don't know what he can do," Joe said. "But we need to find out. Stay with your dad while I get some help. I'll get Mason, too. He shouldn't be alone right now."

Minutes later, the team had been hitched to the buggy and brought around to the front of the house. Joe and Ralph Tomlinson, a cowboy who'd been promoted to foreman after Joe had left the ranch, helped Loren into the buggy, laid him half reclining on a pillow in the rear seat, and covered him with a light blanket. The raised hood on the buggy would keep off the sun.

"I can drive if you want," Tomlinson offered.

"That's all right. Joe can do it," Amelia said. "We'll need you to look after things here."

"I don't want to stay here! I want to go with you and Grandpa!" Mason was crying again. But after Amelia promised to bring him candy if he was good, he stopped crying and went with the friendly cook, who'd agreed to watch him.

Joe took a moment to get the Winchester rifle he carried from his saddle and put it under the buggy seat, as protection from any trouble they might meet. Then he helped his wife into the buggy.

Amelia leaned back and tried to give her father a drink of water from a cup, but he only choked on it. How long could they keep Loren alive if he couldn't eat or drink? That, and a plethora of new worries, nagged at Joe as they drove back toward Blue Moon, headed for Miles City.

Sarah was walking home from the store, holding Blake's hand and Humdinger's leash, when she saw the approaching buggy, coming at a fast clip. Tugging her son and the dog with her, she moved back into the long grass at the roadside to give the rig room to pass safely.

As the buggy came closer, she recognized Joe driving the team. Beside him sat one of the prettiest women she'd ever seen, with doll-like features and russet curls falling below her fashionable hat. She had to be Joe's wife.

In an instant the rig passed her. In another instant, they were speeding away down the road, growing smaller with distance. She'd hoped Joe wouldn't see her, standing there with their son. It appeared that he hadn't. He was too intent on going somewhere in a hurry, maybe to Miles City.

At least, seeing his wife and how pretty she was might make it easier for Sarah to put him out of her mind. She'd never believed in taking things that weren't hers, and that included other women's husbands. She'd told Joe to stay away. It was time she gave the same advice to herself.

Forget him. Whatever had passed between them, it had ended the night he'd kissed her good-bye and ridden away from Ogallala. This new Joe was a stranger, someone she no longer knew. And that was how things would stay.

In Miles City, the doctor, a young man with a hawkish nose and spectacles, examined Loren, looking into his eyes, checking his reflexes and his vital signs. Loren was conscious and still trying to talk, but the words spilling out of his lopsided mouth made no sense. The harder he tried, the more frustrated he became until, at last he gave up and sat slumped on the examining table.

"It does appear to be a stroke," the doctor said. "His heartbeat is irregular, and his blood pressure is somewhat elevated, which may be due to stress. Otherwise . . ." The doctor shrugged. "The human brain is a mystery. We can only guess how severe the damage is. It seems confined to his left side—the face, the weakness in the body. That's typical of a stroke."

"But what can you do for him?" Amelia demanded.

"Unfortunately, there are no miracle cures. For now, all we can do is try to keep him healthy and comfortable and hope he improves over time. I'd like to keep him here, in the infirmary, for a couple of days to get him stabilized and watch for any changes."

"I tried giving him water, but he choked on it," Amelia said. "He's going to need fluids."

"We'll work on getting him to drink," the doctor said. "You should be able to take him home on Friday."

Amelia put her arms around her father and kissed his cheek. Loren responded with a string of garbled profanity. Joe sensed that his father-in-law knew exactly what was going on. He could imagine how trapped and scared the once-powerful man must feel. But there was nothing more that could be done.

Joe walked out into the sunshine with his wife, both of them lost in thought. Their lives had taken an abrupt turn. There were some far-reaching decisions to be made.

"Let's have some lunch at the hotel before we drive home," he said. "It'll be easier to talk there than in the buggy."

They walked into the hotel restaurant. The busy noon lunch hour had passed, so getting a quiet table wasn't a problem. Amelia ordered chicken soup. "I don't really feel like eating," she said.

"Neither do I, but we've got to eat sometime." Joe ordered the same thing, with coffee for him and tea for her. "Are you all right?" he asked her as their beverages arrived.

"I will be." Amelia added milk to her tea and stirred it. "I just need a little time. It's not as if Loren Hollister was ever much of a father to me. But I need to be there for him. At least you won't have to worry about my running off to St. Louis."

"I hadn't even thought of that." Joe took a deep breath, knowing what he needed to say and that it wouldn't be easy. "You can't take care of your father and Mason and run the ranch on your own. As soon as your father's ready to come home, I'll be closing my house and moving back to the ranch with you."

He watched her face as he spoke the words. At first she looked surprised. Then her expression hardened. "No," she said.

"Amelia, you're going to need—"

"No, listen." She cut him off. "I've already thought this through. You could've stayed on the ranch with your family. Instead you chose to go off and live your own life. Now that you're gone, I don't want you back—not in the house and not in my bed. Ralph is an excellent foreman. He's already running things at the ranch. And there's a strong, kindly man, a former buffalo soldier, who tends the animals when they're sick or hurt. I'm sure that if I offered to raise his pay, he'd be willing to come inside and take care of my father—the lifting, the bathing and changing, things I could never do myself. So you see, I'll be fine." She took a sip of her tea and set the cup onto its saucer with a click. "I don't need you, Joe."

"Are you saying you want a divorce?"

She gave him an odd little smile. "Not at all. I like being a respectable married woman who's free to make her own choices. And there's a small matter of property—the house you built, the livestock, and the lumber business, for which you use land that you filed on under my name. Being Mrs. Joe Dollarhide has certain advantages, and I don't want to lose them. And then, of course, there's Mason—" She broke off. "Oh, look. Here comes the waiter. I think maybe I could eat a little something after all."

Forcing himself to eat, Joe watched as his wife calmly finished her chicken soup.

Who was this woman?

Over the years, he'd let himself believe that he'd married a helpless little doll. But the wife who sat across the table from him was strong-willed and calculating, even cold.

He could understand that she had no great love for her father, who'd left her at a young age, then married her off at the first opportunity. Joe could even understand her lack of feelings for a husband who'd put his ambition ahead of their marriage. But was he seeing something new in her—or was he seeing what had been there all along?

They finished their lunch and, after stopping to buy a peppermint stick for Mason, made the long, tense drive back to the ranch. When Joe pulled the buggy up to the house, he saw Mason on the porch. Ralph Tomlinson was with him. Joe had paid little attention to the hired help since leaving the ranch. But as Tomlinson came down the steps to give Amelia a hand and take the buggy, Joe couldn't help but notice his rugged good looks, and the way his gaze lingered on her as he helped her to the ground. Did the foreman have something to do with Amelia's refusal to let her husband come home?

Did it really matter anymore?

Joe turned the buggy over to Tomlinson, mounted the porch, and scooped Mason into his arms. "Daddy, where's Grandpa?" the boy asked. "Why isn't he with you?"

"Your grandpa is really sick, son," Joe said. "The doctor is taking care of him. He'll be home in a few days."

"Will he be better?"

Joe shook his head. *Damn, but this was hard.* "No, son, he'll still be sick. But your mother wants to take care of him at home. You can help her by being good and doing whatever she asks. All right?"

"Uh-huh." He wriggled free and ran to his mother to get the promised peppermint stick. For Joe, there was nothing to do now but leave.

"I'll be here to drive you on Friday," he said to Amelia.

"No need," she responded with a smile. "I'm sure I can find someone here to do it."

She was baiting him. Joe bit back a curse. "I'll be here. Plan on it."

Without saying more, he left the porch, collected his horse from the corral, replaced the rifle in its scabbard, and took the road home.

By now it was late in the day. The sun hung low above the

prairie, already touching the clouds with pale color. A red-tailed hawk circled overhead. In a nearby pasture, longhorns grazed on the rich late-summer grass.

The scene provided a peaceful end to what had been a crushing day. First seeing Sarah and meeting their son, then Loren's stroke, the emotional trip to Miles City, and the abrupt change in his wife. In the weeks ahead, he would have no choice except to deal with it all, as fairly and rationally as he could.

The most important thing would be seeing that Mason was all right, and after that, making sure that Sarah was not in any way involved. He was already fighting the temptation to go to her and tell her about the sham his marriage had become. But that would be out of the question. He was a married man, and his wife had made it clear that she had no intention of setting him free.

If there was a chance he could prove adultery with Tomlinson . . . but no, Amelia was the mother of his precious son. Even at the price of his freedom, he couldn't leave that stain on his family.

And unless he could marry Sarah and claim their son, the only honorable choice would be to do as she'd insisted—leave them alone.

That Friday he drove Amelia to Miles City to pick up her father. The morning was clear, the air pleasantly crisp with the first hint of autumn, but the atmosphere between Joe and his wife was one of tense silence. Going through Blue Moon in the buggy, they passed the school and its adjoining house. Risking a sidelong glance, he saw a clothesline hung with laundry in the side yard. The big yellow dog was lolling on the porch. But Sarah and Blake were nowhere to be seen. And that was just as well, Joe told himself. The sight of them would have taken his thoughts where they had no right to go.

Farther on, beyond the town, the road passed along the boundary of the Calder ranch. Everything past the line of the long buck fence, all the way to the horizon and beyond, belonged to Benteen Calder. In the distance, past the sweeping pastures, where herds of fat cattle grazed, the imposing white house, with its pillared front, rose like a castle overlooking a kingdom. Unseen from here were the outbuildings, the pens and corrals, the bunkhouses, the line shacks, and the homesteads where Calder employees lived with their families.

Joe was wealthy in his own right—in fact, he probably had more cash in the bank than Benteen did. He had long since stopped envying the Calders for their vast land holdings. But the fact that he'd never gotten satisfaction for the old wrong Benteen had done him still rankled.

Someday, he vowed, he would find a legal way to get even—a way that would leave Benteen beaten and fuming. Right now, with so much chaos in his domestic life, the thought provided Joe with a welcome distraction.

In Miles City, they met with the doctor and loaded Loren in the buggy for the trip home. He was somewhat better. He could use his right hand and walk a few steps with someone to support his weakened left side. He could take liquids through the right side of his mouth, although he couldn't yet feed himself. His speech, though still garbled and confused, could be at least partly understood.

But his father-in-law reminded Joe of an animal brought down by hunters, mortally wounded, its eyes glazing over as it waited to die. The fire of life had fled from Loren Hollister. He had lost all will to go on—and Joe could in no way blame him.

They helped him into the back seat of the buggy, under the hood. Amelia climbed in beside him, leaving Joe alone in the front to drive the team.

It was midday by the time they reached the ranch. Abraham, the gentle giant whom Amelia had promoted from ranch hand to nurse, was waiting on the porch. He came down the steps, lifted Loren out of the buggy, and carried him into the house.

A cowboy was waiting to take care of the buggy and the team. Joe handed him the reins and followed Amelia into the house. Abraham had placed Loren in his favorite armchair. Loren's mouth worked until one unmistakable word emerged.

"*Whiskey.*"

Amelia poured three fingers into a glass and helped him drink it. As soon as it was gone, he managed another word. "*More.*"

Amelia handed the glass to Abraham. "You saw how I had to help him," she said. "Give him all he wants."

Just then Mason came in from the kitchen. He took one look at his grandfather and burst into heartbroken sobs. "Grandpa . . . no!" he wailed.

Joe stepped forward and lifted his son in his arms. "Let me take him today," he said to Amelia.

"Fine. Just have him home in time for bed."

"How about it, son? Do you want to spend the day with me?" It was a safe question. Mason always loved spending time with Joe.

"Uh-huh." Mason smiled through his tears.

"Then let's go." Joe carried his son outside, retrieved his horse from the corral, and rode off holding Mason in front of him on the saddle. He had work to do, but Mason enjoyed tagging along to see the cattle, the horses, and the sawmill. Joe also planned to talk with the boy about his grandfather's condition, what he could expect, and how to help.

The rest of the day passed pleasantly enough. As darkness fell, Joe took his son back to the ranch and turned him over to his mother at the front door. He'd known better than to get entangled in the family problems there. Still, he couldn't escape the tension and worry. As he rode away, headed home, it was as if the events of the past few days had come circling in to roost like black vultures on a snag.

Reaching the spot where the trail to his place turned off the main road, he swung his horse aside, then hesitated. There was nothing to do at the house except read for a while and then go to bed. But with so much weighing on his mind, he was liable to spend the whole night tossing and turning.

Maybe a drink and a little socializing at the saloon in Blue Moon would settle his nerves. With luck, there would even be a poker game going on. Losing a few dollars to some happy cowboy might prove a welcome distraction.

By the time he tied his horse to the hitching rail outside the saloon, along with four others, two with bedrolls and gear on their saddles, the moon was high in the sky. Although he'd sworn not to do it, he couldn't help looking in the direction of the school and Sarah's house, which was just visible at this distance. He could see no light through the high windows. Sarah and Blake would likely be asleep.

At the bar, Joe settled for a single whiskey before joining the lively poker game around the large, round table. He played a few hands, won a little cash, lost a little more. Never mind. It was just a way to pass the time before riding home and trying to get some rest.

Usually he knew the other men in the game. Tonight, he recognized two cowboys who worked for the Calders; but two of the men at the table were strangers, rough types whose unwashed clothes and unshaven faces marked them as trail bums. At least their money was good. And they were both winning more when, abruptly, they exchanged glances and quit the game. One of the men, the bigger one, ambled outside. The other man had a quick shot of whiskey at the bar, then followed him.

Joe played a few more minutes before he realized he was tiring of the game. He pocketed his meager winnings, crossed the room, and opened the door to leave.

The moment he stepped outside, he sensed that something was wrong. An instant later he realized what it was.

There'd been four horses, besides his own, at the hitching rail. All four horses, including the pair loaded with gear, were still there. But where were the two men who'd left earlier? Thinking they might be relieving themselves in the shadows, Joe checked around the saloon. He found no trace of them.

Why would they leave their horses here and set out on foot unless—

His heart slammed.

Sarah!

CHAPTER SEVENTEEN

*T*HE DOG WOKE SARAH FROM A RESTLESS SLUMBER. SHE COULD HEAR him by the front door, not barking but growling, as if to warn her that something evil was outside.

She slipped out of bed and put on her robe. The house was dark, but squares of moonlight shone through the high windows.

"What is it, boy?" She laid a hand on the dog. His thick hair bristled in a line that went all the way down his back. He growled again, low in his throat.

That was when she heard gruff voices, muffled by the door, then a knock and a voice.

"Ma'am, my boy here is hurt. We need your help."

Sarah almost answered, then thought better of it. The saloon was still open down the road. If the man outside really needed help—and some instinct told her not to believe him—he could go there.

"Open the door, teacher lady. We know you're in there." The second voice was a different one. Two men, at least. Maybe more. If they got in, she would be no match for them. The knock on the door became a pounding.

"Mama, who's out there?" Blake had come down from the loft to stand behind her. Whatever happened, she had to keep him safe. If only she had a gun—but she'd long since sold the .44 that Joe had given her. She'd needed the money to pay her rent back in Ogallala.

"Mama?" Blake tugged at her robe.

Sarah touched a finger to his lips. "Take Hummy. Go out the side door and sneak through the open place in the passageway, where the woodpile is. Then run around the back and hide in the shed. Don't come out until I call you. Understand?"

Wide-eyed, the boy nodded. "But who will protect you, Mama?"

"I'll be fine. Make sure they don't see you. Run!"

Blake raced off with the dog behind him. The pounding on the door had grown louder. What if the unwelcome guests tried to kick the door in? The wood was thick, but the cheap hinges wouldn't hold out long. She could've kept Humdinger with her, but she'd wanted him to stay with Blake. If the men had guns, they wouldn't hesitate to shoot a dog; and if, God forbid, they were to find Blake, the big yellow mutt would give his life to protect his young master.

"Go away. I've got a gun and I know how to use it," she lied, trying to distract them while her son hid.

"That's what they all say." There was a rough laugh. "Just open the damned door and be nice to us, sweetheart. That's all we want. Then we'll go away and leave you with happy memories."

The words were punctuated by a crashing blow to the door. The hinges creaked in the frame as the men kicked and rammed against the wood. Sarah had nothing heavy enough to brace the door. A few more blows, and they'd be inside. Did they have guns? Did they plan to kill her?

As the screws splintered away from the frame, she plunged out the side door, and raced into the passageway. Going out the side opening could lead the men to her son. But once they were inside the house, she might be able to get out through the schoolroom, without being seen. Then she could get to Blake and run for help.

It was a good plan, but she'd forgotten one thing. She'd locked the door between the passageway and the classroom to make sure Blake didn't go exploring in there. The key was in the cupboard.

The two men crashed into the house and cornered her in the passageway. She was dragged, kicking, twisting, and biting, into the bedroom and flung onto the bed.

One man held her down while the other man undid his dirty trousers and yanked up her nightgown. Still struggling, she willed herself not to cry out. Whatever happened, she would not let Blake hear his mother scream.

Sarah could smell his filthy, whiskey-laden breath as he leaned over her, grinning. She braced herself for the unthinkable.

"Stop right there, you bastards. Let her go and back off, before I blow your brains out." Silhouetted against the moonlight, Joe stood in the doorway to the bedroom, the Winchester rifle in his hands cocked and aimed. Caught off guard, the men reeled backward, the bigger one clutching his unbuttoned trousers. "That's it," Joe said in an icy voice. "Back off and raise your hands. One false move and I'll enjoy pulling this trigger."

The men, still wearing their gun belts, did as they were ordered. "We didn't mean no harm, mister," the bigger man whined. "We was only funnin'."

"Shut up and keep your hands where I can see them." Joe kept his eyes on the pair. "Are you all right, Sarah?"

"I am now." She pushed her nightgown down and stood, shaken and fighting tears of rage.

"Get their pistols," Joe said. "And, you two, don't you dare touch her!"

Sarah slid the pistols out of the men's holsters. Close-up, the odor of their bodies made her want to vomit, but she willed herself to stay calm. So the pair had been armed after all. Maybe they'd planned to shoot her once they'd had their fun.

"Where's Blake?" Joe asked.

"I sent him out back with the dog. He should be safe."

"Go to him. He'll be scared. I'll take care of our friends here."

After leaving the pistols in the cupboard, Sarah hurried out through the front door. Unmindful of her bare feet, she raced around the house. She found Blake in the shed, hiding under the buggy, with Humdinger guarding him. She called her son out and hugged him. "Are we safe now, Mama?" he asked.

She held him close, trembling with all the emotions she'd held back—terror, rage, and relief. "Yes, my big, brave boy, we're safe," she said.

*　*　*

The was no sheriff in Blue Moon and no jail. Unless he wanted to shoot the monsters who'd nearly raped Sarah, Joe would have to make do with forcing them to shed their boots and clothes. Barefoot, naked, and shivering in the night breeze, they were set free to go back to the horses they'd tethered outside the saloon and leave town, with a warning that worse would happen if they ever came back.

As they mounted and disappeared down the road, Joe piled their possessions on a patch of bare earth, doused them with lamp oil from the kitchen, and set them ablaze. Then he turned and went back into the house, where he found Sarah sitting on the edge of the bed, holding her son on her lap. The dog crouched at her feet.

Without a word, he put the rifle aside, sat down beside them, and gathered them into the circle of his arms. Fiercely protective, he held them tight. They nestled against him, making no effort to pull away. They were his—his woman and his son. He felt it in his mind, in his heart, and in his soul. And he knew that he wouldn't rest until he could make them his in the eyes of the world.

"You can't stay here tonight," he said. "You and Blake are coming with me, to my place."

She stiffened and pulled away from him. "I know you mean well. But that wouldn't look good for us, Joe. And I don't need to tell you why."

He let her go, knowing that she was right. Even under these conditions, keeping up appearances mattered.

"I understand," he said. "But I'm not leaving you here alone with a broken door. Go on back to bed. I'll stay and keep watch."

"There's no need for that. I can use one of the guns that those men left. And there's the dog."

"Don't argue with me, Sarah. I'm not leaving you alone, even if it means I have to spend the night on the porch."

She hesitated, then sighed. "All right. You can put your horse in the shed. But there's no way I'll be able to sleep. I'll fire up the stove and make us some coffee. And you"—she turned to her son—"back to bed now."

"Can I sleep in your bed? I want to be close to Hummy."

"Fine. And Hummy can sleep on the rug. But just for tonight."

As the boy climbed into the bed, Joe went out to his horse, which he'd ridden the short distance from the saloon. In the shed, he removed the saddle and bridle and left Flint a bucket of water from the outside pump before going back inside.

The door was hanging from one broken hinge. Joe took a moment to lift it into place against the frame.

"Thanks." Sarah had lit a lamp in the kitchen, fired up the stove, and was measuring coffee into a pot. "And thanks for coming to my rescue."

"It was pure luck that I was here. If those animals had hurt you, they wouldn't be alive right now." Joe battled the urge to walk up behind her, wrap her in his arms, and kiss the back of her neck. "I'll send a man to fix your door in the morning."

"No need. I'm sure the folks in charge of the school will take care of it." She set the pot to boil on the stove.

"I can get it done sooner and better. When my man's finished with that door, a buffalo stampede won't be able to break it down."

That brought a smile to her lips. She sank onto a kitchen chair to wait while the coffee boiled. The lamplight cast the lines and shadows around her eyes into stark relief. She hadn't had it easy, his Sarah. Having her baby and raising him alone had taken its toll in hardship and worry. But she was even more beautiful than he remembered.

"Tell me about your family," she said. "I saw you riding with your little boy, and then later I saw you with your wife, in the buggy. She was so pretty. I'd like to know more about your life with them."

Where to begin—and to end? Joe knew what Sarah was trying to do. Talking about his wife and son would raise the protective barrier between them and lay out the reasons why they had to treat each other as strangers. But Joe had different intentions. If there was any chance that he and Sarah could move on from here, he must have no secrets from her.

As she set the mug of coffee before him on the table and took a seat across from him, he began. It would be tempting to leave out the parts of his story that were hard to tell and would be even harder for Sarah to hear. But there was no other way. She needed to know it all.

She listened as his best friend, her violet eyes soft and knowing. Now and again she stopped him to ask a question, but only to understand, not to judge.

By the time he finished, her eyes were moist. "You could have become a doctor, Sarah," he said. "You could have lived your dream. What happened to stop you was my fault."

She gave him a wistful smile. "What happened was Blake. And I wouldn't have missed being his mother for all the fancy medical degrees in the world."

"But if I'd known, I'd have come back and married you. Our whole lives would have been different."

"You have another son," she said. "A wonderful little boy who loves you. Would you have chosen not to have him?"

Without waiting for an answer, she stood. "I can't tell you what to do with the rest of your life, Joe. But until you decide, Blake and I can't be part of it. I won't have you coming by to see us and then going back to your real family. I'm going to bed now. You can stay here or leave before sunrise. But when I wake up in the morning, I want you gone."

Joe had also risen to his feet. "I understand, and I'll be leaving before first light," he said. "But I still plan to have your door fixed. I hope you'll allow me that."

"I'd appreciate it, of course. And thank you again for the rescue."

She turned away to go. Only then, as her face caught the light, did he see the tear flowing down her cheek. He moved into her path, blocking her way to the bedroom. His hands cupped her face.

"*No . . .*" she whispered. But she didn't resist as he bent toward her and claimed her lips in a long, tender kiss. She softened against him, her mouth molding to his, her body arching upward as she stretched on tiptoe, her heart pounding against his, her breasts soft through the robe and nightgown. Joe was already aroused and wanting her. But he knew better than to take their kiss any further. Nothing was going to happen. Not until, and not unless, he could put things right.

Knowing he must, he eased himself away from her. "Good night, Sarah," he murmured. "But know this. You haven't seen the last of me."

With a little gasp, she spun away, fled to her bedroom, and closed the door behind her.

True to his word, Joe was gone when Sarah came into the kitchen the next morning. The only sign that he'd been there was the empty coffee mug on the counter and the charred pile of leather boots, belts, and brass buckles that remained from the fire he'd lit in the front yard.

By the time breakfast was over, a taciturn, middle-aged man driving a wagon had shown up to fix the door. Laying out a pair of iron hinges and several long screws, as well as a sliding iron bolt to serve as a lock, he set to work.

He was just finishing the job when a one-horse buggy pulled up to the house. The driver was Lorna Calder.

"What on earth?" She climbed down from the buggy and secured the horse to a post. A basket, covered with a checkered cloth, was slung over one arm. "Sarah, are you and your boy all right?"

"We're fine." Sarah had no wish to upset her friend by making a fuss over the break-in. "I'm just having the door repaired after a couple of drunks from the saloon broke it in."

"Sarah! What happened? And what's this?" She nodded toward the torched remains of the men's clothes.

"It's . . . a long story. I didn't want you to be concerned."

"Well, I certainly am concerned!" Lorna said, stepping around the workman's clutter on the front porch. "Let's go inside, and you can tell me about it."

"Of course. I've got hot water on the stove. I'll make us some tea."

After checking on Blake, who was in the backyard with Humdinger, gathering scrap lumber for the doghouse he wanted to build, Sarah followed Lorna into the kitchen and started the tea.

Lorna lifted the cloth that covered the contents of the basket.

"The blueberries are ripe, so I made some muffins," she said. "I hope you like them."

"I'll love them, and so will Blake. Thank you so much." Sarah put the fresh muffins in a bowl and returned the empty basket. "The tea will be ready in a few minutes."

"That's fine," Lorna said. "What I really want is to hear what happened to you. Please sit down and tell me."

Sarah gave her an abbreviated version of last night's events, leaving out how close the two ruffians had come to raping her and the memory of Joe's searing kiss. "So, as you see, Blake and I are fine," she said. "And Joe sent one of his men to reinforce the door."

"And that pile of burned things in the yard?"

"I didn't see what happened. But I think Joe had the men strip down, then ran them off, and set their clothes on fire."

"Oh, my goodness!" Lorna laughed. "That must've been quite a sight. I trust they won't be coming back this way."

"I hope not. But since you're on the women's committee for Blue Moon, maybe you can suggest that we choose a sheriff and build a jail. We need some law in this town." Sarah poured some tea and split one of the generously sized muffins for them to share.

"Actually, that's one of the reasons I'm here," Lorna said. "As the new teacher, you'll be essential to the committee. Our monthly meeting will be next Saturday. We've been using the classroom since it was built. If that's not a problem, and if you're free, we'd love to have you join us."

"Oh . . . my, that's so kind of you."

"But why are you so surprised, Sarah? Of course we'd want you on our committee. You're going to make a real difference in Blue Moon."

Sarah laughed nervously. "It's just that, when I lived in Ogallala, people turned their backs on me. This is such a change. And it bothers me some that my acceptance here is based on a lie. I'm not really a widow. And the father of my boy is a man who's known all over the county. What if somebody finds out?"

"Your secret is safe with me, Sarah. But understand that Montana is a place of new beginnings. One of the ladies in our group was a prostitute in Miles City before she married a cowboy from the Calder ranch. She's a lovely person, and I keep her secret, too. But everybody's got their stories. People don't tend to judge here. So how about it? Will you join us?"

Sarah sighed. "Later, for sure. But I just got here. And with all this"—she gestured toward the door—"and now, with Joe showing up, I'm wondering if it was a mistake for me to come here."

"I had an idea this might be about Joe," Lorna said. "Do you still have feelings for him?"

"It doesn't matter. Joe is married. He's got a beautiful wife and a darling little boy. I've seen them both. I know they live apart— he told me that. But married is married. And if Blake were to learn the truth . . ." Sarah shook her head. "The only thing I know is that I mustn't let Joe come near us."

Lorna reached across the table and took Sarah's hand. "I can only offer you one piece of advice. Give it time. If you run now, you'll never know what might have worked out. But if you stay and build a life, as a teacher and a mother, good things are bound to happen—good things that you deserve. People here are waiting to be your friends, Sarah. Will you give Blue Moon a chance? Think about it, at least."

Lorna said good-bye with a hug and drove away in her buggy. Her friend was right, Sarah told herself. She couldn't let her feelings for Joe keep her from building a life here. For now, she resolved, she would do her best to be a good teacher, a good mother, and a useful member of the community. As for the future, she could only trust it to luck and fate.

After a long day in Miles City, Joe rode homeward under the late-afternoon sun. Chilly nights had painted the oaks and maples on the hillsides with a crimson blush, but the Indian summer days were warm. He had taken off his leather jacket and laid it across the saddle as he rode.

Passing through Blue Moon, he turned his gaze away from the

school and the adjoining house. Two weeks ago, in the gray dawn of that morning when he'd left Sarah's place, he had made himself a promise. He would not seek out Sarah, or his son, again until he could go to them with honor, as a free man.

Even then, he'd known that the cost of his freedom would be high. Just how high, he'd been in the process of finding out. After talking with his lawyer and with the bank in Miles City, he was surprised at how wealthy he'd become. That was the good news. Other news was less encouraging.

Amelia was holding the cards and, unless he could trap her in adultery, she was under no obligation to give him a divorce. His only chance would be to play on her avarice and offer her half of his land, livestock, cash, and business holdings. Financially, the blow would be devastating. But some things were worth more than money. A life with Sarah and their son was at the top of the list.

He passed the outskirts of Blue Moon and rode on, surrounded by open fields on both sides of the road. A flock of geese flew in to settle on a harvested grain field. They would spend the night resting and feeding among the stubble before lifting off at dawn to fly on south.

The Hollister ranch was a little less than an hour from here. Joe didn't look forward to broaching the subject of divorce with Amelia. She was bound to want her proverbial pound of flesh before she listened to his offer. What he did look forward to was riding up to the house and seeing Mason race across the porch to meet him. Joe would give Amelia almost anything in exchange for his freedom. But he would insist on access to Mason. He would never walk away from his boy—not for any price.

Unlike Benteen Calder, who'd placed the value of his cattle above the cost of a man's life, Joe had learned that some things were worth more than money. Of course, Benteen had it all. The herd of 2,000 cattle he'd first driven to Montana had increased to more than 20,000 head of longhorns and other breeds. He had more land than he could ride around in three days. He had a magnificent home; and his marriage to Lorna was the envy of every man who knew them.

But Benteen's wealth hadn't come as a reward for being kind and fair. He'd acquired all that he possessed through ruthless drive and ambition. Joe was still looking for a way to best the man and see him cut down to size. But that would have to wait. Right now, he had more urgent matters on his mind.

He rode through the ranch gate and up to the house. By the time he'd dismounted, Mason was out the front door and running across the porch to meet him. A movement from the corner of the house caught Joe's eye as Ralph Tomlinson slipped out the kitchen door and disappeared around the corner of the house.

What did it matter? Joe scooped the boy up and carried him to the front door, where Amelia was waiting.

"Come in, Joe." She looked pretty in a yellow gown, her hair tied back with a matching ribbon. "I'd invite you for supper, but we've already eaten. Can I get you a drink?"

"Don't bother." Joe lowered his son to the floor. "I just came by to see Mason and to pay my respects to your father—and to talk with you, if you have a few minutes."

She tossed her hair, a gesture he remembered from their courting days. "Your timing's perfect. I need to talk with you as well," she said. "I'll meet you on the front porch, after you've seen Daddy."

"Grandpa's really sick." Mason tugged at Joe's hand. "But you can go in and see him. I'll show you where he is."

Joe let Mason lead him down the hall to Loren's bedroom. Amelia's father lay in his bed, freshly washed and wearing a clean nightshirt. His head and shoulders were supported by pillows. Abraham hovered nearby, a bowl of soup, a spoon, and a crumpled napkin in his huge hands.

"Hello, Loren," Joe said.

Loren's mouth moved, but the sound that emerged was less than a word. He'd lost weight since the stroke. His frame was skeletal beneath the bedding. His cheeks were hollow, his eyes like burned-out coals in the sunken pits of their sockets.

"The ranch looks good. You don't need to worry about that." Joe was groping for words. What could one say to a man who'd given up on life?

Loren's mouth moved again, but Joe couldn't understand what he was saying. He gave Abraham a questioning look.

"He said to thank you for coming," Abraham translated. "And he wants you to look after Amelia and Mason."

"I'll do my best." Joe took the thin, lifeless fingers in his in the semblance of a handshake. "I'll go now and let you rest." He turned to Abraham. "Is it all right if Mason stays with you for a little while? I need to talk to his mother."

"You bet." The big man gave him a smile. "We're good friends, Mason and me. He even helps me look after his grandpa. Come on, Mason, let's go to the kitchen. I think there's a couple of cookies in there just waiting for us."

Joe found his way back to the front porch, where he found Amelia on the swing, her skirt spread prettily around her. He pulled up a chair so he could sit facing her. He'd come prepared to lay out the terms of the divorce he wanted. But she'd mentioned that she needed to talk to him. It might be wise to hold back until he'd heard what she had to say.

They sat in silence for a moment, the twilight deepening around them. "We both mentioned we wanted to talk," Joe said. "How about we start with ladies first?"

She sighed and nodded. "My father is dying, Joe. He doesn't have much time left."

"I guessed as much when I saw him. I'm sorry."

"Don't be. I'm not. He walked away when I was a baby, and he didn't really want me when my mother sent me here. You know that he didn't waste any time in marrying me off."

"He's your father, Amelia. That has to mean something."

"Actually, it does." She swung her feet to the porch and turned to face him. "I'm his only child. When he dies, I'll inherit this ranch. Except that, since I'm a married woman, you, as my husband, will be the one who owns and runs it."

Her words startled Joe. In figuring his assets today in Miles City, he hadn't thought to include the Hollister ranch because it belonged to Loren. While the ranch was nowhere near as large as the Calder spread, it was still a sizable property. The land was rich in grass and water, with a fine house on it and plenty of livestock. For anyone who owned it, the place would be a prize.

"Hear me out," she said. "You and I haven't been happy together for a long time. I'm sure you remember what I told you the day we left Daddy at the doctor's—that I wanted to stay married. But I've been rethinking my position. I want this ranch for myself and for Mason. But if we're still married when my father dies, the ranch will go to you and me—which means it would actually go to you."

Joe stared at his wife. What was Amelia implying? Was it what he thought—what he barely dared to hope?

"This is what I'm proposing," she said. "Give me a quick divorce now, while Daddy is still alive. That way, I can inherit the ranch as a single woman. In return, I'll deed you all the property you acquired in my name. We can make a clean break and move on—both of us."

"And what about Mason?" Joe asked. "The rest is fine. But there's no way I'm giving up my son."

"I can't see any need for change," she said as if the question had meant nothing. "As the future heir to this ranch, I'd like him to be raised here, of course. But he'd still be your son. You could still see him and have him with you—just as you do now."

"And if you remarry?" Joe almost mentioned Ralph Tomlinson, then thought better of it.

She shook her head. "If I needed a husband, I would just keep you. At least you haven't been around enough to give me much trouble. No, this ranch will be mine—and Mason's. I won't share it with any man. And I won't have a man telling me what to do. I've had enough of that. So what will it be, Joe? I saw my lawyer in Miles City earlier this week. We drew up the papers. I have them right here. All you need to do is sign."

A large, brown envelope lay on the seat of the swing, partly covered by her skirt. Picking it up, she thrust it toward Joe. "Here. Take it. There's a pen and ink in the study. Once you've signed, I'll file the papers with the court, and we'll be done."

Taking the envelope, Joe struggled to find his voice. This was a new Amelia, as clearheaded and ruthless as any man. He found himself admiring her, almost liking her. But he didn't want to stay married to her. "Fine," he said, "but I'm not signing anything until I've read this document."

"Of course you aren't," she said, getting up. "Come on inside. I'll light the lamp in the study so you can see every word."

Thirty minutes later, Joe said good night to Mason, mounted his horse, and rode away a free man. He felt the loss of a marriage he'd entered in good faith, but the twinge of regret was nothing compared to the euphoria of having resolved his life with the stroke of a pen.

He fought against the urge to gallop back to town, knock on Sarah's door, and sweep her into his arms. Years ago, his impetuous act had ruined her plans and almost ruined her life. This time would be different.

He would wait a decent interval after the divorce was final. Then he would court her the way a lady deserved to be courted—with flowers, little gifts, picnics, dinners, and sweet words. He would take the time to know his son, teach him to ride, fish, and shoot. Maybe his two boys would even get to know each other. Only when the way was clear and everything felt right, would he ask Sarah to marry him.

His beautiful Sarah had endured shame, disappointment, poverty, and hard work, much of which was his fault. Now that he was free, he would make it up to her. He would treat her like the magnificent woman she was—the woman who had always been first in his heart.

CHAPTER EIGHTEEN

November 23, 1891
Back to the beginning . . .

*B*Y THE NEXT MORNING THE STORM HAD MOVED ON. THE FIRST glimmer of dawn revealed a clear sky, the stars fading, the wind so frigid that Joe's breath emerged in white puffs as he hitched the two big draft horses to the sleigh. The snow, which lay almost two feet deep in the drifts, would be impassable for a buggy and dangerous for a mounted rider. But the sleigh, which Joe had built after the first hard Montana winter, would glide over the snow behind the massive bay horses, who wore special coverings to protect their hooves and keep them from slipping.

When the sleigh was ready to go, Joe went back into the house for a last-minute cup of hot coffee. Sarah was waiting in the kitchen. She handed him the steaming mug. "You don't need to do this," she said. "We don't need more land."

He gulped the coffee, feeling the heat travel down through his body. "Neither does Benteen. But if I can get to the bank and buy that parcel ahead of him, it'll leave him with a black eye—and we'll own one of the sweetest little ranches in the county."

"Or maybe we won't. Maybe you'll be wasting your time. Just be careful. That's all I ask." She took the empty cup, set it on the counter, and waited for his kiss.

He gathered her in his arms. Because he knew Sarah was worried, he allowed extra time to make the kiss long and deep. He loved the feel of her, the taste of her, and the fire she ignited in his body. They had married six years ago, after a proper courtship. Over time, they'd become true soul mates. To their disappointment, they'd had no more children. But Blake, who was bright, strong, and compassionate, was a joy every day of Joe's life. And Mason would always be part of his family.

Sarah had taught school for just one year before her marriage. But she was still in demand as a midwife, nurse, and tutor. Joe understood her need to be of use. It was one of the reasons he loved her so much.

When he went outside again, the big yellow dog, gray-muzzled now, was waiting on the porch, probably hoping for a ride.

Joe scratched the shaggy head. "Not this time, old boy," he said. "It's too cold for you, and I've got some serious business in town."

He pulled on his thick gloves, gave the sleigh a shake to free the iced runners, and climbed onto the seat. After pulling a warm buffalo robe over his lap, he took the reins. The horses strained against their collars and the sleigh began to move. Glancing back, he saw Sarah and Blake on the porch with the dog. Joe gave them a wave before the sleigh carried him from their sight.

The year he'd married Sarah, Joe had hired a crew to widen and grade the road up the hill to his house. The job had been expensive but well worth the price in terms of ease and safety. Even so, with the wind blowing the snow into drifts across the road, the way down was treacherous. He took a long breath of relief when the team and sleigh finally reached level ground. From here it would be a matter of pushing through snow along the road, all the way to Miles City.

Joe's errand, and the race to beat Benteen Calder, had been triggered by a tragedy. This past Thursday evening, Blaise Ransom, Joe's former boss and as fine a man as Joe had ever known, had been thrown from his horse and killed instantly when his head struck the rocky ground. He'd left behind a widow and two teenaged sons.

Joe had attended the funeral service on Sunday. Sarah had been needed elsewhere, so he'd gone alone. After the burial, he'd approached Blaise's widow, Florence, to offer his condolences. "I always thought the world of Blaise," he'd told her. "If you and the boys ever need anything—anything at all—don't hesitate to ask for my help."

Florence, as Joe remembered, had been dry-eyed; but her plain, thin face had been etched with strain. She had always been strong, but the loss of her husband had pushed her to the limit.

"Thank you, Joe, but we won't be staying," she'd told him. "I'm not spending another Montana winter here without Blaise. I have a sister in Ohio. I can move there, have good neighbors, and get enough money from the ranch to buy a house and send the boys to college."

"You're selling the ranch? How much are you asking? I'll buy it from you."

"It's not that simple," she'd told him. "On Friday, when we took Blaise's body to the undertaker in Miles City, I went to the bank, signed a quit claim deed to the ranch, agreed on the minimum price I'd accept, and left the paperwork with the land office. I didn't know how long it might take to find a buyer, and with winter on the way, I didn't want to be stuck here, waiting for a sale."

"That shouldn't be a problem," Joe had said. "I can go into Miles City first thing tomorrow, transfer the cash from my account, and have it in your hands before you leave."

Florence had sighed. "I'd be happy to sell you this ranch, Joe, but as I said, it's not that simple. There's another buyer ahead of you. Benteen Calder came by yesterday and made an offer on the place."

So, the bastard hadn't even waited until Blaise was in the ground. That was Benteen for you—and he hadn't even shown up at the funeral service.

"Did you sign anything?" Joe asked.

"No. I told Benteen that I'd left everything in the hands of the bank. Whoever got there first, with an acceptable offer and ready cash, could buy the ranch."

"How much did Benteen offer you?"

She'd told him. The offer was fair but not generous.

"I can raise that by ten percent."

"Fine, Joe. But it's out of my hands. If Benteen makes it to the bank before you submit your offer, you'll be too late."

"Won't the bank wait for other offers to come in?" Joe had asked.

"I told them I needed a quick sale. They'll take the first offer that's over my asking price."

"Then I'll plan to be at the bank as soon as the doors open. Wish me luck."

"Either way, I need the money, but I'd rather see the ranch in your hands than in Benteen's." Florence had squeezed Joe's arm before turning away to greet other friends.

By the time the sun's first rays streaked the eastern sky, Joe was passing through Blue Moon. The snow in the road was undisturbed except for where the biting wind had blown ripples in the surface. The only sign of life was the young married man who taught at the school, clearing a path to the classroom door. Apart from the wind, the scrape of his shovel was the only sound. Even the sleigh moved in silence. Frozen breath coated the whiskers of the big bay horses.

As Joe estimated the time to Miles City, he was aware of one advantage he might have. Unless someone had told him, Benteen wouldn't know about the second offer on the ranch. With luck, he would take his time getting on the road and getting to the bank—only to discover that the property had been snatched away from him. That was the victory Joe hoped for—the kind of victory he'd been craving since the day Benteen had ridden off and left him to die in that wash.

He was coming up on the boundary of the Calder ranch now. Beyond the fence line, the pastures were a vast sea of glistening white. Cattle, their bodies dark smudges against the winter landscape, bunched together for warmth. They'd be hungry, but soon the Calder ranch hands would be out hauling loads of hay to feed them. Back on Joe's land, his own cowboys would be doing the same. By this time of year, most of the mature animals had been rounded up, sold off, and loaded into railroad cars for the long ride to Chicago. Those left to winter over on the land were calves, yearlings, and breeding stock, all vital to the future.

Joe found himself wondering how Amelia was faring with the snow on her ranch—probably fine, he told himself. He'd expected to see her at the funeral, since the Ransoms were her neighbors. She hadn't shown up, but then Amelia had never been much for sympathy.

Loren had died a few weeks after her divorce from Joe, leaving her as sole heir to the Hollister ranch. With the help of her foreman, she'd done a competent job of running the place. In an odd sort of way, Joe was proud of the woman his former wife had become. True to her intent, she'd never remarried. He suspected that she and Ralph Tomlinson were lovers, but that was none of his business. As long as Mason was growing into a strong, active, keen-minded boy, and Joe was allowed to spend time with him, nothing else mattered.

Joe passed the gate to the Calder ranch. In the distance, the grand house crowned the bluff like an alabaster carving, bright in the morning sun. The gate was closed, with no tracks of any kind leading out to the main road. Either Benteen hadn't left yet, or he'd braved the storm and gone last night, to be there for the Monday morning opening of the bank.

If Benteen was already in Miles City, and if he made it to the bank first, Joe would have no choice except to take the loss, act as if nothing had happened, and wait for another chance. But he wouldn't have to like it. Twelve years was long enough to wait for satisfaction. He knew he ought to move on. But that didn't mean he was ready to give up.

With wind blowing the surface of the snow, the road was slow going, but with his powerful team, Joe was making steady progress. By now the sun was well above the horizon. A glance at his pocket watch told him the time was coming up on 9:00. The bank opened at 10:00. Miles City should be a little over an hour away. Even if Benteen had arrived in town ahead of him, it might still be possible to beat him to the door of the bank. He pushed the horses as fast as he dared, their huge hooves and strong legs plowing through the drifts.

A few yards ahead, on the right-hand side of the road was a large, snow-covered lump. He was about to drive on past it, but then slowed the team for a closer look. He knew the road well. Nothing like this had been here before. What if some traveler had been trapped in last night's freezing storm?

Anxious as he was to get to Miles City, Joe knew he couldn't move on without taking a moment to investigate. Stopping, he shoved the buffalo robe off his lap and climbed out of the sleigh. He could see no movement, no visible tracks anywhere. Whatever he was looking at had been here long enough for the blowing snow to cover it all.

Pushing through knee-deep snow, he reached the roadside and gave the mound a light kick. His boot struck something solid. Bending, he brushed away the snow with one gloved hand— enough to reveal what lay beneath. It was a dead horse, partly frozen and still wearing its saddle. It had been shot through the head.

Puzzling, Joe walked around the horse, half expecting to find some poor soul lying there, dead of cold. Instead, what he saw was a hollow space next to the horse's belly. Partly filled in by blowing snow, it was the size and shape of a huddled body. As his view of the scene changed with the angle of the sun, he could make out faint tracks, almost hidden by drifting snow. They were leading away from the horse, in the direction of Miles City.

As he freed the sleigh runners, climbed back onto the seat, and urged the team forward, his cold-numbed mind struggled to make sense of what he'd just seen. What had happened here, when had it happened, and where was the missing rider?

Piecing the clues together, the best he could figure was that someone had taken this road last night before the weather moved in. The storm had worsened. The horse had slipped, broken its leg, and had to be put down. Unable to forge ahead in the blinding snow, the rider had hunkered down next to the horse, using its body for warmth and protection, until sometime toward morning, when the storm had cleared enough for him to get up and continue on foot.

Could the rider have been Benteen?

Could someone at the funeral have overheard Joe's conversation with Florence Ransom and passed him the word that there was a second offer on the ranch?

Not every man could make it to Miles City on foot, in the deep snow, after spending a night in the freezing cold. But Benteen Calder was as tough and determined as any man alive. If anybody could do it, he could.

Time was getting short. Joe leaned over the reins, urging the horses faster.

Twenty minutes later, he spotted a figure ahead of him, in the road, stumbling along through the snow, half falling forward, then staggering up and pushing on again, making progress a few steps at a time.

Even at a distance, Joe recognized the rangy, broad-shouldered frame of Benteen Calder.

With less need to hurry now, he slowed the team and pulled up alongside the struggling man.

Benteen glared up at him. His hat was missing, but he'd tied a scarf around the lower part of his face and over his ears. Where the scarf didn't cover, his hair and heavy eyebrows were coated with frost. His face was gray, his bloodshot eyes rheumy and rimmed with red. Under the thick sheepskin coat he wore, his body was stooped with fatigue.

He looked like walking death.

"Nice day for a stroll, isn't it, Benteen?" Joe said.

Benteen muttered a vile oath.

"I found your horse," Joe said. "Tough luck."

Benteen swore again, tugging the scarf down to his chin. His lips were blue. "Damn you, Dollarhide. One more word and, so help me, I'll draw my pistol and shoot you dead. I know what you're thinking. When you're done tormenting me, you'll drive off and leave me to freeze to death, just like I left you to die in that wash on the cattle drive. It's been twelve years, and you've still got that damned burr under your saddle." He cleared his throat and spat in the snow. "I heard about the offer you made on the Ransom place."

Joe didn't ask him how he knew. "I offered ten percent more than you did," he said. "Florence deserves as much as she can get for that ranch. And when I get to the bank, that's what she'll be getting."

"But I offered first, and I'll beat your price if I have to double it! I want that land, and damn it, you're not going to steal it from me." Tugging off a glove, he reached under his coat for the pistol he wore at his hip. But it was frozen in its holster.

Joe watched as Benteen struggled to free the weapon. He had his rifle under the seat of the sleigh, but he left it in place, acting on the hunch that he wouldn't need it.

After a moment of trying, Benteen wrenched the pistol out of the holster and leveled it at Joe. "I'm taking that sleigh," he said. "You can walk. Get down."

Joe could see that the pistol was clogged with ice. The hammer was frozen in place, and Benteen's cold, numbed hand was too weak to aim and fire. Now Benteen could see it, too. With a curse, he flung the useless pistol into the snow.

"All right, you bastard!" he snarled. "Go on then. Get out of here. But I won't forget this. I'll see that you pay, even if it's in hell."

Joe looked at his rival, standing knee-deep in snow, shaking with cold and fury. Benteen's skin was colorless. His clothes were coated with snow. Left to walk the rest of the way to town, a distance of several miles, he could die of exposure. Even if Benteen lived to reach Miles City, he could still perish from pneumonia. Joe thought of Lorna. He thought of Benteen's young son, Webb, and how much they needed him. This wasn't what he wanted. Beating Benteen Calder at fair play was one thing. But Joe had never meant to cause his death.

"Well," Benteen's voice quivered with false bravado, "what are you waiting for? Get going."

Joe shook his head. "Benteen Calder, I swear you are the stubbornest sonofabitch on God's green earth! Just climb in the damned sleigh, before I lose my patience and leave you here to freeze."

This time Benteen didn't argue. He slogged through the snow and, with the last of his strength, hauled himself onto the back seat of the sleigh. Joe handed him the buffalo robe. He wrapped himself in it and sat in silence, a shivering bundle of rage and wounded pride, as the sleigh began to move.

By the time they reached Miles City, Benteen was doing better. He'd stopped shivering and could find no frostbite damage to his hands, face, or ears. As they passed the bank, they saw that it was open, but there was no reason to hurry now.

"Do you need to see a doctor?" Joe asked as they pulled the sleigh up on a side street. "It might be a good idea to have him check your feet."

"What are you now, my mother?" Benteen groused. "All I need is a hot cup of coffee and I'll be fine."

After giving the horses some oats and water, they walked around the corner to the hotel and ordered coffee in big, steaming mugs. They drank in silence, letting the hot, black liquid warm their bodies. Benteen was being civil enough, but the question of who had the right to buy the Ransom ranch hung between them like an unspoken threat. Now that they were here, and the bank was open, Joe knew that it would have to be settled.

It stood to reason that Joe had won the race to buy the property. After all, he'd gotten here on his own power, with Benteen as his rescued passenger.

But Benteen had left earlier. If he hadn't lost his horse, he would've arrived in town last night. Joe might have won, but only because of his rival's bad luck.

Was that fair? Did the question of fairness even matter?

Hadn't crushing Benteen's pride by saving his life been enough to balance the scale?

Joe could think of only one way to resolve the question.

"I have a proposition," he said. "Hear me out."

"I'm listening." Benteen's eyes narrowed. The color had returned to his face, but he still looked like some wild mountain man who'd wandered in from a blizzard.

"What if we were to buy the ranch together, as partners? That way, Florence would get her money right away. We could even put in something extra for her."

Benteen's eyebrows met in a scowl. He shook his head. "I don't see the advantage to that. I need that land—all of it—to run my cattle next spring."

"The thing is, this way would give us time," Joe said. "If, by spring, you need the land more than I do, you could buy me out. Or I could do the same with you. Meanwhile, neither of us would have to tie up the full amount. Florence would get her money, the ranch would be protected from other buyers, and we wouldn't have to fight over it now."

"Well, I don't know. . . ." Benteen wiped a trickle of snow melt off his face.

"Damn it, Benteen. I won, fair and square. I'm doing you a favor. Which would you rather have, half a ranch or none at all?"

Benteen hesitated for the space of a long breath, then sighed. "What the hell? I'm too tired to argue. Let's go to the bank, get it done, and go home."

They left change for their coffee on the table, walked out of the hotel, and went next door to the bank.

The counter for the land office was in the rear of the building, the young clerk a stranger. "What can I do for you, gentlemen?" he asked.

"We've come to purchase the Blaise Ransom ranch property," Joe told him. "His widow left the signed papers here. We'll be buying it jointly."

The clerk frowned behind his thick glasses. "I know the parcel you're talking about. But I'm afraid it's just been sold. The new owner is in the manager's office right now, signing the papers and transferring the funds."

Joe glanced at Benteen. The man looked as if he'd been gut kicked. "What the hell . . . ?" he muttered.

Joe managed to find his voice. "Can you tell us who the buyer is?" he asked.

"Certainly." The clerk glanced at a paper in front of him. "The new owner of the Ransom property is Mrs. Amelia Hollister Dollarhide."

Joe felt the shock like a stab in the back. Before he could recover, the door to the manager's office opened, and Amelia stepped out. Dressed in a stylishly warm sable coat and a smart little hat, she nodded as she passed Joe and Benteen.

"Gentlemen." She gave them a knowing smile, walked to the front of the bank, and out the door.

A long beat of silence passed. Then Benteen threw up his hands. "To hell with her. To hell with it all. Come on, Dollarhide. As a thanks for saving me, I'll buy you breakfast. Then we can hit the road."

Joe pulled the sleigh up in front of his house and turned the horses and rig over to a stable hand. Half-frozen, bone-tired, and bear hungry, he mounted the front steps. The drive home from Miles City, with a side trip to let Benteen Calder off at his home, had used up the rest of the day. He hadn't eaten since the breakfast he'd shared with Benteen at the hotel. All he wanted tonight was a good meal, a hot bath, and a warm, loving woman in his bed.

Sarah came out onto the porch, a woolen shawl around her shoulders. The savory aroma of roast beef drifted through the open doorway before she closed it behind her to keep the heat inside the house.

Joe mounted the steps two at a time, stomped the snow off his boots, tugged off his gloves, and opened his coat. Sarah flew across the porch to nestle against him, warming him with her body as he wrapped the front of the coat around them both.

"My stars, you're freezing!" she said.

He laughed, his arms tightening around her. "But not for long. You always know how to warm me up."

Her arms stole around him under the coat, pulling him tight against her. "Did you buy the ranch?" she asked.

"I did not."

She looked up at him. "You don't sound unhappy about it. Did Benteen beat you to the bank?"

"No, he didn't." Joe found himself grinning.

"So what happened? Who bought the ranch?"

He bent and kissed her warm lips. "That," he said, "is a very long story. I'll tell you over supper. How's Blake?"

"I kept him home today because of the snow. He's doing his schoolwork," she said. "I know you must be hungry. I can have supper on the table in a few minutes."

She pulled away from him a little, but he drew her back, holding her inside his coat. "This feels good. Let's just stay like this for a minute. Then we can go inside."

They stood at the rail, holding each other. In the west, the sun was going down, streaking the sky with glorious ribbons of flame, mauve, and indigo. They watched as the colors faded into twilight.

This was all that mattered, Joe thought. Not owning more land, and not even getting even with Benteen Calder. *More* was an empty word when you already had it all.

He might not have the most, but he had the best. As far as Joe was concerned, he was the richest man in Montana.

EPILOGUE

Summer, ten years later

"*R*ACE YOU TO THE GATE!"

With those words the two riders were off, horses thundering the length of the grassy pasture. Seated on his aging buckskin, Joe watched his two sons from beyond the fence—Blake, lean, dark, and quick like his father; Mason, younger and huskier, with chestnut hair and his mother's green eyes. They were evenly matched, as were their horses, first one leading, then the other, until they finished the race in a dead heat, pulled up at the fence, then turned and went back to working cattle.

Joe had always hoped that if he raised his boys together, they would be friends. He had been honest about their relationship from the start, reasoning that letting them grow into understanding would be kinder than surprising them when they were older. He'd never regretted that decision, but as for the two being friends . . .

Joe shook his head as they rode off in different directions. It wasn't that his sons were enemies. In most respects, they got along fine. But they were fierce competitors, each one always trying to outdo the other.

Mason still lived on the Hollister ranch with his mother, who was already teaching him the business. But the ranch had been a lonely place for a growing boy. He'd spent a good share of his time at Joe's, where he had his own room, his own horse, dogs to play with, and a loving stepmother who treated him like her own son.

It was Joe who'd taught the boys to fish, to hunt, and to cowboy. But even when they were young, everything had to be a contest—who could catch the most fish, shoot the biggest buck and skin it the fastest, who could be the best at roping a steer or breaking a horse. Joe had little doubt that the competition would continue for the rest of their lives.

"I see they're at it again." Sarah had ridden up beside him on her palomino mare. With her, on a pinto pony, was their daughter, Kristin, who'd come as a delightful surprise nine years ago. Fair like her mother, she was pretty, smart, and almost as competitive as the boys.

"I'll bet I could beat both of them if you'd let me race," she said. "And I'll bet I could rope a calf, too, if you'd let me go on roundup."

"Wait till you're older," Joe said. "Those brothers of yours play rough. You could get hurt. And those cowboys on the roundup, the way they talk, they're no fit company for a young lady."

Kristin tossed her braids. "I wouldn't care. And I don't want to be a young lady. Boys have all the fun."

Joe reached out and gave her a hug, then gave Sarah a longer one. Time went by so fast. Before he knew it, the boys would be grown and making their own way—like Benteen's son Webb, who was already a man. Everything seemed to be changing in this part of Montana. Blue Moon was a real town now, and a new land rush was happening as immigrant homesteaders moved in to take advantage of free farmland.

Joe was still in his thirties, but he had seen so much, so many changes, that sometimes he felt old. What new things were coming? He was in no hurry to find out. The best time was now, on this land, with these precious people. It was enough.